HOMAGE TO CATALONIA

GEORGE ORWELL

HOMAGE TO CATALONIA

W. Books

This is a W. Books publication, a division of Grupo Ciranda Cultural.

Text: George Orwell
First Publication: 1938
Graphic Design: Linea Editora
Cover Design and Illustrations: © Sweet Cherry Publishing Limited, 2024

Dados Internacionais de Catalogação na Publicação (CIP) de acordo com ISBD

O79h Orwell, George.

Homage to Catalonia / George Orwell. - Jandira, SP : W. Books, 2025.
240 p. : 12,80cm x 19,70cm. - (Classics).

ISBN: 978-65-5294-067-4

1. Literatura inglesa. 2. Clássicos. 3. Séries. 4. Filmes. 5. Inglês. I. Título. II. Série.

CDD 823.91
2024-2424 CDU 821.111-3

Elaborada por Lucio Feitosa - CRB-8/8803

Índice para catálogo sistemático:
1. Literatura inglesa 823.91
2. Literatura inglesa 821.111-3

www.cirandacultural.com.br

CONTENTS

Answer not a fool according to his folly, lest thou be like unto him.

Answer a fool according to his folly, lest he be wise in his own conceit.

—Proverbs XXVI. 5-6

CHAPTER 1

In the Lenin Barracks in Barcelona, the day before I joined the militia, I saw an Italian militiaman standing in front of the officers' table.

He was a tough-looking youth of twenty-five or six, with reddish-yellow hair and powerful shoulders. His peaked leather cap was pulled fiercely over one eye. He was standing in profile to me, his chin on his breast, gazing with a puzzled frown at a map which one of the officers had open on the table. Something in his face deeply moved me. It was the face of a man who would commit murder and throw away his life for a friend—the kind of face you would expect in an Anarchist, though as likely as not he was a Communist. There were both candour and ferocity in it; also the pathetic reverence that illiterate people have for their supposed superiors. Obviously he could not make head or tail of the map; obviously he regarded map-reading as a stupendous intellectual feat. I hardly know why, but I have seldom seen anyone—any man, I mean—to whom I have taken such an immediate liking. While they were talking round the table some remark brought it out that I was a foreigner. The Italian raised his head and said quickly:

‘_*Italiano*?_’

I answered in my bad Spanish: ‘_No, Inglés. *Y tú*?_’

‘_*Italiano*_.’

As we went out he stepped across the room and gripped my hand very hard. Queer, the affection you can feel for a stranger! It was as though his spirit and mine had momentarily succeeded in bridging the gulf of language and tradition and meeting in utter intimacy. I hoped he liked me as well as I liked him. But I also knew that to retain my first impression of him I must not see him again; and needless to say I never did see him again. One was always making contacts of that kind in Spain.

I mention this Italian militiaman because he has stuck vividly in my memory. With his shabby uniform and fierce pathetic face he typifies for me the special atmosphere of that time. He is bound up with all my memories of that period of the war—the red flags in Barcelona, the gaunt trains full of shabby soldiers creeping to the front, the grey war-stricken towns farther up the line, the muddy, ice-cold trenches in the mountains.

This was in late December 1936, less than seven months ago as I write, and yet it is a period that has already receded into enormous distance. Later events have obliterated it much more completely than they have obliterated 1935, or 1905, for that matter. I had come to Spain with some notion of writing newspaper articles, but I had joined the militia almost immediately, because at that time and in that atmosphere it seemed the only conceivable thing to do. The Anarchists were still in virtual control of Catalonia and the revolution was still in full swing. To anyone who had been there since the beginning it probably seemed even in December or January that the revolutionary period was ending; but when one came straight from England the aspect of Barcelona was something startling and overwhelming. It was the first time that I had ever been in a town where the working class was in the saddle.

Practically every building of any size had been seized by the workers and was draped with red flags or with the red and black flag of the Anarchists; every wall was scrawled with the hammer and sickle and with the initials of the revolutionary parties; almost every church had been gutted and its images burnt. Churches here and there were being systematically demolished by gangs of workmen. Every shop and *café* had an inscription saying that it had been collectivized; even the bootblacks had been collectivized and their boxes painted red and black. Waiters and shop-walkers looked you in the face and treated you as an equal. Servile and even ceremonial forms of speech had temporarily disappeared. Nobody said '_*Señor*_' or '_*Don*_' or even '_*Usted*_'; everyone called everyone else '_Comrade_' and '_Thou_', and said '_*Salud!*_' instead of '_*Buenos días*_'. Tipping was forbidden by law since the time of *Primo de Rivera*; almost my first experience was receiving a lecture from a hotel manager for trying to tip a lift-boy. There were no private motor-cars, they had all been commandeered, and all the trams and taxis and much of the other transport were painted red and black. The revolutionary posters were everywhere, flaming from the walls in clean reds and blues that made the few remaining advertisements look like daubs of mud. Down the *Ramblas*, the wide central artery of the town where crowds of people streamed constantly to and fro, the loudspeakers were bellowing revolutionary songs all day and far into the night. And it was the aspect of the crowds that was the queerest thing of all. In outward appearance it was a town in which the wealthy classes had practically ceased to exist. Except for a small number of women and foreigners there were no 'well-dressed' people at all. Practically everyone wore rough working-class clothes, or blue overalls, or some variant of the militia uniform. All this was queer and moving. There was much in it that I did not understand, in some ways I did not even like it, but I recognized it immediately as a state of affairs worth fighting for. Also I believed that things were as they appeared, that this was really a workers' State and that the entire bourgeoisie had either fled, been killed, or voluntarily come over to the workers' side; I did not realize that great numbers of well-to-do bourgeois were simply lying low and disguising themselves as proletarians for the time being.

Together with all this there was something of the evil atmosphere of war. The town had a gaunt untidy look, roads and buildings were in poor repair, the streets at night were dimly lit for fear of air-raids, the shops were mostly shabby and half-empty. Meat was scarce and milk practically unobtainable, there was a shortage of coal, sugar, and petrol, and a really serious shortage of bread. Even at this period the bread-queues were often hundreds of yards long. Yet so far as one could judge the people were contented and hopeful. There was no unemployment, and the price of living was still extremely low; you saw very few conspicuously destitute people, and no beggars except the gipsies. Above all, there was a belief in the revolution and the future, a feeling of having suddenly emerged into an era of equality and freedom. Human beings were trying to behave as human beings and not as cogs in the capitalist machine. In the barbers' shops were Anarchist notices (the barbers were mostly Anarchists) solemnly explaining that barbers were no longer slaves. In the streets were coloured posters appealing to prostitutes to stop being prostitutes. To anyone from the hard-boiled, sneering civilization of the English-speaking races there was something rather pathetic in the literalness with which these idealistic Spaniards took the hackneyed phrases of revolution. At that time revolutionary ballads of the naivest kind, all about proletarian brotherhood and the wickedness of Mussolini, were being sold on the streets for a few centimes each. I have often seen an illiterate militiaman buy one of these ballads, laboriously spell out the words, and then, when he had got the hang of it, begin singing it to an appropriate tune.

All this time I was at the Lenin Barracks, ostensibly in training for the front. When I joined the militia I had been told that I should be sent to the front the next day, but in fact I had to wait while a fresh _centuria_ was got ready. The workers' militias, hurriedly raised by the trade unions at the beginning of the war, had not yet been organized on an ordinary army basis. The units of command were the 'section', of about thirty men, the _centuria_, of about a hundred men, and the 'column', which in practice meant any large number of men. The Lenin Barracks was a block of splendid stone buildings with a riding-school and enormous cobbled courtyards; it had been a cavalry barracks and had been captured during the July fighting. My _centuria_ slept in one of the stables, under the stone mangers where the names of the cavalry chargers were still inscribed. All the horses had been seized and sent to the front, but the whole place still smelt of horse-piss and rotten oats. I was at the barracks about a week. Chiefly I remember the horsy smells, the quavering bugle-calls (all our buglers were amateurs—I first learned the Spanish bugle-calls by listening to them outside the Fascist lines), the tramp-tramp of hobnailed boots in the barrack yard, the long morning parades in the wintry sunshine, the wild games of football, fifty a side, in the gravelled riding-school. There were perhaps a thousand men at the barracks, and a score or so of women, apart from the militiamen's wives who did the cooking. There were still women serving in the militias, though not very many. In the early battles they had fought side by side with the men as a matter of course. It is a thing that seems natural in time of revolution. Ideas were changing already, however. The militiamen had to be kept out of the riding-school while the women were drilling there because they laughed at the women and put them off. A few months earlier no one would have seen anything comic in a woman handling a gun.

The whole barracks was in the state of filth and chaos to which the militia reduced every building they occupied and which seems to be one of the by-products of revolution. In every corner you came upon piles of smashed furniture, broken saddles, brass cavalry-helmets, empty sabre-scabbards, and decaying food. There was frightful wastage of food, especially bread. From my barrack-room alone a basketful of bread was thrown away at every meal—a disgraceful thing when the civilian population was short of it. We ate at long trestle-tables out of permanently greasy tin pannikins, and drank out of a dreadful thing called a _porrón_. A _porrón_ is a sort of glass bottle with a pointed spout from which a thin jet of wine spurts out whenever you tip it up; you can thus drink from a distance, without touching it with your lips, and it can be passed from hand to hand. I went on strike and demanded a drinking-cup as soon as I saw a _porrón_ in use. To my eye the things were altogether too like bed-bottles, especially when they were filled with white wine.

By degrees they were issuing the recruits with uniforms, and because this was Spain everything was issued piecemeal, so that it was never quite certain who had received what, and various of the things we most needed, such as belts and cartridge-boxes, were not issued till the last moment, when the train was actually waiting to take us to the front. I have spoken of the militia 'uniform', which probably gives a wrong impression. It was not exactly a uniform. Perhaps a 'multiform' would be the proper name for it. Everyone's clothes followed the same general plan, but they were never quite the same in any two cases. Practically everyone in the army wore corduroy knee-breeches, but there the uniformity ended. Some wore puttees, others corduroy gaiters, others leather leggings or high boots. Everyone wore a zipper jacket, but some of the jackets were of leather, others of wool and of every conceivable colour. The kinds of cap were about as numerous as their wearers. It was usual to adorn the front of your cap with a party badge, and in addition nearly every man wore a red or red and black handkerchief round his throat. A militia column at that time was an extraordinary-looking rabble. But the clothes had to be issued as this or that factory rushed them out, and they were not bad clothes considering the circumstances. The shirts and socks were wretched cotton things, however, quite useless against cold. I hate to think of what the militiamen must have gone through in the earlier months before anything was organized. I remember coming upon a newspaper of only about two months earlier in which one of the P.O.U.M. leaders, after a visit to the front, said that he would try to see to it that 'every militiaman had a blanket'. A phrase to make you shudder if you have ever slept in a trench.

On my second day at the barracks there began what was comically called 'instruction'. At the beginning there were frightful scenes of chaos. The recruits were mostly boys of sixteen or seventeen from the back streets of Barcelona, full of revolutionary ardour but completely ignorant of the meaning of war. It was impossible even to get them to stand in line. Discipline did not exist; if a man disliked an order he would step out of the ranks and argue fiercely with the officer. The lieutenant who instructed us was a stout, fresh-faced, pleasant young man who had previously been a Regular Army officer, and still looked like one, with his smart carriage and spick-and-span uniform. Curiously enough he was a sincere and ardent Socialist. Even more than the men themselves he insisted upon complete social equality between all ranks. I remember his pained surprise when an ignorant recruit addressed him as '_Señor_'. 'What! _Señor_? Who is that calling me _Señor_? Are we not all comrades?' I doubt whether it made his job any easier. Meanwhile the raw recruits were getting no military training that could be of the slightest use to them. I had been told that foreigners were not obliged to attend 'instruction' (the Spaniards, I noticed, had a pathetic belief that all foreigners knew more of military matters than themselves), but naturally I turned out with the others. I was very anxious to learn how to use a machine-gun; it was a weapon I had never had a chance to handle. To my dismay I found that we were taught nothing about the use of weapons. The so-called instruction was simply parade-ground drill of the most antiquated, stupid kind; right turn, left turn, about turn, marching at attention in column of threes and all the rest of that useless nonsense which I had learned when I was fifteen years old.

It was an extraordinary form for the training of a *guerilla* army to take. Obviously if you have only a few days in which to train a soldier, you must teach him the things he will most need; how to take cover, how to advance across open ground, how to mount guards and build a parapet—above all, how to use his weapons. Yet this mob of eager children, who were going to be thrown into the front line in a few days' time, were not even taught how to fire a rifle or pull the pin out of a bomb. At the time I did not grasp that this was because there were no weapons to be had. In the P.O.U.M. militia the shortage of rifles was so desperate that fresh troops reaching the front always had to take their rifles from the troops they relieved in the line. In the whole of the Lenin Barracks there were, I believe, no rifles except those used by the sentries.

After a few days, though still a complete rabble by any ordinary standard, we were considered fit to be seen in public, and in the mornings we were marched out to the public gardens on the hill beyond the *Plaza de España*. This was the common drill-ground of all the party militias, besides the *Carabineros* and the first contingents of the newly formed Popular Army. Up in the public gardens it was a strange and heartening sight. Down every path and alley-way, amid the formal flower-beds, squads and companies of men marched stiffly to and fro, throwing out their chests and trying desperately to look like soldiers. All of them were unarmed and none completely in uniform, though on most of them the militia uniform was breaking out in patches here and there. The procedure was always very much the same. For three hours we strutted to and fro (the Spanish marching step is very short and rapid), then we halted, broke the ranks, and flocked thirstily to a little grocer's shop which was half-way down the hill and was doing a roaring trade in cheap wine. Everyone was very friendly to me. As an Englishman I was something of a curiosity, and the *Carabinero* officers made much of me and stood me drinks. Meanwhile, whenever I could get our lieutenant into a corner, I was clamouring to be instructed in the use of a machine-gun. I used to drag my Hugo's dictionary out of my pocket and start on him in my villainous Spanish:

> '_*Yo sé manejar fusil. No sé manejar ametralladora. Quiero apprender ametralladora. Quándo vamos apprender ametralladora?*_'

The answer was always a harassed smile and a promise that there should be machine-gun instruction _*mañana*_. Needless to say _*mañana*_ never came. Several days passed and the recruits learned to march in step and spring to attention almost smartly, but if they knew which end of a rifle the bullet came out of, that was all they knew. One day an armed *Carabinero* strolled up to us when we were halting and allowed us to examine his rifle. It turned out that in the whole of my section no one except myself even knew how to load the rifle, much less how to take aim.

All this time I was having the usual struggles with the Spanish language. Apart from myself there was only one Englishman at the barracks, and nobody even among the officers spoke a word of French. Things were not made easier for me by the fact that when my companions spoke to one another they generally spoke in Catalan. The only way I could get along was to carry everywhere a small dictionary which I whipped out of my pocket in moments of crisis. But I would sooner be a foreigner in Spain than in most countries. How easy it is to make friends in Spain! Within a day or two there was a score of militiamen who called me by my Christian name, showed me the ropes, and overwhelmed me with hospitality. I am not writing a book of propaganda and I do not want to idealize the P.O.U.M. militia. The whole militia-system had serious faults, and the men themselves were a mixed lot, for by this time voluntary recruitment was falling off and many of the best men were already at the front or dead. There was always among us a certain percentage who were completely useless. Boys of fifteen were being brought up for enlistment by their parents, quite openly for the sake of the ten *pesetas* a day which was the militiaman's wage; also for the sake of the bread which the militia received in plenty and could smuggle home to their parents. But I defy anyone to be thrown as I was among the Spanish working class—I ought perhaps to say the Catalan working class, for apart from a few Aragónese and Andalusians I mixed only with Catalans—and not be struck by their essential decency; above all, their straightforwardness and generosity. A Spaniard's generosity, in the ordinary sense of the word, is at times almost embarrassing. If you ask him for a cigarette he will force the whole packet upon you. And beyond this there is generosity in a deeper sense, a real largeness of spirit, which I have met with again and again in the most unpromising circumstances. Some of the journalists and other foreigners who travelled in Spain during the war have declared that in secret the Spaniards were bitterly jealous of foreign aid. All I can say is that I never observed anything of the kind. I remember that a few days before I left the barracks a group of men returned on leave from the front. They were talking excitedly about their experiences and were full of enthusiasm for some French troops who had been next to them at Huesca. The French were very brave, they said; adding enthusiastically: ‘_Más valientes que nosotros_’—’Braver than we are!’ Of course I demurred, whereupon they explained that the French knew more of the art of war—were more expert with bombs, machine-guns, and so forth. Yet the remark was significant. An Englishman would cut his hand off sooner than say a thing like that.

Every foreigner who served in the militia spent his first few weeks in learning to love the Spaniards and in being exasperated by certain of their characteristics. In the front line my own exasperation sometimes reached the pitch of fury. The Spaniards are good at many things, but not at making war. All foreigners alike are appalled by their inefficiency, above all their maddening unpunctuality. The one Spanish word that no foreigner can avoid learning is _mañana_—'tomorrow' (literally, 'the morning'). Whenever it is conceivably possible, the business of today is put off until _mañana_. This is so notorious that even the Spaniards themselves make jokes about it. In Spain nothing, from a meal to a battle, ever happens at the appointed time. As a general rule things happen too late, but just occasionally—just so that you shan't even be able to depend on their happening late—they happen too early. A train which is due to leave at eight will normally leave at any time between nine and ten, but perhaps once a week, thanks to some private whim of the engine-driver, it leaves at half past seven. Such things can be a little trying. In theory I rather admire the Spaniards for not sharing our Northern time-neurosis; but unfortunately I share it myself.

After endless rumours, _mañanas_, and delays we were suddenly ordered to the front at two hours' notice, when much of our equipment was still unissued. There were terrible tumults in the quartermaster's store; in the end numbers of men had to leave without their full equipment. The barracks had promptly filled with women who seemed to have sprung up from the ground and were helping their men-folk to roll their blankets and pack their kit-bags. It was rather humiliating that I had to be shown how to put on my new leather cartridge-boxes by a Spanish girl, the wife of Williams, the other English militiaman. She was a gentle, dark-eyed, intensely feminine creature who looked as though her life-work was to rock a cradle, but who as a matter of fact had fought bravely in the street-battles of July. At this time she was carrying a baby which was born just ten months after the outbreak of war and had perhaps been begotten behind a barricade.

The train was due to leave at eight, and it was about ten past eight when the harassed, sweating officers managed to marshal us in the barrack square. I remember very vividly the torchlit scene—the uproar and excitement, the red flags flapping in the torchlight, the massed ranks of militiamen with their knapsacks on their backs and their rolled blankets worn bandolier-wise across the shoulder; and the shouting and the clatter of boots and tin pannikins, and then a tremendous and finally successful hissing for silence; and then some political commissar standing beneath a huge rolling red banner and making us a speech in Catalan. Finally they marched us to the station, taking the longest route, three or four miles, so as to show us to the whole town. In the *Ramblas* they halted us while a borrowed band played some revolutionary tune or other. Once again the conquering-hero stuff—shouting and enthusiasm, red flags and red and black flags everywhere, friendly crowds thronging the pavement to have a look at us, women waving from the windows. How natural it all seemed then; how remote and improbable now! The train was packed so tight with men that there was barely room even on the floor, let alone on the seats. At the last moment Williams's wife came rushing down the platform and gave us a bottle of wine and a foot of that bright red sausage which tastes of soap and gives you diarrhoea. The train crawled out of Catalonia and on to the plateau of Aragón at the normal wartime speed of something under twenty kilometres an hour.

CHAPTER 2

Barbastro, though a long way from the front line, looked bleak and chipped. Swarms of militiamen in shabby uniforms wandered up and down the streets, trying to keep warm. On a ruinous wall I came upon a poster dating from the previous year and announcing that 'six handsome bulls' would be killed in the arena on such and such a date. How forlorn its faded colours looked! Where were the handsome bulls and the handsome bull-fighters now? It appeared that even in Barcelona there were hardly any bullfights nowadays; for some reason all the best matadors were Fascists.

They sent my company by lorry to Sietamo, then westward to Alcubierre, which was just behind the line fronting Zaragoza. Sietamo had been fought over three times before the Anarchists finally took it in October, and parts of it were smashed to pieces by shell-fire and most of the houses pockmarked by rifle-bullets. We were 1500 feet above sea-level now. It was beastly cold, with dense mists that came swirling up from nowhere. Between Sietamo and Alcubierre the lorry-driver lost his way (this was one of the regular features of the war) and we were wandering for hours in the mist. It was late at night when we reached Alcubierre. Somebody shepherded us through morasses of mud into a mule-stable where we dug ourselves down into the chaff and promptly fell asleep. Chaff is not bad to sleep in when it is clean, not so good as hay but better than straw. It was only in the morning light that I discovered that the chaff was full of breadcrusts, torn newspapers, bones, dead rats, and jagged milk tins.

We were near the front line now, near enough to smell the characteristic smell of war—in my experience a smell of excrement and decaying food. Alcubierre had never been shelled and was in a better state than most of the villages immediately behind the line. Yet I believe that even in peacetime you could not travel in that part of Spain without being struck by the peculiar squalid misery of the Aragónese villages. They are built like fortresses, a mass of mean little houses of mud and stone huddling round the church, and even in spring you see hardly a flower anywhere; the houses have no gardens, only back-yards where ragged fowls skate over the beds of mule-dung. It was vile weather, with alternate mist and rain. The narrow earth roads had been churned into a sea of mud, in places two feet deep, through which the lorries struggled with racing wheels and the peasants led their clumsy carts which were pulled by strings of mules, sometimes as many as six in a string, always pulling tandem. The constant come-and-go of troops had reduced the village to a state of unspeakable filth. It did not possess and never had possessed such a thing as a lavatory or a drain of any kind, and there was not a square yard anywhere where you could tread without watching your step. The church had long been used as a latrine; so had all the fields for a quarter of a mile round. I never think of my first two months at war without thinking of wintry stubble fields whose edges are crusted with dung.

Two days passed and no rifles were issued to us. When you had been to the *Comite de Guerra* and inspected the row of holes in the wall-holes made by rifle-volleys, various Fascists having been executed there—you had seen all the sights that Alcubierre contained. Up in the front line things were obviously quiet; very few wounded were coming in. The chief excitement was the arrival of Fascist deserters, who were brought under guard from the front line. Many of the troops opposite us on this part of the line were not Fascists at all, merely wretched conscripts who had been doing their military service at the time when war broke out and were only too anxious to escape. Occasionally small batches of them took the risk of slipping across to our lines. No doubt more would have done so if their relatives had not been in Fascist territory. These deserters were the first 'real' Fascists I had ever seen. It struck me that they were indistinguishable from ourselves, except that they wore khaki overalls. They were always ravenously hungry when they arrived—natural enough after a day or two of dodging about in no man's land, but it was always triumphantly pointed to as a proof that the Fascist troops were starving. I watched one of them being fed in a peasant's house. It was somehow rather a pitiful sight. A tall boy of twenty, deeply windburnt, with his clothes in rags, crouched over the fire shovelling a pannikinful of stew into himself at desperate speed; and all the while his eyes flitted nervously round the ring of militiamen who stood watching him. I think he still half-believed that we were bloodthirsty 'Reds' and were going to shoot him as soon as he had finished his meal; the armed man who guarded him kept stroking his shoulder and making reassuring noises. On one memorable day fifteen deserters arrived in a single batch. They were led through the village in triumph with a man riding in front of them on a white horse. I managed to take a rather blurry photograph which was stolen from me later.

On our third morning in Alcubierre the rifles arrived. A sergeant with a coarse dark-yellow face was handing them out in the mule-stable. I got a shock of dismay when I saw the thing they gave me. It was a German Mauser dated 1896—more than forty years old! It was rusty, the bolt was stiff, the wooden barrel-guard was split; one glance down the muzzle showed that it was corroded and past praying for. Most of the rifles were equally bad, some of them even worse, and no attempt was made to give the best weapons to the men who knew how to use them. The best rifle of the lot, only ten years old, was given to a half-witted little beast of fifteen, known to everyone as the _maricón_ (Nancy-boy). The sergeant gave us five minutes' 'instruction', which consisted in explaining how you loaded a rifle and how you took the bolt to pieces. Many of the militiamen had never had a gun in their hands before, and very few, I imagine, knew what the sights were for. Cartridges were handed out, fifty to a man, and then the ranks were formed and we strapped our kits on our backs and set out for the front line, about three miles away.

The _*centuria*_, eighty men and several dogs, wound raggedly up the road. Every militia column had at least one dog attached to it as a mascot. One wretched brute that marched with us had had P.O.U.M. branded on it in huge letters and slunk along as though conscious that there was something wrong with its appearance. At the head of the column, beside the red flag, Georges Kopp, the stout Belgian _*commandante*_, was riding a black horse; a little way ahead a youth from the brigand-like militia cavalry pranced to and fro, galloping up every piece of rising ground and posing himself in picturesque attitudes at the summit. The splendid horses of the Spanish cavalry had been captured in large numbers during the revolution and handed over to the militia, who, of course, were busy riding them to death.

The road wound between yellow infertile fields, untouched since last year's harvest. Ahead of us was the low sierra that lies between Alcubierre and Zaragoza. We were getting near the front line now, near the bombs, the machine-guns, and the mud. In secret I was frightened. I knew the line was quiet at present, but unlike most of the men about me I was old enough to remember the Great War, though not old enough to have fought in it. War, to me, meant roaring projectiles and skipping shards of steel; above all it meant mud, lice, hunger, and cold. It is curious, but I dreaded the cold much more than I dreaded the enemy. The thought of it had been haunting me all the time I was in Barcelona; I had even lain awake at nights thinking of the cold in the trenches, the stand-to's in the grisly dawns, the long hours on sentry-go with a frosted rifle, the icy mud that would slop over my boot-tops. I admit, too, that I felt a kind of horror as I looked at the people I was marching among. You cannot possibly conceive what a rabble we looked. We straggled along with far less cohesion than a flock of sheep; before we had gone two miles the rear of the column was out of sight. And quite half of the so-called men were children—but I mean literally children, of sixteen years old at the very most. Yet they were all happy and excited at the prospect of getting to the front at last. As we neared the line the boys round the red flag in front began to utter shouts of '_*Visca* P.O.U.M.!_' '_*Fascistas—maricones*_!' and so forth—shouts which were meant to be war-like and menacing, but which, from those childish throats, sounded as pathetic as the cries of kittens. It seemed dreadful that the defenders of the Republic should be this mob of ragged children carrying worn-out rifles which they did not know how to use. I remember wondering what would happen if a Fascist aeroplane passed our way whether the airman would even bother to dive down and give us a burst from his machine-gun. Surely even from the air he could see that we were not real soldiers?

As the road struck into the sierra we branched off to the right and climbed a narrow mule-track that wound round the mountain-side. The hills in that part of Spain are of a queer formation, horseshoe-shaped with flattish tops and very steep sides running down into immense ravines. On the higher slopes nothing grows except stunted shrubs and heath, with the white bones of the limestone sticking out everywhere. The front line here was not a continuous line of trenches, which would have been impossible in such mountainous country; it was simply a chain of fortified posts, always known as 'positions', perched on each hill-top. In the distance you could see our 'position' at the crown of the horseshoe; a ragged barricade of sand-bags, a red flag fluttering, the smoke of dug-out fires. A little nearer, and you could smell a sickening sweetish stink that lived in my nostrils for weeks afterwards. Into the cleft immediately behind the position all the refuse of months had been tipped—a deep festering bed of breadcrusts, excrement, and rusty tins.

The company we were relieving were getting their kits together. They had been three months in the line; their uniforms were caked with mud, their boots falling to pieces, their faces mostly bearded. The captain commanding the position, Levinski by name, but known to everyone as Benjamin, and by birth a Polish Jew, but speaking French as his native language, crawled out of his dug-out and greeted us. He was a short youth of about twenty-five, with stiff black hair and a pale eager face which at this period of the war was always very dirty. A few stray bullets were cracking high overhead. The position was a semi-circular enclosure about fifty yards across, with a parapet that was partly sand-bags and partly lumps of limestone. There were thirty or forty dug-outs running into the ground like rat-holes. Williams, myself, and Williams's Spanish brother-in-law made a swift dive for the nearest unoccupied dug-out that looked habitable. Somewhere in front an occasional rifle banged, making queer rolling echoes among the stony hills. We had just dumped our kits and were crawling out of the dug-out when there was another bang and one of the children of our company rushed back from the parapet with his face pouring blood. He had fired his rifle and had somehow managed to blow out the bolt; his scalp was torn to ribbons by the splinters of the burst cartridge-case. It was our first casualty, and, characteristically, self-inflicted.

In the afternoon we did our first guard and Benjamin showed us round the position. In front of the parapet there ran a system of narrow trenches hewn out of the rock, with extremely primitive loopholes made of piles of limestone. There were twelve sentries, placed at various points in the trench and behind the inner parapet.

In front of the trench was the barbed wire, and then the hillside slid down into a seemingly bottomless ravine; opposite were naked hills, in places mere cliffs of rock, all grey and wintry, with no life anywhere, not even a bird. I peered cautiously through a loophole, trying to find the Fascist trench.

'Where are the enemy?'

Benjamin waved his hand expansively. 'Over zere.' (Benjamin spoke English—terrible English.)

'But _where?_'

According to my ideas of trench warfare the Fascists would be fifty or a hundred yards away. I could see nothing—seemingly their trenches were very well concealed. Then with a shock of dismay I saw where Benjamin was pointing; on the opposite hill-top, beyond the ravine, seven hundred metres away at the very least, the tiny outline of a parapet and a red-and-yellow flag—the Fascist position. I was indescribably disappointed. We were nowhere near them! At that range our rifles were completely useless. But at this moment there was a shout of excitement. Two Fascists, greyish figurines in the distance, were scrambling up the naked hill-side opposite. Benjamin grabbed the nearest man's rifle, took aim, and pulled the trigger. Click! A dud cartridge; I thought it a bad omen.

The new sentries were no sooner in the trench than they began firing a terrific fusillade at nothing in particular. I could see the Fascists, tiny as ants, dodging to and fro behind their parapet, and sometimes a black dot which was a head would pause for a moment, impudently exposed. It was obviously no use firing. But presently the sentry on my left, leaving his post in the typical Spanish fashion, sidled up to me and began urging me to fire. I tried to explain that at that range and with these rifles you could not hit a man except by accident. But he was only a child, and he kept motioning with his rifle towards one of the dots, grinning as eagerly as a dog that expects a pebble to be thrown. Finally I put my sights up to seven hundred and let fly. The dot disappeared. I hope it went near enough to make him jump. It was the first time in my life that I had fired a gun at a human being.

Now that I had seen the front I was profoundly disgusted. They called this war! And we were hardly even in touch with the enemy! I made no attempt to keep my head below the level of the trench. A little while later, however, a bullet shot past my ear with a vicious crack and banged into the parados behind. Alas! I ducked. All my life I had sworn that I would not duck the first time a bullet passed over me; but the movement appears to be instinctive, and almost everybody does it at least once.

CHAPTER 3

In trench warfare five things are important: firewood, food, tobacco, candles, and the enemy. In winter on the Zaragoza front they were important in that order, with the enemy a bad last. Except at night, when a surprise-attack was always conceivable, nobody bothered about the enemy. They were simply remote black insects whom one occasionally saw hopping to and fro. The real preoccupation of both armies was trying to keep warm.

I ought to say in passing that all the time I was in Spain I saw very little fighting. I was on the Aragón front from January to May, and between January and late March little or nothing happened on that front, except at Teruel. In March there was heavy fighting round Huesca, but I personally played only a minor part in it. Later, in June, there was the disastrous attack on Huesca in which several thousand men were killed in a single day, but I had been wounded and disabled before that happened. The things that one normally thinks of as the horrors of war seldom happened to me. No aeroplane ever dropped a bomb anywhere near me, I do not think a shell ever exploded within fifty yards of me, and I was only in hand-to-hand fighting once (once is once too often, I may say). Of course I was often under heavy machine-gun fire, but usually at longish ranges. Even at Huesca you were generally safe enough if you took reasonable precautions.

Up here, in the hills round Zaragoza, it was simply the mingled boredom and discomfort of stationary warfare. A life as uneventful as a city clerk's, and almost as regular. Sentry-go, patrols, digging;

digging, patrols, sentry-go. On every hill-top, Fascist or Loyalist, a knot of ragged, dirty men shivering round their flag and trying to keep warm. And all day and night the meaningless bullets wandering across the empty valleys and only by some rare improbable chance getting home on a human body.

Often I used to gaze round the wintry landscape and marvel at the futility of it all. The inconclusiveness of such a kind of war! Earlier, about October, there had been savage fighting for all these hills; then, because the lack of men and arms, especially artillery, made any large-scale operation impossible, each army had dug itself in and settled down on the hill-tops it had won. Over to our right there was a small outpost, also P.O.U.M., and on the spur to our left, at seven o'clock of us, a P.S.U.C. position faced a taller spur with several small Fascist posts dotted on its peaks. The so-called line zigzagged to and fro in a pattern that would have been quite unintelligible if every position had not flown a flag. The P.O.U.M. and P.S.U.C. flags were red, those of the Anarchists red and black; the Fascists generally flew the monarchist flag (red-yellow-red), but occasionally they flew the flag of the Republic (red-yellow-purple).[1] The scenery was stupendous, if you could forget that every mountain-top was occupied by troops and was therefore littered with tin cans and crusted with dung. To the right of us the *sierra* bent south-eastwards and made way for the wide, veined valley that stretched across to Huesca. In the middle of the plain a few tiny cubes sprawled like a throw of dice; this was the town of *Robres*, which was in Loyalist possession. Often in the mornings the valley was hidden under seas of cloud, out of which the hills rose flat and blue, giving the landscape a strange resemblance to a photographic

---

[1] An errata note found in Orwell's papers after his death: "Am not now completely certain that I ever saw Fascists flying the republican flag, though I _think_ they sometimes flew it with a small imposed swastika."

negative. Beyond Huesca there were more hills of the same formation as our own, streaked with a pattern of snow which altered day by day. In the far distance the monstrous peaks of the Pyrenees, where the snow never melts, seemed to float upon nothing. Even down in the plain everything looked dead and bare. The hills opposite us were grey and wrinkled like the skins of elephants. Almost always the sky was empty of birds. I do not think I have ever seen a country where there were so few birds. The only birds one saw at any time were a kind of magpie, and the coveys of partridges that startled one at night with their sudden whirring, and, very rarely, the flights of eagles that drifted slowly over, generally followed by rifle-shots which they did not deign to notice.

At night and in misty weather, patrols were sent out in the valley between ourselves and the Fascists. The job was not popular, it was too cold and too easy to get lost, and I soon found that I could get leave to go out on patrol as often as I wished. In the huge jagged ravines there were no paths or tracks of any kind; you could only find your way about by making successive journeys and noting fresh landmarks each time. As the bullet flies the nearest Fascist post was seven hundred metres from our own, but it was a mile and a half by the only practicable route. It was rather fun wandering about the dark valleys with the stray bullets flying high overhead like redshanks whistling. Better than night-time were the heavy mists, which often lasted all day and which had a habit of clinging round the hill-tops and leaving the valleys clear. When you were anywhere near the Fascist lines you had to creep at a snail's pace; it was very difficult to move quietly on those hill-sides, among the crackling shrubs and tinkling limestones. It was only at the third or fourth attempt that I managed to find my way to the Fascist lines. The mist was very thick, and I crept up to the barbed wire to listen. I could hear the Fascists talking and singing inside. Then to my alarm I heard several of them coming down the hill towards me. I cowered behind a bush that suddenly seemed very small, and tried to cock my rifle without noise. However, they branched off and did not come within sight of me. Behind the bush where I was hiding I came upon various relics of the earlier fighting—a pile of empty cartridge-cases, a leather cap with a bullet-hole in it, and a red flag, obviously one of our own. I took it back to the position, where it was unsentimentally torn up for cleaning-rags.

I had been made a corporal, or _*cabo*_, as it was called, as soon as we reached the front, and was in command of a guard of twelve men. It was no sinecure, especially at first. The _*centuria*_ was an untrained mob composed mostly of boys in their teens. Here and there in the militia you came across children as young as eleven or twelve, usually refugees from Fascist territory who had been enlisted as militiamen as the easiest way of providing for them. As a rule they were employed on light work in the rear, but sometimes they managed to worm their way to the front line, where they were a public menace. I remember one little brute throwing a hand-grenade into the dug-out fire 'for a joke'. At Monte Pocero I do not think there was anyone younger than fifteen, but the average age must have been well under twenty. Boys of this age ought never to be used in the front line, because they cannot stand the lack of sleep which is inseparable from trench warfare. At the beginning it was almost impossible to keep our position properly guarded at night. The wretched children of my section could only be roused by dragging them out of their dug-outs feet foremost, and as soon as your back was turned they left their posts and slipped into shelter; or they would even, in spite of the frightful cold, lean up against the wall of the trench and fall fast asleep. Luckily the enemy were very unenterprising. There were nights when it seemed to me that our position could be stormed by twenty Boy Scouts armed with airguns, or twenty Girl Guides armed with battledores, for that matter.

At this time and until much later the Catalan militias were still on the same basis as they had been at the beginning of the war. In the early days of Franco's revolt the militias had been hurriedly raised by the various trade unions and political parties; each was essentially a political organization, owing allegiance to its party as much as to the central Government. When the Popular Army, which was a 'non-political' army organized on more or less ordinary lines, was raised at the beginning of 1937, the party militias were theoretically incorporated in it. But for a long time the only changes that occurred were on paper; the new Popular Army troops did not reach the Aragón front in any numbers till June, and until that time the militia-system remained unchanged. The essential point of the system was social equality between officers and men. Everyone from general to private drew the same pay, ate the same food, wore the same clothes, and mingled on terms of complete equality. If you wanted to slap the general commanding the division on the back and ask him for a cigarette, you could do so, and no one thought it curious. In theory at any rate each militia was a democracy and not a hierarchy. It was understood that orders had to be obeyed, but it was also understood that when you gave an order you gave it as comrade to comrade and not as superior to inferior. There were officers and N.C.O.s but there was no military rank in the ordinary sense; no titles, no badges, no heel-clicking and saluting. They had attempted to produce within the militias a sort of temporary working model of the classless society. Of course there was no perfect equality, but there was a nearer approach to it than I had ever seen or than I would have thought conceivable in time of war.

But I admit that at first sight the state of affairs at the front horrified me. How on earth could the war be won by an army of this type? It was what everyone was saying at the time, and though it was true it was also unreasonable. For in the circumstances the militias could not have been much better than they were. A modern mechanized army does not spring up out of the ground, and if the Government had waited until it had trained troops at its disposal, Franco would never have been resisted. Later it became the fashion to decry the militias, and therefore to pretend that the faults which were due to lack of training and weapons were the result of the equalitarian system. Actually, a newly raised draft of militia was an undisciplined mob not because the officers called the private 'Comrade' but because raw troops are _always_ an undisciplined mob. In practice the democratic 'revolutionary' type of discipline is more reliable than might be expected. In a workers' army discipline is theoretically voluntary. It is based on class-loyalty, whereas the discipline of a bourgeois conscript army is based ultimately on fear. (The Popular Army that replaced the militias was midway between the two types.) In the militias the bullying and abuse that go on in an ordinary army would never have been tolerated for a moment. The normal military punishments existed, but they were only invoked for very serious offences. When a man refused to obey an order you did not immediately get him punished; you first appealed to him in the name of comradeship. Cynical people with no experience of handling men will say instantly that this would never 'work', but as a matter of fact it does 'work' in the long run. The discipline of even the worst drafts of militia visibly improved as time went on. In January the job of keeping a dozen raw recruits up to the mark almost turned my hair grey. In May for a short while I was acting-lieutenant in command of about thirty men, English and Spanish. We had all been under fire for months, and I never had the slightest difficulty in getting an order obeyed or in getting men to volunteer for a dangerous job. 'Revolutionary' discipline depends on political consciousness—on an understanding of _why_ orders must be obeyed; it takes time to diffuse this, but it also takes time to drill a man into an automaton on the barrack-square. The journalists who sneered at the militia-system seldom remembered that the militias had to hold the line while the Popular Army was training in the rear. And it is a tribute to the strength of 'revolutionary' discipline that the militias stayed in the field at all. For until about June 1937 there was nothing to keep them there, except class loyalty. Individual deserters could be shot—were shot, occasionally—but if a thousand men had decided to walk out of the line together there was no force to stop them. A conscript army in the same circumstances—with its battle-police removed—would have melted away. Yet the militias held the line, though God knows they won very few victories, and even individual desertions were not common. In four or five months in the P.O.U.M. militia I only heard of four men deserting, and two of those were fairly certainly spies who had enlisted to obtain information. At the beginning the apparent chaos, the general lack of training, the fact that you often had to argue for five minutes before you could get an order obeyed, appalled and infuriated me. I had British Army ideas, and certainly the Spanish militias were very unlike the British Army. But considering the circumstances they were better troops than one had any right to expect.

Meanwhile, firewood—always firewood. Throughout that period there is probably no entry in my diary that does not mention firewood, or rather the lack of it. We were between two and three thousand feet above sea-level, it was mid winter and the cold was unspeakable. The temperature was not exceptionally low, on many nights it did not even freeze, and the wintry sun often shone for an hour in the middle of the day; but even if it was not really cold, I assure you that it seemed so. Sometimes there were shrieking winds that tore your cap off and twisted your hair in all directions, sometimes there were mists that poured into the trench like a liquid and seemed to penetrate your bones; frequently it rained, and even a quarter of an hour's rain was enough to make conditions intolerable. The thin skin of earth over the limestone turned promptly into a slippery grease, and as you were always walking on a slope it was impossible to keep your footing. On dark nights I have often fallen half a dozen times in twenty yards; and this was dangerous, because it meant that the lock of one's rifle became jammed with mud. For days together clothes, boots, blankets, and rifles were more or less coated with mud. I had brought as many thick clothes as I could carry, but many of the men were terribly underclad. For the whole garrison, about a hundred men, there were only twelve great-coats, which had to be handed from sentry to sentry, and most of the men had only one blanket. One icy night I made a list in my diary of the clothes I was wearing. It is of some interest as showing the amount of clothes the human body can carry. I was wearing a thick vest and pants, a flannel shirt, two pull-overs, a woollen jacket, a pigskin jacket, corduroy breeches, puttees, thick socks, boots, a stout trench-coat, a muffler, lined leather gloves, and a woollen cap. Nevertheless I was shivering like a jelly. But I admit I am unusually sensitive to cold.

Firewood was the one thing that really mattered. The point about the firewood was that there was practically no firewood to be had. Our miserable mountain had not even at its best much vegetation, and for months it had been ranged over by freezing militiamen, with the result that everything thicker than one's finger had long since been burnt. When we were not eating, sleeping, on guard, or on fatigue-duty we were in the valley behind the position, scrounging for fuel. All my memories of that time are memories of scrambling up and down the almost perpendicular slopes, over the jagged limestone that knocked one's boots to pieces, pouncing eagerly on tiny twigs of wood. Three people searching for a couple of hours could collect enough fuel to keep the dug-out fire alight for about an hour. The eagerness of our search for firewood turned us all into botanists. We classified according to their burning qualities every plant that grew on the mountainside; the various heaths and grasses that were good to start a fire with but burnt out in a few minutes, the wild rosemary and the tiny whin bushes that would burn when the fire was well alight, the stunted oak tree, smaller than a gooseberry bush, that was practically unburnable. There was a kind of dried-up reed that was very good for starting fires with, but these grew only on the hill-top to the left of the position, and you had to go under fire to get them. If the Fascist machine-gunners saw you they gave you a drum of ammunition all to yourself. Generally their aim was high and the bullets sang overhead like birds, but sometime they crackled and chipped the limestone uncomfortably close, whereupon you flung yourself on your face. You went on gathering reeds, however; nothing mattered in comparison with firewood.

Beside the cold the other discomforts seemed petty. Of course all of us were permanently dirty. Our water, like our food, came on mule-back from Alcubierre, and each man's share worked out at about a quart a day. It was beastly water, hardly more transparent than milk. Theoretically it was for drinking only, but I always stole a pannikinful for washing in the mornings. I used to wash one day and shave the next; there was never enough water for both. The position stank abominably, and outside the little enclosure of the barricade there was excrement everywhere. Some of the militiamen habitually defecated in the trench, a disgusting thing when one had to walk round it in the darkness. But the dirt never worried me. Dirt is a thing people make too much fuss about. It is astonishing how quickly you get used to doing without a handkerchief and to eating out of the tin pannikin in which you also wash. Nor was sleeping in one's clothes any hardship after a day or two. It was of course impossible to take one's clothes and especially one's boots off at night; one had to be ready to turn out instantly in case of an attack. In eighty nights I only took my clothes off three times, though I did occasionally manage to get them off in the daytime. It was too cold for lice as yet, but rats and mice abounded. It is often said that you don't find rats and mice in the same place, but you do when there is enough food for them.

In other ways we were not badly off. The food was good enough and there was plenty of wine. Cigarettes were still being issued at the rate of a packet a day, matches were issued every other day, and there was even an issue of candles. They were very thin candles, like those on a Christmas cake, and were popularly supposed to have been looted from churches. Every dug-out was issued daily with three inches of candle, which would bum for about twenty minutes. At that time it was still possible to buy candles, and I had brought several pounds of them with me. Later on the famine of matches and candles made life a misery. You do not realize the importance of these things until you lack them. In a night-alarm, for instance, when everyone in the dug-out is scrambling for his rifle and treading on everybody else's face, being able to strike a light may make the difference between life and death. Every militiaman possessed a tinder-lighter and several yards of yellow wick. Next to his rifle it was his most important possession. The tinder-lighters had the great advantage that they could be struck in a wind, but they would only smoulder, so that they were no use for lighting a fire. When the match famine was at its worst our only way of producing a flame was to pull the bullet out of a cartridge and touch the cordite off with a tinder-lighter.

It was an extraordinary life that we were living—an extraordinary way to be at war, if you could call it war. The whole militia chafed against the inaction and clamoured constantly to know why we were not allowed to attack. But it was perfectly obvious that there would be no battle for a long while yet, unless the enemy started it. Georges Kopp, on his periodical tours of inspection, was quite frank with us. 'This is not a war,' he used to say, 'it is a comic opera with an occasional death.' As a matter of fact the stagnation on the Aragón front had political causes of which I knew nothing at that time; but the purely military difficulties—quite apart from the lack of reserves of men—were obvious to anybody.

To begin with, there was the nature of the country. The front line, ours and the Fascists', lay in positions of immense natural strength, which as a rule could only be approached from one side. Provided a few trenches have been dug, such places cannot be taken by infantry, except in overwhelming numbers. In our own position or most of those round us a dozen men with two machine-guns could have held off a battalion. Perched on the hill-tops as we were, we should have made lovely marks for artillery; but there was no artillery. Sometimes I used to gaze round the landscape and long—oh, how passionately!—for a couple of batteries of guns. One could have destroyed the enemy positions one after another as easily as smashing nuts with a hammer. But on our side the guns simply did not exist. The Fascists did occasionally manage to bring a gun or two from Zaragoza and fire a very few shells, so few that they never even found the range and the shells plunged harmlessly into the empty ravines. Against machine-guns and without artillery there are only three things you can do: dig yourself in at a safe distance—four hundred yards, say—advance across the open and be massacred, or make small-scale night-attacks that will not alter the general situation. Practically the alternatives are stagnation or suicide.

And beyond this there was the complete lack of war materials of every description. It needs an effort to realize how badly the militias were armed at this time. Any public school O.T.C. in England is far more like a modern army than we were. The badness of our weapons was so astonishing that it is worth recording in detail.

For this sector of the front the entire artillery consisted of four trench-mortars with _fifteen rounds_ for each gun. Of course they were far too precious to be fired and the mortars were kept in Alcubierre. There were machine-guns at the rate of approximately one to fifty men; they were oldish guns, but fairly accurate up to three or four hundred yards. Beyond this we had only rifles, and the majority of the rifles were scrap-iron. There were three types of rifle in use. The first was the long Mauser. These were seldom less than twenty years old, their sights were about as much use as a broken speedometer, and in most of them the rifling was hopelessly corroded; about one rifle in ten was not bad, however. Then there was the short Mauser, or mousqueton, really a cavalry weapon. These were more popular than the others because they were lighter to carry and less nuisance in a trench, also because they were comparatively new and looked efficient. Actually they were almost useless. They were made out of reassembled parts, no bolt belonged to its rifle, and three-quarters of them could be counted on to jam after five shots. There were also a few Winchester rifles. These were nice to shoot with, but they were wildly inaccurate, and as their cartridges had no clips they could only be fired one shot at a time. Ammunition was so scarce that each man entering the line was only issued with fifty rounds, and most of it was exceedingly bad. The Spanish-made cartridges were all refills and would jam even the best rifles. The Mexican cartridges were better and were therefore reserved for the machine-guns. Best of all was the German-made ammunition, but as this came only from prisoners and deserters there was not much of it. I always kept a clip of German or Mexican ammunition in my pocket for use in an emergency. But in practice when the emergency came I seldom fired my rifle; I was too frightened of the beastly thing jamming and too anxious to reserve at any rate one round that would go off.

We had no tin hats, no bayonets, hardly any revolvers or pistols, and not more than one bomb between five or ten men. The bomb in use at this time was a frightful object known as the 'F.A.I. bomb', it having been produced by the Anarchists in the early days of the war. It was on the principle of a Mills bomb, but the lever was held down not by a pin but a piece of tape. You broke the tape and then got rid of the bomb with the utmost possible speed. It was said of these bombs that they were 'impartial'; they killed the man they were thrown at and the man who threw them. There were several other types, even more primitive but probably a little less dangerous—to the thrower, I mean. It was not till late March that I saw a bomb worth throwing.

And apart from weapons there was a shortage of all the minor necessities of war. We had no maps or charts, for instance. Spain has never been fully surveyed, and the only detailed maps of this area were the old military ones, which were almost all in the possession of the Fascists. We had no range-finders, no telescopes, no periscopes, no field-glasses except for a few privately-owned pairs, no flares or Very lights, no wire-cutters, no armourers' tools, hardly even any cleaning materials. The Spaniards seemed never to have heard of a pull-through and looked on in surprise when I constructed one. When you wanted your rifle cleaned you took it to the sergeant, who possessed a long brass ramrod which was invariably bent and therefore scratched the rifling. There was not even any gun oil. You greased your rifle with olive oil, when you could get hold of it; at different times I have greased mine with vaseline, with cold cream, and even with bacon-fat. Moreover, there were no lanterns or electric torches—at this time there was not, I believe, such a thing as an electric torch throughout the whole of our sector of the front, and you could not buy one nearer than Barcelona, and only with difficulty even there.

As time went on, and the desultory rifle-fire rattled among the hills, I began to wonder with increasing scepticism whether anything would ever happen to bring a bit of life, or rather a bit of death, into this cock-eyed war. It was pneumonia that we were fighting against, not against men. When the trenches are more than five hundred yards apart no one gets hit except by accident. Of course there were casualties, but the majority of them were self-inflicted. If I remember rightly, the first five men I saw wounded in Spain were all wounded by our own weapons—I don't mean intentionally, but owing to accident or carelessness. Our worn-out rifles were a danger in themselves. Some of them had a nasty trick of going off if the butt was tapped on the ground; I saw a man shoot himself through the hand owing to this. And in the darkness the raw recruits were always firing at one another. One evening when it was barely even dusk a sentry let fly at me from a distance of twenty yards; but he missed me by a yard—goodness knows how many times the Spanish standard of marksmanship has saved my life. Another time I had gone out on patrol in the mist and had carefully warned the guard commander beforehand. But in coming back I stumbled against a bush, the startled sentry called out that the Fascists were coming, and I had the pleasure of hearing the guard commander order everyone to open rapid fire in my direction. Of course I lay down and the bullets went harmlessly over me. Nothing will convince a Spaniard, at least a young Spaniard, that fire-arms are dangerous. Once, rather later than this, I was photographing some machine-gunners with their gun, which was pointed directly towards me.

'Don't fire,' I said half-jokingly as I focused the camera.

'Oh no, we won't fire.'

The next moment there was a frightful roar and a stream of bullets tore past my face so close that my cheek was stung by grains of cordite. It was unintentional, but the machine-gunners considered it a great joke. Yet only a few days earlier they had seen a mule-driver accidentally shot by a political delegate who was playing the fool with an automatic pistol and had put five bullets in the mule-driver's lungs.

The difficult passwords which the army was using at this time were a minor source of danger. They were those tiresome double passwords in which one word has to be answered by another. Usually they were of an elevating and revolutionary nature, such as

Cultura—progreso, or _Seremos—invencibles_, and it was often impossible to get illiterate sentries to remember these highfalutin' words. One night, I remember, the password was _Cataluña—heroica_, and a moonfaced peasant lad named Jaime Domenech approached me, greatly puzzled, and asked me to explain.

'_Heroica_—what does _heroica_ mean?'

I told him that it meant the same as _valiente_. A little while later he was stumbling up the trench in the darkness, and the sentry challenged him:

> '_Alto! Cataluña_!'

'_Valiente!_' yelled Jaime, certain that he was saying the right thing.

Bang!

However, the sentry missed him. In this war everyone always did miss everyone else, when it was humanly possible.

CHAPTER 4

When I had been about three weeks in the line a contingent of twenty or thirty men, sent out from England by the I.L.P., arrived at Alcubierre, and in order to keep the English on this front together Williams and I were sent to join them. Our new position was at Monte Oscuro, several miles farther west and within sight of Zaragoza.

The position was perched on a sort of razor-back of limestone with dug-outs driven horizontally into the cliff like sand-martins'nests. They went into the ground for prodigious distances, and inside they were pitch dark and so low that you could not even kneel in them, let alone stand. On the peaks to the left of us there were two more P.O.U.M. positions, one of them an object of fascination to every man in the line, because there were three militiawomen there who did the cooking. These women were not exactly beautiful, but it was found necessary to put the position out of bounds to men of other companies. Five hundred yards to our right there was a P.S.U.C. post at the bend of the Alcubierre road. It was just here that the road changed hands. At night you could watch the lamps of our supply-lorries winding out from Alcubierre and, simultaneously, those of the Fascists coming from Zaragoza. You could see Zaragoza itself, a thin string of lights like the lighted portholes of a ship, twelve miles south-westward. The Government troops had gazed at it from that distance since August 1936, and they are gazing at it still.

There were about thirty of ourselves, including one Spaniard (Ramon, Williams's brother-in-law), and there were a dozen Spanish machine-gunners. Apart from the one or two inevitable nuisances—for, as everyone knows, war attracts riff-raff—the English were an exceptionally good crowd, both physically and mentally. Perhaps the best of the bunch was Bob Smillie—the grandson of the famous miners' leader—who afterwards died such an evil and meaningless death in Valencia. It says a lot for the Spanish character that the English and the Spaniards always got on well together, in spite of the language difficulty. All Spaniards, we discovered, knew two English expressions. One was 'O.K., baby', the other was a word used by the Barcelona whores in their dealings with English sailors, and I am afraid the compositors would not print it.

Once again there was nothing happening all along the line: only the random crack of bullets and, very rarely, the crash of a Fascist mortar that sent everyone running to the top trench to see which hill the shells were bursting on. The enemy was somewhat closer to us here, perhaps three or four hundred yards away. Their nearest position was exactly opposite ours, with a machine-gun nest whose loopholes constantly tempted one to waste cartridges. The Fascists seldom bothered with rifle-shots, but sent bursts of accurate machine-gun fire at anyone who exposed himself. Nevertheless it was ten days or more before we had our first casualty. The troops opposite us were Spaniards, but according to the deserters there were a few German N.C.O.S. among them. At some time in the past there had also been Moors there—poor devils, how they must have felt the cold!—for out in no man's land there was a dead Moor who was one of the sights of the locality. A mile or two to the left of us the line ceased to be continuous and there was a tract of country, lower-lying and thickly wooded, which belonged neither to the Fascists nor ourselves. Both we and they used to make daylight patrols there. It was not bad fun in a Boy Scoutish way, though I never saw a Fascist patrol nearer than several hundred yards. By a lot of crawling on your belly you could work your way partly through the Fascist lines and could even see the farm-house flying the monarchist flag, which was the local Fascist headquarters. Occasionally we gave it a rifle-volley and then slipped into cover before the machine-guns could locate us. I hope we broke a few windows, but it was a good eight hundred metres away, and with our rifles you could not make sure of hitting even a house at that range.

The weather was mostly clear and cold; sometimes sunny at midday, but always cold. Here and there in the soil of the hill-sides you found the green beaks of wild crocuses or irises poking through; evidently spring was coming, but coming very slowly. The nights were colder than ever. Coming off guard in the small hours we used to rake together what was left of the cook-house fire and then stand in the red-hot embers. It was bad for your boots, but it was very good for your feet. But there were mornings when the sight of the dawn among the mountain-tops made it almost worth while to be out of bed at godless hours. I hate mountains, even from a spectacular point of view. But sometimes the dawn breaking behind the hill-tops in our rear, the first narrow streaks of gold, like swords slitting the darkness, and then the growing light and the seas of carmine cloud stretching away into inconceivable distances, were worth watching even when you had been up all night, when your legs were numb from the knees down, and you were sullenly reflecting that there was no hope of food for another three hours. I saw the dawn oftener during this campaign than during the rest of my life put together—or during the part that is to come, I hope.

We were short-handed here, which meant longer guards and more fatigues. I was beginning to suffer a little from the lack of sleep which is inevitable even in the quietest kind of war. Apart from guard-duties and patrols there were constant night-alarms and stand-to's, and in any case you can't sleep properly in a beastly hole in the ground with your feet aching with the cold. In my first three or four months in the line I do not suppose I had more than a dozen periods of twenty-four hours that were completely without sleep; on the other hand I certainly did not have a dozen nights of full sleep. Twenty or thirty hours' sleep in a week was quite a normal amount. The effects of this were not so bad as might be expected; one grew very stupid, and the job of climbing up and down the hills grew harder instead of easier, but one felt well and one was constantly hungry—heavens, how hungry! All food seemed good, even the eternal haricot beans which everyone in Spain finally learned to hate the sight of. Our water, what there was of it, came from miles away, on the backs of mules or little persecuted donkeys. For some reason the Aragón peasants treated their mules well but their donkeys abominably. If a donkey refused to go it was quite usual to kick him in the testicles. The issue of candles had ceased, and matches were running short. The Spaniards taught us how to make olive oil lamps out of a condensed milk tin, a cartridge-clip, and a bit of rag. When you had any olive oil, which was not often, these things would burn with a smoky flicker, about a quarter candle power, just enough to find your rifle by.

There seemed no hope of any real fighting. When we left Monte Pocero I had counted my cartridges and found that in nearly three weeks I had fired just three shots at the enemy. They say it takes a thousand bullets to kill a man, and at this rate it would be twenty years before I killed my first Fascist. At Monte Oscuro the lines were closer and one fired oftener, but I am reasonably certain that I never hit anyone. As a matter of fact, on this front and at this period of the war the real weapon was not the rifle but the megaphone. Being unable to kill your enemy you shouted at him instead. This method of warfare is so extraordinary that it needs explaining.

Wherever the lines were within hailing distance of one another there was always a good deal of shouting from trench to trench. From ourselves: '_*Fascistas—maricones!*_' From the Fascists: '_*Viva España*! *Viva* Franco!_'—or, when they knew that there were

English opposite them: 'Go home, you English! We don't want foreigners here!' On the Government side, in the party militias, the shouting of propaganda to undermine the enemy morale had been developed into a regular technique. In every suitable position men, usually machine-gunners, were told off for shouting-duty and provided with megaphones. Generally they shouted a set-piece, full of revolutionary sentiments which explained to the Fascist soldiers that they were merely the hirelings of international capitalism, that they were fighting against their own class, etc., etc., and urged them to come over to our side. This was repeated over and over by relays of men; sometimes it continued almost the whole night. There is very little doubt that it had its effect; everyone agreed that the trickle of Fascist deserters was partly caused by it. If one comes to think of it, when some poor devil of a sentry—very likely a Socialist or Anarchist trade union member who has been conscripted against his will—is freezing at his post, the slogan 'Don't fight against your own class!' ringing again and again through the darkness is bound to make an impression on him. It might make just the difference between deserting and not deserting. Of course such a proceeding does not fit in with the English conception of war. I admit I was amazed and scandalized when I first saw it done. The idea of trying to convert your enemy instead of shooting him! I now think that from any point of view it was a legitimate manoeuvre. In ordinary trench warfare, when there is no artillery, it is extremely difficult to inflict casualties on the enemy without receiving an equal number yourself. If you can immobilize a certain number of men by making them desert, so much the better; deserters are actually more useful to you than corpses, because they can give information. But at the beginning it dismayed all of us; it made us fed that the Spaniards were not taking this war of theirs sufficiently seriously. The man who did the shouting at the P.S.U.C. post down on our right was an artist at the job. Sometimes, instead of shouting revolutionary slogans he simply told the Fascists how much better we were fed than they were. His account of the Government rations was apt to be a little imaginative. 'Buttered toast!'—you could hear his voice echoing across the lonely valley—'We're just sitting down to buttered toast over here! Lovely slices of buttered toast!' I do not doubt that, like the rest of us, he had not seen butter for weeks or months past, but in the icy night the news of buttered toast probably set many a Fascist mouth watering. It even made mine water, though I knew he was lying.

One day in February we saw a Fascist aeroplane approaching. As usual, a machine-gun was dragged into the open and its barrel cocked up, and everyone lay on his back to get a good aim. Our isolated positions were not worth bombing, and as a rule the few Fascist aeroplanes that passed our way circled round to avoid machine-gun fire. This time the aeroplane came straight over, too high up to be worth shooting at, and out of it came tumbling not bombs but white glittering things that turned over and over in the air. A few fluttered down into the position. They were copies of a Fascist newspaper, the _Heraldo de Aragón_, announcing the fall of Málaga.

That night the Fascists made a sort of abortive attack. I was just getting down into kip, half dead with sleep, when there was a heavy stream of bullets overhead and someone shouted into the dug-out: 'They're attacking!' I grabbed my rifle and slithered up to my post, which was at the top of the position, beside the machine-gun. There was utter darkness and diabolical noise. The fire of, I think five machine-guns was pouring upon us, and there was a series of heavy crashes caused by the Fascists flinging bombs over their own parapet in the most idiotic manner. It was intensely dark. Down in the valley to the left of us I could see the greenish flash of rifles where a small party of Fascists, probably a patrol, were chipping in. The bullets were flying round us in the darkness, crack-zip-crack. A few shells came whistling over, but they fell nowhere near us and (as usual in this war) most of them failed to explode. I had a bad moment when yet another machine-gun opened fire from the hill-top in our rear—actually a gun that had been brought up to support us, but at the time it looked as though we were surrounded. Presently our own machine-gun jammed, as it always did jam with those vile cartridges, and the ramrod was lost in the impenetrable darkness. Apparently there was nothing that one could do except stand still and be shot at. The Spanish machine-gunners disdained to take cover, in fact exposed themselves deliberately, so I had to do likewise. Petty though it was, the whole experience was very interesting. It was the first time that I had been properly speaking under fire, and to my humiliation I found that I was horribly frightened. You always, I notice, feel the same when you are under heavy fire—not so much afraid of being hit as afraid because you don't know where you will be hit. You are wondering all the while just where the bullet will nip you, and it gives your whole body a most unpleasant sensitiveness.

After an hour or two the firing slowed down and died away. Meanwhile we had had only one casualty. The Fascists had advanced a couple of machine-guns into no man's land, but they had kept a safe distance and made no attempt to storm our parapet. They were in fact not attacking, merely wasting cartridges and making a cheerful noise to celebrate the fall of Málaga. The chief importance of the affair was that it taught me to read the war news in the papers with a more disbelieving eye. A day or two later the newspapers and the radio published reports of a tremendous attack with cavalry and tanks (up a perpendicular hill-side!) which had been beaten off by the heroic English.

When the Fascists told us that Málaga had fallen we set it down as a lie, but next day there were more convincing rumours, and it must have been a day or two later that it was admitted officially. By degrees the whole disgraceful story leaked out—how the town had been evacuated without firing a shot, and how the fury of the

Italians had fallen not upon the troops, who were gone, but upon the wretched civilian population, some of whom were pursued and machine-gunned for a hundred miles. The news sent a sort of chill all along the line, for, whatever the truth may have been, every man in the militia believed that the loss of Málaga was due to treachery. It was the first talk I had heard of treachery or divided aims. It set up in my mind the first vague doubts about this war in which, hitherto, the rights and wrongs had seemed so beautifully simple.

In mid February we left Monte Oscuro and were sent, together with all the P.O.U.M. troops in this sector, to make a part of the army besieging Huesca. It was a fifty-mile lorry journey across the wintry plain, where the clipped vines were not yet budding and the blades of the winter barley were just poking through the lumpy soil. Four kilometres from our new trenches Huesca glittered small and clear like a city of dolls' houses. Months earlier, when Sietamo was taken, the general commanding the Government troops had said gaily: 'Tomorrow we'll have coffee in Huesca.' It turned out that he was mistaken. There had been bloody attacks, but the town did not fall, and 'Tomorrow we'll have coffee in Huesca' had become a standing joke throughout the army. If I ever go back to Spain I shall make a point of having a cup of coffee in Huesca.

CHAPTER 5

On the eastern side of Huesca, until late March, nothing happened—almost literally nothing. We were twelve hundred metres from the enemy. When the Fascists were driven back into Huesca the Republican Army troops who held this part of the line had not been over-zealous in their advance, so that the line formed a kind of pocket. Later it would have to be advanced—a ticklish job under fire—but for the present the enemy might as well have been nonexistent; our sole preoccupation was keeping warm and getting enough to eat. As a matter of fact there were things in this period that interested me greatly, and I will describe some of them later. But I shall be keeping nearer to the order of events if I try here to give some account of the internal political situation on the Government side.

At the beginning I had ignored the political side of the war, and it was only about this time that it began to force itself upon my attention. If you are not interested in the horrors of party politics, please skip; I am trying to keep the political parts of this narrative in separate chapters for precisely that purpose. But at the same time it would be quite impossible to write about the Spanish war from a purely military angle. It was above all things a political war. No event in it, at any rate during the first year, is intelligible unless one has some grasp of the inter-party struggle that was going on behind the Government lines.

When I came to Spain, and for some time afterwards, I was not only uninterested in the political situation but unaware of it. I knew there was a war on, but I had no notion what kind of a war. If you had asked me why I had joined the militia I should have answered: 'To fight against Fascism,' and if you had asked me what I was fighting for, I should have answered: 'Common decency.' I had accepted the _News Chronicle-New Statesman_ version of the war as the defence of civilization against a maniacal outbreak by an army of Colonel Blimps in the pay of Hitler. The revolutionary atmosphere of Barcelona had attracted me deeply, but I had made no attempt to understand it. As for the kaleidoscope of political parties and trade unions, with their tiresome names—P.S.U.C., P.O.U.M., F.A.I., C.N.T., U.G.T., J.C.I., J.S.U., A.I.T.—they merely exasperated me. It looked at first sight as though Spain were suffering from a plague of initials. I knew that I was serving in something called the P.O.U.M. (I had only joined the P.O.U.M. militia rather than any other because I happened to arrive in Barcelona with I.L.P. papers), but I did not realize that there were serious differences between the political parties. At Monte Pocero, when they pointed to the position on our left and said: 'Those are the Socialists' (meaning the P.S.U.C.), I was puzzled and said: 'Aren't we all Socialists?' I thought it idiotic that people fighting for their lives should _have_ separate parties; my attitude always was, 'Why can't we drop all this political nonsense and get on with the war?' This of course was the correct 'anti-Fascist' attitude which had been carefully disseminated by the English newspapers, largely in order to prevent people from grasping the real nature of the struggle. But in Spain, especially in Catalonia, it was an attitude that no one could or did keep up indefinitely. Everyone, however unwillingly, took sides sooner or later. For even if one cared nothing for the political parties and their conflicting 'lines', it was too obvious that one's own destiny was involved. As a militiaman one was a soldier against Franco, but one was also a pawn in an enormous struggle that was being fought out between two political theories. When I scrounged for firewood on the mountainside and wondered whether this was really a war or whether the News Chronicle had made it up, when I dodged the Communist machine-guns in the Barcelona riots, when I finally fled from Spain with the police one jump behind me—all these things happened to me in that particular way because I was serving in the P.O.U.M. militia and not in the P.S.U.C. So great is the difference between two sets of initials!

To understand the alignment on the Government side one has got to remember how the war started. When the fighting broke out on 18 July it is probable that every anti-Fascist in Europe felt a thrill of hope. For here at last, apparently, was democracy standing up to Fascism. For years past the so-called democratic countries had been surrendering to Fascism at every step. The Japanese had been allowed to do as they liked in Manchuria. Hitler had walked into power and proceeded to massacre political opponents of all shades. Mussolini had bombed the Abyssinians while fifty-three nations (I think it was fifty-three) made pious noises 'off'. But when Franco tried to overthrow a mildly Left-wing Government the Spanish people, against all expectation, had risen against him. It seemed—possibly it was—the turning of the tide.

But there were several points that escaped general notice. To begin with, Franco was not strictly comparable with Hitler or Mussolini. His rising was a military mutiny backed up by the aristocracy and the Church, and in the main, especially at the beginning, it was an attempt not so much to impose Fascism as to restore feudalism. This meant that Franco had against him not only the working class but also various sections of the liberal bourgeoisie—the very people who are the supporters of Fascism when it appears in a more modern form. More important than this was the fact that the Spanish working class did not, as we might conceivably do in England, resist Franco in the name of 'democracy' and the _status quo_; their resistance was accompanied by—one might almost say it consisted of—a definite revolutionary outbreak. Land was seized by the peasants; many factories and most of the transport were seized by the trade unions; churches were wrecked and the priests driven out or killed. The _Daily Mail_, amid the cheers of the Catholic clergy, was able to represent Franco as a patriot delivering his country from hordes of fiendish 'Reds'.

For the first few months of the war Franco's real opponent was not so much the Government as the trade unions. As soon as the rising broke out the organized town workers replied by calling a general strike and then by demanding—and, after a struggle, getting—arms from the public arsenals. If they had not acted spontaneously and more or less independently it is quite conceivable that Franco would never have been resisted. There can, of course, be no certainty about this, but there is at least reason for thinking it. The Government had made little or no attempt to forestall the rising, which had been foreseen for a long time past, and when the trouble started its attitude was weak and hesitant, so much so, indeed, that Spain had three premiers in a single day.[2] Moreover, the one step that could save the immediate situation, the arming of the workers, was only taken unwillingly and in response to violent popular clamour. However, the arms were distributed, and in the big towns of eastern Spain the Fascists were defeated by a huge effort, mainly of the working class, aided by some of the armed forces (Assault Guards, etc.) who had remained loyal. It was the kind of effort that could probably only be made by people who were fighting with a revolutionary intention—i.e. believed that they were fighting for something better than the status quo. In the various centres of revolt it is thought that three thousand people died in the streets in a single day. Men and women armed only with sticks of dynamite rushed across the open squares and stormed stone buildings held by trained soldiers with

[2] Quiroga, Barrios, and Giral. The first two refused to distribute arms to the trade unions.

machine-guns. Machine-gun nests that the Fascists had placed at strategic spots were smashed by rushing taxis at them at sixty miles an hour. Even if one had heard nothing of the seizure of the land by the peasants, the setting up of local Soviets, etc., it would be hard to believe that the Anarchists and Socialists who were the backbone of the resistance were doing this kind of thing for the preservation of capitalist democracy, which especially in the Anarchist view was no more than a centralized swindling machine.

Meanwhile the workers had weapons in their hands, and at this stage they refrained from giving them up. (Even a year later it was computed that the Anarcho-Syndicalists in Catalonia possessed 30,000 rifles.) The estates of the big pro-Fascist landlords were in many places seized by the peasants. Along with the collectivization of industry and transport there was an attempt to set up the rough beginnings of a workers' government by means of local committees, workers' patrols to replace the old pro-capitalist police forces, workers' militias based on the trade unions, and so forth. Of course the process was not uniform, and it went further in Catalonia than elsewhere. There were areas where the institutions of local government remained almost untouched, and others where they existed side by side with revolutionary committees. In a few places independent Anarchist communes were set up, and some of them remained in being till about a year later, when they were forcibly suppressed by the Government. In Catalonia, for the first few months, most of the actual power was in the hands of the Anarcho-syndicalists, who controlled most of the key industries. The thing that had happened in Spain was, in fact, not merely a civil war, but the beginning of a revolution. It is this fact that the anti-Fascist press outside Spain has made it its special business to obscure. The issue has been narrowed down to 'Fascism versus democracy' and the revolutionary aspect concealed as much as possible. In England, where the Press is more centralized and the public more easily deceived than elsewhere, only two versions of the Spanish war have had any publicity to speak of: the Right-wing version of Christian patriots versus Bolsheviks dripping with blood, and the Left-wing version of gentlemanly republicans quelling a military revolt. The central issue has been successfully covered up.

There were several reasons for this. To begin with, appalling lies about atrocities were being circulated by the pro-Fascist press, and well-meaning propagandists undoubtedly thought that they were aiding the Spanish Government by denying that Spain had 'gone Red'. But the main reason was this: that, except for the small revolutionary groups which exist in all countries, the whole world was determined, upon preventing revolution in Spain. In particular the Communist Party, with Soviet Russia behind it, had thrown its whole weight against the revolution. It was the Communist thesis that revolution at this stage would be fatal and that what was to be aimed at in Spain was not workers' control, but bourgeois democracy. It hardly needs pointing out why 'liberal' capitalist opinion took the same line. Foreign capital was heavily invested in Spain. The Barcelona Traction Company, for instance, represented ten millions of British capital; and meanwhile the trade unions had seized all the transport in Catalonia. If the revolution went forward there would be no compensation, or very little; if the capitalist republic prevailed, foreign investments would be safe. And since the revolution had got to be crushed, it greatly simplified things to pretend that no revolution had happened. In this way the real significance of every event could be covered up; every shift of power from the trade unions to the central Government could be represented as a necessary step in military reorganization. The situation produced was curious in the extreme. Outside Spain few people grasped that there was a revolution; inside Spain nobody doubted it. Even the P.S.U.C. newspapers. Communist-controlled and more or less committed to an antirevolutionary policy, talked about 'our glorious revolution'. And meanwhile the Communist press in foreign countries was shouting that there was no sign of revolution anywhere; the seizure of factories, setting up of workers' committees, etc., had not happened—or, alternatively, had happened, but 'had no political significance'. According to the _Daily Worker_ (6 August 1936) those who said that the Spanish people were fighting for social revolution, or for anything other than bourgeois democracy, were' downright lying scoundrels'. On the other hand, Juan Lopez, a member of the Valencia Government, declared in February 1937 that 'the Spanish people are shedding their blood, not for the democratic Republic and its paper Constitution, but for...a revolution'. So it would appear that the downright lying scoundrels included members of the Government for which we were bidden to fight. Some of the foreign anti-Fascist papers even descended to the pitiful lie of pretending that churches were only attacked when they were used as Fascist fortresses. Actually churches were pillaged everywhere and as a matter of course, because it was perfectly well understood that the Spanish Church was part of the capitalist racket. In six months in Spain I only saw two undamaged churches, and until about July 1937 no churches were allowed to reopen and hold services, except for one or two Protestant churches in Madrid.

But, after all, it was only the beginning of a revolution, not the complete thing. Even when the workers, certainly in Catalonia and possibly elsewhere, had the power to do so, they did not overthrow or completely replace the Government. Obviously they could not do so when Franco was hammering at the gate and sections of the middle class were on their side. The country was in a transitional state that was capable either of developing in the direction of Socialism or of reverting to an ordinary capitalist republic. The peasants had most of the land, and they were likely to keep it, unless Franco won; all large industries had been collectivized, but whether they remained collectivized, or whether capitalism was reintroduced, would depend finally upon which group gained control. At the beginning both the Central Government and the *Generalite de Cataluña* (the semi-autonomous Catalan Government) could definitely be said to represent the working class. The Government was headed by *Caballero*, a Left-wing Socialist, and contained ministers representing the U.G.T. (Socialist trade unions) and the C.N.T. (Syndicalist unions controlled by the Anarchists). The *Catalan Generalite* was for a while virtually superseded by an anti-Fascist Defence Committee[3] consisting mainly of delegates from the trade unions. Later the Defence Committee was dissolved and the *Generalite* was reconstituted so as to represent the unions and the various Left-wing parties. But every subsequent reshuffling of the Government was a move towards the Right. First the P.O.U.M. was expelled from the *Generalite*; six months later *Caballero* was replaced by the Right-wing Socialist *Negrin*; shortly afterwards the C.N.T. was eliminated from the Government; then the U.G.T.; then the C.N.T. was turned out of the *Generalite*; finally, a year after the outbreak of war and revolution, there remained a Government composed entirely of Right-wing Socialists, Liberals, and Communists.

The general swing to the Right dates from about October-November 1936, when the U.S.S.R. began to supply arms to the Government and power began to pass from the Anarchists to the Communists. Except Russia and Mexico no country had had the decency to come to the rescue of the Government, and Mexico, for obvious reasons, could not supply arms in large quantities. Consequently the Russians were in a position to dictate terms. There is very little doubt that these terms were, in substance, 'Prevent revolution or you get no weapons', and that the first move

[3] Comité Central de Milicias Antifascistas. Delegates were chosen in proportion to the membership of their organizations. Nine delegates represented the trade unions, three the Catalan Liberal parties, and two the various Marxist parties (P.O.U.M., Communists, and others).

against the revolutionary elements, the expulsion of the P.O.U.M. from the *Catalan Generalite*, was done under orders from the U.S.S.R. It has been denied that any direct pressure was exerted by the Russian Government, but the point is not of great importance, for the Communist parties of all countries can be taken as carrying out Russian policy, and it is not denied that the Communist Party was the chief mover first against the P.O.U.M., later against the Anarchists and against *Caballero*'s section of the Socialists, and, in general, against a revolutionary policy. Once the U.S.S.R. had intervened the triumph of the Communist Party was assured.

To begin with, gratitude to Russia for the arms and the fact that the Communist Party, especially since the arrival of the International Brigades, looked capable of winning the war, immensely raised the Communist prestige. Secondly, the Russian arms were supplied via the Communist Party and the parties allied to them, who saw to it that as few as possible got to their political opponents.[4] Thirdly, by proclaiming a non-revolutionary policy the Communists were able to gather in all those whom the extremists had scared. It was easy, for instance, to rally the wealthier peasants against the collectivization policy of the Anarchists. There was an enormous growth in the membership of the party, and the influx was largely from the middle class-shopkeepers, officials, army officers, well-to-do peasants, etc., etc. The war was essentially a triangular struggle. The fight against Franco had to continue, but the simultaneous aim of the Government was to recover such power as remained in the hands of the trade unions. It was done by a series of small moves—a policy of pin-pricks, as somebody called it—and on the whole very cleverly. There was no general and obvious counter-revolutionary move, and

---

[4] This is why there were so few Russian arms on the Aragón front, where the troops were predominantly Anarchist. Until April 1937 the only Russian weapon I saw—with the exception of some aeroplanes which may or may not have been Russian—was a solitary sub-machinegun.

until May 1937 it was scarcely necessary to use force. The workers could always be brought to heel by an argument that is almost too obvious to need stating: 'Unless you do this, that, and the other we shall lose the war.' In every case, needless to say, it appeared that the thing demanded by military necessity was the surrender of something that the workers had won for themselves in 1936. But the argument could hardly fail, because to lose the war was the last thing that the revolutionary parties wanted; if the war was lost democracy and revolution. Socialism and Anarchism, became meaningless words. The Anarchists, the only revolutionary party that was big enough to matter, were obliged to give way on point after point. The process of collectivization was checked, the local committees were got rid of, the workers patrols were abolished and the pre-war police forces, largely reinforced and very heavily armed, were restored, and various key industries which had been under the control of the trade unions were taken over by the Government (the seizure of the Barcelona Telephone Exchange, which led to the May fighting, was one incident in this process); finally, most important of all, the workers' militias, based on the trade unions, were gradually broken up and redistributed among the new Popular Army, a 'non-political' army on semi-bourgeois lines, with a differential pay rate, a privileged officer-caste, etc., etc. In the special circumstances this was the really decisive step; it happened later in Catalonia than elsewhere because it was there that the revolutionary parties were strongest. Obviously the only guarantee that the workers could have of retaining their winnings was to keep some of the armed forces under their own control. As usual, the breaking-up of the militias was done in the name of military efficiency; and no one denied that a thorough military reorganization was needed. It would, however, have been quite possible to reorganize the militias and make them more efficient while keeping them under direct control of the trade unions; the main purpose of the change was to make sure that the Anarchists did not possess an army of their own. Moreover, the democratic spirit of the militias made them breeding-grounds for revolutionary ideas. The Communists were well aware of this, and inveighed ceaselessly and bitterly against the P.O.U.M. and Anarchist principle of equal pay for all ranks. A general 'bourgeoisification', a deliberate destruction of the equalitarian spirit of the first few months of the revolution, was taking place. All happened so swiftly that people making successive visits to Spain at intervals of a few months have declared that they seemed scarcely to be visiting the same country; what had seemed on the surface and for a brief instant to be a workers' State was changing before one's eyes into an ordinary bourgeois republic with the normal division into rich and poor. By the autumn of 1937 the 'Socialist' Negrin was declaring in public speeches that 'we respect private property', and members of the *Cortes* who at the beginning of the war had had to fly the country because of their suspected Fascist sympathies were returning to Spain.

The whole process is easy to understand if one remembers that it proceeds from the temporary alliance that Fascism, in certain forms, forces upon the bourgeois and the worker. This alliance, known as the Popular Front, is in essential an alliance of enemies, and it seems probable that it must always end by one partner swallowing the other. The only unexpected feature in the Spanish situation—and outside Spain it has caused an immense amount of misunderstanding—is that among the parties on the Government side the Communists stood not upon the extreme Left, but upon the extreme Right. In reality this should cause no surprise, because the tactics of the Communist Party elsewhere, especially in France, have made it clear that Official Communism must be regarded, at any rate for the time being, as an antirevolutionary force. The whole of Comintern policy is now subordinated (excusably, considering the world situation) to the defence of U.S.S.R., which depends upon a system of military alliances. In particular, the U.S.S.R. is in alliance with France, a capitalist-imperialist country. The alliance is of little use to Russia unless French capitalism is strong, therefore Communist policy in France has got to be anti-revolutionary. This means not only that French Communists now march behind the tricolour and sing the Marseillaise, but, what is more important, that they have had to drop all effective agitation in the French colonies. It is less than three years since Thorez, the Secretary of the French Communist Party, was declaring that the French workers would never be bamboozled into fighting against their German comrades;[5] he is now one of the loudest-lunged patriots in France. The clue to the behaviour of the Communist Party in any country is the military relation of that country, actual or potential, towards the U.S.S.R. In England, for instance, the position is still uncertain, hence the English Communist Party is still hostile to the National Government, and, ostensibly, opposed to rearmament. If, however, Great Britain enters into an alliance or military understanding with the U.S.S.R., the English Communist, like the French Communist, will have no choice but to become a good patriot and imperialist; there are premonitory signs of this already. In Spain the Communist 'line' was undoubtedly influenced by the fact that France, Russia's ally, would strongly object to a revolutionary neighbour and would raise heaven and earth to prevent the liberation of Spanish Morocco. The Daily Mail, with its tales of red revolution financed by Moscow, was even more wildly wrong than usual. In reality it was the Communists above all others who prevented revolution in Spain. Later, when the Right-wing forces were in full control, the Communists showed themselves willing to go a great deal further than the Liberals in hunting down the revolutionary leaders.[6]

---

5 In the Chamber of Deputies, March 1935.

6 For the best account of the interplay between the parties on the Government side, see Franz Borkenau's _The Spanish Cockpit_. This is by a long way the ablest book that has yet appeared on the Spanish war.

I have tried to sketch the general course of the Spanish revolution during its first year, because this makes it easier to understand the situation at any given moment. But I do not want to suggest that in February I held all of the opinions that are implied in what I have said above. To begin with, the things that most enlightened me had not yet happened, and in any case my sympathies were in some ways different from what they are now. This was partly because the political side of the war bored me and I naturally reacted against the viewpoint of which I heard most—i.e. the P.O.U.M.-I.L.P. viewpoint. The Englishmen I was among were mostly I.L.P. members, with a few C.P. members among them, and most of them were much better educated politically than myself. For weeks on end, during the dull period when nothing was happening round Huesca, I found myself in the middle of a political discussion that practically never ended. In the draughty evil-smelling barn of the farm-house where we were billeted, in the stuffy blackness of dug-outs, behind the parapet in the freezing midnight hours, the conflicting party 'lines' were debated over and over. Among the Spaniards it was the same, and most of the newspapers we saw made the inter-party feud their chief feature. One would have had to be deaf or an imbecile not to pick up some idea of what the various parties stood for.

From the point of view of political theory there were only three parties that mattered, the P.S.U.C., the P.O.U.M., and the C.N.T.-F.A.I., loosely described as the Anarchists. I take the P.S.U.C. first, as being the most important; it was the party that finally triumphed, and even at this time it was visibly in the ascendant.

It is necessary to explain that when one speaks of the P.S.U.C. 'line' one really means the Communist Party 'line'. The P.S.U.C. (*Partido Socialista Unificado de Cataluña*) was the Socialist Party of Catalonia; it had been formed at the beginning of the war by the fusion of various Marxist parties, including the Catalan Communist Party, but it was now entirely under Communist control and was affiliated to the Third International. Elsewhere in Spain no formal unification between Socialists and Communists had taken place, but the Communist viewpoint and the Right-wing Socialist viewpoint could everywhere be regarded as identical. Roughly speaking, the P.S.U.C. was the political organ of the U.G.T. (*Union General de Trabajadores*), the Socialist trade unions. The membership of these unions throughout Spain now numbered about a million and a half. They contained many sections of the manual workers, but since the outbreak of war they had also been swollen by a large influx of middle-class members, for in the early 'revolutionary' days people of all kinds had found it useful to join either the U.G.T. or the C.N.T. The two blocks of unions overlapped, but of the two the C.N.T. was more definitely a working-class organization. The P.S.U.C. was therefore a party partly of the workers and partly of the small bourgeoisie—the shopkeepers, the officials, and the wealthier peasants.

The P.S.U.C. 'line' which was preached in the Communist and pro-Communist press throughout the world, was approximately this:

'At present nothing matters except winning the war; without victory in the war all else is meaningless. Therefore this is not the moment to talk of pressing forward with the revolution. We can't afford to alienate the peasants by forcing Collectivization upon them, and we can't afford to frighten away the middle classes who were fighting on our side. Above all for the sake of efficiency we must do away with revolutionary chaos. We must have a strong central government in place of local committees, and we must have a properly trained and fully militarized army under a unified command. Clinging on to fragments of workers' control and parroting revolutionary phrases is worse than useless; it is not merely obstructive, but even counterrevolutionary, because it leads to divisions which can be used against us by the Fascists. At this stage we are not fighting for the dictatorship of the proletariat, we are fighting for parliamentary democracy. Whoever tries to turn the civil war into a social revolution is playing into the hands of the Fascists and is in effect, if not in intention, a traitor.'

The P.O.U.M. 'line' differed from this on every point except, of course, the importance of winning the war. The P.O.U.M. (Partido Obrero de Unificación Marxista) was one of those dissident Communist parties which have appeared in many countries in the last few years as a result of the opposition to 'Stalinism'; i.e. to the change, real or apparent, in Communist policy. It was made up partly of ex-Communists and partly of an earlier party, the Workers' and Peasants' Bloc. Numerically it was a small party,[7] with not much influence outside Catalonia, and chiefly important because it contained an unusually high proportion of politically conscious members. In Catalonia its chief stronghold was Lérida. It did not represent any block of trade unions. The P.O.U.M. militiamen were mostly C.N.T. members, but the actual party-members generally belonged to the U.G.T. It was, however, only in the C.N.T. that the P.O.U.M. had any influence.

The P.O.U.M. 'line' was approximately this:

'It is nonsense to talk of opposing Fascism by bourgeois "democracy". Bourgeois "democracy" is only another name for capitalism, and so is Fascism; to fight against Fascism on behalf of "democracy" is to fight against one form of capitalism on behalf of a second which is liable to turn into the first at any moment. The only real alternative to Fascism is workers' control. If you set up any less goal than this, you will either hand the victory to Franco, or, at best, let in Fascism by the back door. Meanwhile the workers must cling to every scrap of what they have won; if they yield anything to the

[7] The figures for the P.O.U.M. membership are given as: July 1936, 10,000; December 1936, 70,000; June 1937, 40,000. But these are from P.O.U.M. sources; a hostile estimate would probably divide them by four. The only thing one can say with any certainty about the membership of the Spanish political parties is that every party overestimates its own numbers.

semi-bourgeois Government they can depend upon being cheated. The workers' militias and police-forces must be preserved in their present form and every effort to "bourgeoisify" them must be resisted. If the workers do not control the armed forces, the armed forces will control the workers. The war and the revolution are inseparable.'

The Anarchist viewpoint is less easily defined. In any case the loose term 'Anarchists' is used to cover a multitude of people of very varying opinions. The huge block of unions making up the C.N.T. (*Confederacion Nacional de Trabajadores*), with round about two million members in all, had for its political organ the F.A.I. (*Federacion Anarquista Iberica*), an actual Anarchist organization. But even the members of the F.A.I., though always tinged, as perhaps most Spaniards are, with the Anarchist philosophy, were not necessarily Anarchists in the purest sense. Especially since the beginning of the war they had moved more in the direction of ordinary Socialism, because circumstances had forced them to take part in centralized administration and even to break all their principles by entering the Government. Nevertheless they differed fundamentally from the Communists in so much that, like the P.O.U.M., they aimed at workers' control and not a parliamentary democracy. They accepted the P.O.U.M. slogan: 'The war and the revolution are inseparable', though they were less dogmatic about it. Roughly speaking, the C.N.T.-F.A.I. stood for: (1) Direct control over industry by the workers engaged in each industry, e.g. transport, the textile factories, etc.; (2) Government by local committees and resistance to all forms of centralized authoritarianism; (3) Uncompromising hostility to the bourgeoisie and the Church. The last point, though the least precise, was the most important. The Anarchists were the opposite of the majority of so-called revolutionaries in so much that though their principles were rather vague their hatred of privilege and injustice was perfectly genuine. Philosophically, Communism and Anarchism are poles apart. Practically—i.e. in the form of society aimed at—the difference is mainly one of emphasis, but it is quite irreconcilable. The Communist's emphasis is always on centralism and efficiency, the Anarchist's on liberty and equality. Anarchism is deeply rooted in Spain and is likely to outlive Communism when the Russian influence is withdrawn. During the first two months of the war it was the Anarchists more than anyone else who had saved the situation, and much later than this the Anarchist militia, in spite of their indiscipline, were notoriously the best fighters among the purely Spanish forces. From about February 1937 onwards the Anarchists and the P.O.U.M. could to some extent be lumped together. If the Anarchists, the P.O.U.M., and the Left wing of the Socialists had had the sense to combine at the start and press a realistic policy, the history of the war might have been different. But in the early period, when the revolutionary parties seemed to have the game in their hands, this was impossible. Between the Anarchists and the Socialists there were ancient jealousies, the P.O.U.M., as Marxists, were sceptical of Anarchism, while from the pure Anarchist standpoint the 'Trotskyism' of the P.O.U.M. was not much preferable to the 'Stalinism' of the Communists. Nevertheless the Communist tactics tended to drive the two parties together. When the P.O.U.M. joined in the disastrous fighting in Barcelona in May, it was mainly from an instinct to stand by the C.N.T., and later, when the P.O.U.M. was suppressed, the Anarchists were the only people who dared to raise a voice in its defence.

So, roughly speaking, the alignment of forces was this. On the one side the C.N.T.-F.A.I., the P.O.U.M., and a section of the Socialists, standing for workers' control: on the other side the Right-wing Socialists, Liberals, and Communists, standing for centralized government and a militarized army.

It is easy to see why, at this time, I preferred the Communist viewpoint to that of the P.O.U.M. The Communists had a definite practical policy, an obviously better policy from the point of view of the common sense which looks only a few months ahead. And certainly the day-to-day policy of the P.O.U.M., their propaganda and so forth, was unspeakably bad; it must have been so, or they would have been able to attract a bigger mass-following. What clinched everything was that the Communists—so it seemed to me—were getting on with the war while we and the Anarchists were standing still. This was the general feeling at the time. The Communists had gained power and a vast increase of membership partly by appealing to the middle classes against the revolutionaries, but partly also because they were the only people who looked capable of winning the war. The Russian arms and the magnificent defence of Madrid by troops mainly under Communist control had made the Communists the heroes of Spain. As someone put it, every Russian aeroplane that flew over our heads was Communist propaganda. The revolutionary purism of the P.O.U.M., though I saw its logic, seemed to me rather futile. After all, the one thing that mattered was to win the war.

Meanwhile there was the diabolical inter-party feud that was going on in the newspapers, in pamphlets, on posters, in books—everywhere. At this time the newspapers I saw most often were the P.O.U.M. papers _La Batalla_ and _Adelante_, and their ceaseless carping against the 'counter-revolutionary' P.S.U.C. struck me as priggish and tiresome. Later, when I studied the P.S.U.C. and Communist press more closely, I realized that the P.O.U.M. were almost blameless compared with their adversaries. Apart from anything else, they had much smaller opportunities. Unlike the Communists, they had no footing in any press outside their own country, and inside Spain they were at an immense disadvantage because the press censorship was mainly under Communist control, which meant that the P.O.U.M. papers were liable to be suppressed or fined if they said anything damaging. It is also fair to the P.O.U.M. to say that though they might preach endless sermons on revolution and quote Lenin _ad nauseam_, they did not usually indulge in personal libel. Also they kept their polemics mainly to newspaper articles. Their large coloured posters, designed for a wider public (posters are important in Spain, with its large illiterate population), did not attack rival parties, but were simply anti-Fascist or abstractedly revolutionary; so were the songs the militiamen sang. The Communist attacks were quite a different matter. I shall have to deal with some of these later in this book. Here I can only give a brief indication of the Communist line of attack.

On the surface the quarrel between the Communists and the P.O.U.M. was one of tactics. The P.O.U.M. was for immediate revolution, the Communists not. So far so good; there was much to be said on both sides. Further, the Communists contended that the P.O.U.M. propaganda divided and weakened the Government forces and thus endangered the war; again, though finally I do not agree, a good case could be made out for this. But here the peculiarity of Communist tactics came in. Tentatively at first, then more loudly, they began to assert that the P.O.U.M. was splitting the Government forces not by bad judgement but by deliberate design. The P.O.U.M. was declared to be no more than a gang of disguised Fascists, in the pay of Franco and Hitler, who were pressing a pseudo-revolutionary policy as a way of aiding the Fascist cause. The P.O.U.M. was a 'Trotskyist' organization and 'Franco's Fifth Column'. This implied that scores of thousands of working-class people, including eight or ten thousand soldiers who were freezing in the front-line trenches and hundreds of foreigners who had come to Spain to fight against Fascism, often sacrificing their livelihood and their nationality by doing so, were simply traitors in the pay of the enemy. And this story was spread all over Spain by means of posters, etc., and repeated over and over in the Communist and pro-Communist press of the whole world. I could fill half a dozen books with quotations if I chose to collect them.

This, then, was what they were saying about us: we were Trotskyists, Fascists, traitors, murderers, cowards, spies, and so forth. I admit it was not pleasant, especially when one thought of some of the people who were responsible for it. It is not a nice thing to see a Spanish boy of fifteen carried down the line on a stretcher, with a dazed white face looking out from among the blankets, and to think of the sleek persons in London and Paris who are writing pamphlets to prove that this boy is a Fascist in disguise. One of the most horrible features of war is that all the war-propaganda, all the screaming and lies and hatred, comes invariably from people who are not fighting. The P.S.U.C. militiamen whom I knew in the line, the Communists from the International Brigade whom I met from time to time, never called me a Trotskyist or a traitor; they left that kind of thing to the journalists in the rear. The people who wrote pamphlets against us and vilified us in the newspapers all remained safe at home, or at worst in the newspaper offices of Valencia, hundreds of miles from the bullets and the mud. And apart from the libels of the inter-party feud, all the usual war-stuff, the tub-thumping, the heroics, the vilification of the enemy—all these were done, as usual, by people who were not fighting and who in many cases would have run a hundred miles sooner than fight. One of the dreariest effects of this war has been to teach me that the Left-wing press is every bit as spurious and dishonest as that of the Right.[8] I do earnestly feel that on our side—the Government side—this war was different from ordinary, imperialistic wars; but from the nature of the war-propaganda you would never have guessed it. The fighting had barely started when the newspapers of the Right and Left dived simultaneously into the same cesspool of abuse. We all remember

[8] I should like to make an exception of the _Manchester Guardian_. In connexion with this book I have had to go through the files of a good many English papers. Of our larger papers, the _Manchester Guardian_ is the only one that leaves me with an increased respect for its honesty.

the _Daily Mail's_ poster: 'REDS CRUCIFY NUNS', while to the _Daily Worker_ Franco's Foreign Legion was 'composed of murderers, white-slavers, dope-fiends, and the offal of every European country'. As late as October 1937 the _New Statesman_ was treating us to tales of Fascist barricades made of the bodies of living children (a most unhandy thing to make barricades with), and Mr Arthur Bryant was declaring that 'the sawing-off of a Conservative tradesman's legs' was 'a commonplace' in Loyalist Spain. The people who write that kind of stuff never fight; possibly they believe that to write it is a substitute for fighting. It is the same in all wars; the soldiers do the fighting, the journalists do the shouting, and no true patriot ever gets near a front-line trench, except on the briefest of propaganda-tours. Sometimes it is a comfort to me to think that the aeroplane is altering the conditions of war. Perhaps when the next great war comes we may see that sight unprecedented in all history, a jingo with a bullet-hole in him.

As far as the journalistic part of it went, this war was a racket like all other wars. But there was this difference, that whereas the journalists usually reserve their most murderous invective for the enemy, in this case, as time went on, the Communists and the P.O.U.M. came to write more bitterly about one another than about the Fascists. Nevertheless at the time I could not bring myself to take it very seriously. The inter-party feud was annoying and even disgusting, but it appeared to me as a domestic squabble. I did not believe that it would alter anything or that there was any really irreconcilable difference of policy. I grasped that the Communists and Liberals had set their faces against allowing the revolution to go forward; I did not grasp that they might be capable of swinging it _back_.

There was a good reason for this. All this time I was at the front, and at the front the social and political atmosphere did not change. I had left Barcelona in early January and I did not go on leave till late

April; and all this time—indeed, till later—in the strip of Aragón controlled by Anarchist and P.O.U.M. troops, the same conditions persisted, at least outwardly. The revolutionary atmosphere remained as I had first known it. General and private, peasant and militiaman, still met as equals; everyone drew the same pay, wore the same clothes, ate the same food, and called everyone else 'thou' and 'comrade'; there was no boss-class, no menial-class, no beggars, no prostitutes, no lawyers, no priests, no boot-licking, no cap-touching. I was breathing the air of equality, and I was simple enough to imagine that it existed all over Spain. I did not realize that more or less by chance I was isolated among the most revolutionary section of the Spanish working class.

So, when my more politically educated comrades told me that one could not take a purely military attitude towards the war, and that the choice lay between revolution and Fascism, I was inclined to laugh at them. On the whole I accepted the Communist viewpoint, which boiled down to saying: 'We can't talk of revolution till we've won the war', and not the P.O.U.M. viewpoint, which boiled down to saying: 'We must go forward or we shall go back.' When later on I decided that the P.O.U.M. were right, or at any rate righter than the Communists, it was not altogether upon a point of theory. On paper the Communist case was a good one; the trouble was that their actual behaviour made it difficult to believe that they were advancing it in good faith. The often-repeated slogan: 'The war first and the revolution afterwards', though devoutly believed in by the average P.S.U.C. militiaman, who honestly thought that the revolution could continue when the war had been won, was eyewash. The thing for which the Communists were working was not to postpone the Spanish revolution till a more suitable time, but to make sure that it never happened. This became more and more obvious as time went on, as power was twisted more and more out of working-class hands, and as more and more revolutionaries of every shade were flung into jail. Every move was made in the name of military necessity, because this pretext was, so to speak, ready-made, but the effect was to drive the workers back from an advantageous position and into a position in which, when the war was over, they would find it impossible to resist the reintroduction of capitalism. Please notice that I am saying nothing against the rank-and-file Communists, least of all against the thousands of Communists who died heroically round Madrid. But those were not the men who were directing party policy. As for the people higher up, it is inconceivable that they were not acting with their eyes open.

But, finally, the war was worth winning even if the revolution was lost. And in the end I came to doubt whether, in the long run, the Communist policy made for victory. Very few people seem to have reflected that a different policy might be appropriate at different periods of the war. The Anarchists probably saved the situation in the first two months, but they were incapable of organizing resistance beyond a certain point; the Communists probably saved the situation in October-December, but to win the war outright was a different matter. In England the Communist war-policy has been accepted without question, because very few criticisms of it have been allowed to get into print and because its general line—do away with revolutionary chaos, speed up production, militarize the army—sounds realistic and efficient. It is worth pointing out its inherent weakness.

In order to check every revolutionary tendency and make the war as much like an ordinary war as possible, it became necessary to throw away the strategic opportunities that actually existed. I have described how we were armed, or not armed, on the Aragón front. There is very little doubt that arms were deliberately withheld lest too many of them should get into the hands of the Anarchists, who would afterwards use them for a revolutionary purpose; consequently the big Aragón offensive which would have made Franco draw back from Bilbao, and possibly from Madrid, never happened. But this was comparatively a small matter. What was more important was that once the war had been narrowed down to a 'war for democracy' it became impossible to make any large-scale appeal for working-class aid abroad. If we face facts we must admit that the working class of the world has regarded the Spanish war with detachment. Tens of thousands of individuals came to fight, but the tens of millions behind them remained apathetic. During the first year of the war the entire British public is thought to have subscribed to various 'aid Spain' funds about a quarter of a million pounds—probably less than half of what they spend in a single week on going to the pictures. The way in which the working class in the democratic countries could really have helped her Spanish comrades was by industrial action—strikes and boycotts. No such thing ever even began to happen. The Labour and Communist leaders everywhere declared that it was unthinkable; and no doubt they were right, so long as they were also shouting at the tops of their voices that 'red' Spain was not 'red'. Since 1914-18 'war for democracy' has had a sinister sound. For years past the Communists themselves had been teaching the militant workers in all countries that 'democracy' was a polite name for capitalism. To say first 'Democracy is a swindle', and then 'Fight for democracy!' is not good tactics. If, with the huge prestige of Soviet Russia behind them, they had appealed to the workers of the world in the name not of 'democratic Spain', but of 'revolutionary Spain', it is hard to believe that they would not have got a response.

But what was most important of all, with a non-revolutionary policy it was difficult, if not impossible, to strike at Franco's rear. By the summer of 1937 Franco was controlling a larger population than the Government—much larger, if one counts in the colonies—with about the same number of troops. As everyone knows, with a hostile population at your back it is impossible to keep an army in the field without an equally large army to guard your communications, suppress sabotage, etc. Obviously, therefore, there was no real popular movement in Franco's rear. It was inconceivable that the people in his territory, at any rate the town-workers and the poorer peasants, liked or wanted Franco, but with every swing to the Right the Government's superiority became less apparent. What clinches everything is the case of Morocco. Why was there no rising in Morocco? Franco was trying to set up an infamous dictatorship, and the Moors actually preferred him to the Popular Front Government! The palpable truth is that no attempt was made to foment a rising in Morocco, because to do so would have meant putting a revolutionary construction on the war. The first necessity, to convince the Moors of the Government's good faith, would have been to proclaim Morocco liberated. And we can imagine how pleased the French would have been by that! The best strategic opportunity of the war was flung away in the vain hope of placating French and British capitalism. The whole tendency of the Communist policy was to reduce the war to an ordinary, non-revolutionary war in which the Government was heavily handicapped. For a war of that kind has got to be won by mechanical means, i.e. ultimately, by limitless supplies of weapons; and the Government's chief donor of weapons, the U.S.S.R., was at a great disadvantage, geographically, compared with Italy and Germany. Perhaps the P.O.U.M. and Anarchist slogan: 'The war and the revolution are inseparable', was less visionary than it sounds.

I have given my reasons for thinking that the Communist anti-revolutionary policy was mistaken, but so far as its effect upon the war goes I do not hope that my judgement is right. A thousand times I hope that it is wrong. I would wish to see this war won by any means whatever. And of course we cannot tell yet what may happen. The Government may swing to the Left again, the Moors may revolt of their own accord, England may decide to buy Italy out, the war may be won by straightforward military means—there is no knowing. I let the above opinions stand, and time will show how far I am right or wrong.

But in February 1937 I did not see things quite in this light. I was sick of the inaction on the Aragón front and chiefly conscious that I had not done my fair share of the fighting. I used to think of the recruiting poster in Barcelona which demanded accusingly of passers-by: 'What have _you_ done for democracy?' and feel that I could only answer: 'I have drawn my rations.' When I joined the militia I had promised myself to kill one Fascist—after all, if each of us killed one they would soon be extinct—and I had killed nobody yet, had hardly had the chance to do so. And of course I wanted to go to Madrid. Everyone in the army, whatever his political opinions, always wanted to go to Madrid. This would probably mean exchanging into the International Column, for the P.O.U.M. had now very few troops at Madrid and the Anarchists not so many as formerly.

For the present, of course, one had to stay in the line, but I told everyone that when we went on leave I should, if possible, exchange into the International Column, which meant putting myself under Communist control. Various people tried to dissuade me, but no one attempted to interfere. It is fair to say that there was very little heresy-hunting in the P.O.U.M., perhaps not enough, considering their special circumstances; short of being a pro-Fascist no one was penalized for holding the wrong political opinions. I spent much of my time in the militia in bitterly criticizing the P.O.U.M. 'line', but I never got into trouble for it. There was not even any pressure upon one to become a political member of the party, though I think the majority of the militiamen did so. I myself never joined the party—for which afterwards, when the P.O.U.M. was suppressed, I was rather sorry.

CHAPTER 6

Meanwhile, the daily—more particularly nightly—round, the common task. Sentry-go, patrols, digging; mud, rain, shrieking winds, and occasional snow. It was not till well into April that the nights grew noticeably warmer. Up here on the plateau the March days were mostly like an English March, with bright blue skies and nagging winds. The winter barley was a foot high, crimson buds were forming on the cherry trees (the line here ran through deserted orchards and vegetable gardens), and if you searched the ditches you could find violets and a kind of wild hyacinth like a poor specimen of a bluebell. Immediately behind the line there ran a wonderful, green, bubbling stream, the first transparent water I had seen since coming to the front. One day I set my teeth and crawled into the river to have my first bath in six weeks. It was what you might call a brief bath, for the water was mainly snow-water and not much above freezing-point.

Meanwhile nothing happened, nothing ever happened. The English had got into the habit of saying that this wasn't a war, it was a bloody pantomime. We were hardly under direct fire from the Fascists. The only danger was from stray bullets, which, as the lines curved forward on either side, came from several directions. All the casualties at this time were from strays. Arthur Clinton got a mysterious bullet that smashed his left shoulder and disabled his arm, permanently, I am afraid. There was a little shell-fire, but it was extraordinarily ineffectual. The scream and crash of the shells was actually looked upon as a mild diversion. The Fascists ever dropped their shells on our parapet. A few hundred yards behind us there was a country house, called *La Granja*, with big farm-buildings, which was used as a store, headquarters, and cookhouse for this sector of the line. It was this that the Fascist gunners were trying for, but they were five or six kilometres away and they never aimed well enough to do more than smash the windows and chip the walls. You were only in danger if you happened to be coming up the road when the firing started, and the shells plunged into the fields on either side of you. One learned almost immediately the mysterious art of knowing by the sound of a shell how close it will fall. The shells the Fascists were firing at this period were wretchedly bad. Although they were 150 mm. they only made a crater about six feet wide by four deep, and at least one in four failed to explode. There were the usual romantic tales of sabotage in the Fascist factories and unexploded shells in which, instead of the charge, there was found a scrap of paper saying 'Red Front', but I never saw one. The truth was that the shells were hopelessly old; someone picked up a brass fuse-cap stamped with the date, and it was 1917. The Fascist guns were of the same make and calibre as our own, and the unexploded shells were often reconditioned and fired back. There was said to be one old shell with a nickname of its own which travelled daily to and fro, never exploding.

At night small patrols used to be sent into no man's land to lie in ditches near the Fascist lines and listen for sounds (bugle-calls, motor-horns, and so forth) that indicated activity in Huesca. There was a constant come-and-go of Fascist troops, and the numbers could be checked to some extent from listeners' reports. We always had special orders to report the ringing of church bells. It seemed that the Fascists always heard mass before going into action. In among the fields and orchards there were deserted mud-walled huts which it was safe to explore with a lighted match when you had plugged up the windows. Sometimes you came on valuable pieces of loot such as a hatchet or a Fascist water-bottle (better than ours and greatly sought after). You could explore in the daytime as well, but mostly it had to be done crawling on all fours. It was queer to creep about in those empty, fertile fields where everything had been arrested just at the harvest-moment. Last year's crops had never been touched. The unpruned vines were snaking across the ground, the cobs on the standing maize had gone as hard as stone, the mangels and sugar-beets were hyper-trophied into huge woody lumps. How the peasants must have cursed both armies! Sometimes parties of men went spud-gathering in no man's land. About a mile to the right of us, where the lines were closer together, there was a patch of potatoes that was frequented both by the Fascists and ourselves. We went there in the daytime, they only at night, as it was commanded by our machine-guns. One night to our annoyance they turned out _en masse_ and cleared up the whole patch. We discovered another patch farther on, where there was practically no cover and you had to lift the potatoes lying on your belly—a fatiguing job. If their machine-gunners spotted you, you had to flatten yourself out like a rat when it squirms under a door, with the bullets cutting up the clods a few yards behind you. It seemed worth it at the time. Potatoes were getting very scarce. If you got a sackful you could take them down to the cook-house and swap them for a water-bottleful of coffee.

And still nothing happened, nothing ever looked like happening. 'When are we going to attack? Why don't we attack?' were the questions you heard night and day from Spaniard and Englishman alike. When you think what fighting means it is queer that soldiers want to fight, and yet undoubtedly they do. In stationary warfare there are three things that all soldiers long for: a battle, more cigarettes, and a week's leave. We were somewhat better armed now than before. Each man had a hundred and fifty rounds of ammunition instead of fifty, and by degrees we were being issued with bayonets, steel helmets, and a few bombs. There were constant rumours of forthcoming battles, which I have since thought were deliberately circulated to keep up the spirits of the troops. It did not need much military knowledge to see that there would be no major action on this side of Huesca, at any rate for the time being. The strategic point was the road to Jaca, over on the other side. Later, when the Anarchists made their attacks on the Jaca road, our job was to make 'holding attacks' and force the Fascists to divert troops from the other side.

During all this time, about six weeks, there was only one action on our part of the front. This was when our Shock Troopers attacked the *Manicomio*, a disused lunatic asylum which the Fascists had converted into a fortress. There were several hundred refugee Germans serving with the P.O.U.M. They were organized in a special battalion called the *Batallon de Cheque*, and from a military point of view they were on quite a different level from the rest of the militia—indeed, were more like soldiers than anyone I saw in Spain, except the Assault Guards and some of the International Column. The attack was mucked up, as usual. How many operations in this war, on the Government side, were _not_ mucked up, I wonder? The Shock Troops took the *Manicomio* by storm, but the troops, of I forget which militia, who were to support them by seizing the neighbouring hill that commanded the *Manicomio*, were badly let down. The captain who led them was one of those Regular Army officers of doubtful loyalty whom the Government persisted in employing. Either from fright or treachery he warned the Fascists by flinging a bomb when they were two hundred yards away. I am glad to say his men shot him dead on the spot. But the surprise-attack was no surprise, and the militiamen were mown down by heavy fire and driven off the hill, and at nightfall the Shock Troops had to abandon the *Manicomio*. Through the night the ambulances filed down the abominable road to Sietamo, killing the badly wounded with their joltings.

All of us were lousy by this time; though still cold it was warm enough for that. I have had a big experience of body vermin of various kinds, and for sheer beastliness the louse beats everything I have encountered. Other insects, mosquitoes for instance, make you suffer more, but at least they aren't _resident_ vermin. The human louse somewhat resembles a tiny lobster, and he lives chiefly in your trousers. Short of burning all your clothes there is no known way of getting rid of him. Down the seams of your trousers he lays his glittering white eggs, like tiny grains of rice, which hatch out and breed families of their own at horrible speed. I think the pacifists might find it helpful to illustrate their pamphlets with enlarged photographs of lice. Glory of war, indeed! In war _all_ soldiers are lousy, at least when it is warm enough. The men who fought at Verdun, at Waterloo, at Flodden, at Senlac, at Thermopylae—every one of them had lice crawling over his testicles. We kept the brutes down to some extent by burning out the eggs and by bathing as often as we could face it. Nothing short of lice could have driven me into that ice-cold river.

Everything was running short—boots, clothes, tobacco, soap, candles, matches, olive oil. Our uniforms were dropping to pieces, and many of the men had no boots, only rope-soled sandals. You came on piles of worn-out boots everywhere. Once we kept a dug-out fire burning for two days mainly with boots, which are not bad fuel. By this time my wife was in Barcelona and used to send me tea, chocolate, and even cigars when such things were procurable, but even in Barcelona everything was running short, especially tobacco. The tea was a godsend, though we had no milk and seldom any sugar. Parcels were constantly being sent from England to men in the contingent but they never arrived; food, clothes, cigarettes—everything was either refused by the Post Office or seized in France. Curiously enough, the only firm that succeeded in sending packets of tea—even, on one memorable occasion, a tin of biscuits—to my wife was the Army and Navy Stores. Poor old Army and Navy! They did their duty nobly, but perhaps they might have felt happier if the stuff had been going to Franco's side of the barricade. The shortage of tobacco was the worst of all. At the beginning we had been issued with a packet of cigarettes a day, then it got down to eight cigarettes a day, then to five. Finally there were ten deadly days when there was no issue of tobacco at all. For the first time, in Spain, I saw something that you see every day in London—people picking up fag-ends.

Towards the end of March I got a poisoned hand that had to be lanced and put in a sling. I had to go into hospital, but it was not worth sending me to Sietamo for such a petty injury, so I stayed in the so-called hospital at Monflorite, which was merely a casualty clearing station. I was there ten days, part of the time in bed. The _practicantes_ (hospital assistants) stole practically every valuable object I possessed, including my camera and all my photographs. At the front everyone stole, it was the inevitable effect of shortage, but the hospital people were always the worst. Later, in the hospital at Barcelona, an American who had come to join the International Column on a ship that was torpedoed by an Italian submarine, told me how he was carried ashore wounded, and how, even as they lifted him into the ambulance, the stretcher-bearers pinched his wrist-watch.

While my arm was in the sling I spent several blissful days wandering about the country-side. Monflorite was the usual huddle of mud and stone houses, with narrow tortuous alleys that had been churned by lorries till they looked like the craters of the moon. The church had been badly knocked about but was used as a military store. In the whole neighbourhood there were only two farm-houses of any size, Torre Lorenzo and Torre Fabian, and only two really large buildings, obviously the houses of the landowners who had once lorded it over the countryside; you could see their wealth reflected in the miserable huts of the peasants. Just behind the river, close to the front line, there was an enormous flour-mill with a country-house attached to it. It seemed shameful to see the huge costly machine rusting useless and the wooden flour chutes torn down for firewood. Later on, to get firewood for the troops farther back, parties of men were sent in lorries to wreck the place systematically. They used to smash the floorboards of a room by bursting a hand-grenade in it. *La Granja*, our store and cook-house, had possibly at one time been a convent. It had huge courtyards and out-houses, covering an acre or more, with stabling for thirty or forty horses. The country-houses in that part of Spain are of no interest architecturally, but their farm-buildings, of lime-washed stone with round arches and magnificent roof-beams, are noble places, built on a plan that has probably not altered for centuries. Sometimes it gave you a sneaking sympathy with the Fascist ex-owners to see the way the militia treated the buildings they had seized. In *La Granja* every room that was not in use had been turned into a latrine—a frightful shambles of smashed furniture and excrement. The little church that adjoined it, its walls perforated by shell-holes, had its floor inches deep in dung. In the great courtyard where the cooks ladled out the rations the litter of rusty tins, mud, mule dung, and decaying food was revolting. It gave point to the old army song:

> There are rats, rats,
> Rats as big as cats,
> In the quartermaster's store!

The ones at *La Granja* itself really were as big as cats, or nearly; great bloated brutes that waddled over the beds of muck, too impudent even to run away unless you shot at them.

Spring was really here at last. The blue in the sky was softer, the air grew suddenly balmy. The frogs were mating noisily in the ditches. Round the drinking-pool that served for the village mules I found exquisite green frogs the size of a penny, so brilliant that the young grass looked dull beside them. Peasant lads went out with buckets hunting for snails, which they roasted alive on sheets of tin. As soon as the weather improved the peasants had turned out for the spring ploughing. It is typical of the utter vagueness in which the Spanish agrarian revolution is wrapped that I could not even discover for certain whether the land here was collectivized or whether the peasants had simply divided it up among themselves. I fancy that in theory it was collectivized, this being P.O.U.M. and Anarchist territory. At any rate the landowners were gone, the fields were being cultivated, and people seemed satisfied. The friendliness of the peasants towards ourselves never ceased to astonish me. To some of the older ones the war must have seemed meaningless, visibly it produced a shortage of everything and a dismal dull life for everybody, and at the best of times peasants hate having troops quartered upon them. Yet they were invariably friendly—I suppose reflecting that, however intolerable we might be in other ways, we did stand between them and their one-time landlords. Civil war is a queer thing. Huesca was not five miles away, it was these people's market town, all of them had relatives there, every week of their lives they had gone there to sell their poultry and vegetables. And now for eight months an impenetrable barrier of barbed wire and machine-guns had lain between. Occasionally it slipped their memory. Once I was talking to an old woman who was carrying one of those tiny iron lamps in which the Spaniards bum olive oil. 'Where can I buy a lamp like that?' I said.' In Huesca,' she said without thinking, and then we both laughed. The village girls were splendid vivid creatures with coal-black hair, a swinging walk, and a straightforward, man-to-man demeanour which was probably a by-product of the revolution.

Men in ragged blue shirts and black corduroy breeches, with

broad-brimmed straw hats, were ploughing the fields behind teams of mules with rhythmically flopping ears. Their ploughs were wretched things, only stirring the soil, not cutting anything we should regard as a furrow. All the agricultural implements were pitifully antiquated, everything being governed by the expensiveness of metal. A broken plough-share, for instance, was patched, and then patched again, till sometimes it was mainly patches. Rakes and pitchforks were made of wood. Spades, among a people who seldom possessed boots, were unknown; they did their digging with a clumsy hoe like those used in India. There was a kind of harrow that took one straight back to the later Stone Age. It was made of boards joined together, to about the size of a kitchen table; in the boards hundreds of holes were morticed, and into each hole was jammed a piece of flint which had been chipped into shape exactly as men used to chip them ten thousand years ago. I remember my feelings almost of horror when I first came upon one of these things in a derelict hut in no man's land. I had to puzzle over it for a long while before grasping that it was a harrow. It made me sick to think of the work that must go into the making of such a thing, and the poverty that was obliged to use flint in place of steel. I have felt more kindly towards industrialism ever since. But in the village there were two up-to-date farm tractors, no doubt seized from some big landowner's estate.

Once or twice I wandered out to the little walled graveyard that stood a mile or so from the village. The dead from the front were normally sent to Sietamo; these were the village dead. It was queerly different from an English graveyard. No reverence for the dead here! Everything overgrown with bushes and coarse grass, human bones littered everywhere. But the really surprising thing was the almost complete lack of religious inscriptions on the gravestones, though they all dated from before the revolution. Only once, I think, I saw the 'Pray for the Soul of So-and-So' which is usual on Catholic graves. Most of the inscriptions were purely secular, with ludicrous poems about the virtues of the deceased. On perhaps one grave in four or five there was a small cross or a perfunctory reference to Heaven; this had usually been chipped off by some industrious atheist with a chisel.

It struck me that the people in this part of Spain must be genuinely without religious feeling—religious feeling, I mean, in the orthodox sense. It is curious that all the time I was in Spain I never once saw a person cross himself; yet you would think such a movement would become instinctive, revolution or no revolution. Obviously the Spanish Church will come back (as the saying goes, night and the Jesuits always return), but there is no doubt that at the outbreak of the revolution it collapsed and was smashed up to an extent that would be unthinkable even for the moribund C. of E. in like circumstances. To the Spanish people, at any rate in Catalonia and Aragón, the Church was a racket pure and simple. And possibly Christian belief was replaced to some extent by Anarchism, whose influence is widely spread and which undoubtedly has a religious tinge.

It was the day I came back from hospital that we advanced the line to what was really its proper position, about a thousand yards forward, along the little stream that lay a couple of hundred yards in front of the Fascist line. This operation ought to have been carried out months earlier. The point of doing it now was that the Anarchists were attacking on the Jaca road, and to advance on this side made them divert troops to face us.

We were sixty or seventy hours without sleep, and my memories go down into a sort of blue, or rather a series of pictures. Listening-duty in no man's land, a hundred yards from the Casa Francesa, a fortified farm-house which was part of the Fascist line. Seven hours lying in a horrible marsh, in reedy-smelling water into which one's body subsided gradually deeper and deeper: the reedy smell, the numbing cold, the stars immovable in the black sky, the harsh croaking of the frogs. Though this was April it was the coldest night that I remember in Spain. Only a hundred yards behind us the working-parties were hard at it, but there was utter silence except for the chorus of the frogs. Just once during the night I heard a sound—the familiar noise of a sand-bag being flattened with a spade. It is queer how, just now and again, Spaniards can carry out a brilliant feat of organization. The whole move was beautifully planned. In seven hours six hundred men constructed twelve hundred metres of trench and parapet, at distances of from a hundred and fifty to three hundred yards from the Fascist line, and all so silently that the Fascists heard nothing, and during the night there was only one casualty. There were more next day, of course. Every man had his job assigned to him, even to the cook-house orderlies who suddenly arrived when the work was done with buckets of wine laced with brandy.

And then the dawn coming up and the Fascists suddenly discovering that we were there. The square white block of the Casa Francesa, though it was two hundred yards away, seemed to tower over us, and the machine-guns in its sandbagged upper windows seemed to be pointing straight down into the trench. We all stood gaping at it, wondering why the Fascists didn't see us. Then a vicious swirl of bullets, and everyone had flung himself on his knees and was frantically digging, deepening the trench and scooping out small shelters in the side. My arm was still in bandages, I could not dig, and I spent most of that day reading a detective story—_The Missing Moneylender_ its name was. I don't remember the plot of it, but I remember very clearly the feeling of sitting there reading it; the dampish clay of the trench bottom underneath me, the constant shifting of my legs out of the way as men hurried stopping down the trench, the crack-crack-crack of bullets a foot or two overhead. Thomas Parker got a bullet through the top of his thigh, which, as he said, was nearer to being a D.S.O. than he cared about. Casualties were happening all along the line, but nothing to what there would have been if they had caught us on the move during the night. A deserter told us afterwards that five Fascist sentries were shot for negligence. Even now they could have massacred us if they had had the initiative to bring up a few mortars. It was an awkward job getting the wounded down the narrow, crowded trench. I saw one poor devil, his breeches dark with blood, flung out of his stretcher and gasping in agony. One had to carry wounded men a long distance, a mile or more, for even when a road existed the ambulances never came very near the front line. If they came too near the Fascists had a habit of shelling them—justifiably, for in modern war no one scruples to use an ambulance for carrying ammunition.

And then, next night, waiting at *Torre Fabian* for an attack that was called off at the last moment by wireless. In the barn where we waited the floor was a thin layer of chaff over deep beds of bones, human bones and cows' bones mixed up, and the place was alive with rats. The filthy brutes came swarming out of the ground on every side. If there is one thing I hate more than another it is a rat running over me in the darkness. However, I had the satisfaction of catching one of them a good punch that sent him flying.

And then waiting fifty or sixty yards from the Fascist parapet for the order to attack. A long line of men crouching in an irrigation ditch with their bayonets peeping over the edge and the whites of their eyes shining through the darkness. Kopp and Benjamin squatting behind us with a man who had a wireless receiving-box strapped to his shoulders. On the western horizon rosy gun-flashes followed at intervals of several seconds by enormous explosions. And then a pip-pip-pip noise from the wireless and the whispered order that we were to get out of it while the going was good. We did so, but not quickly enough. Twelve wretched children of the J.C.I. (the Youth League of the P.O.U.M., corresponding to the J.S.U. of the P.S.U.C.) who had been posted only about forty yards from the Fascist parapet, were caught by the dawn and unable to escape. All day they had to lie there, with only tufts of grass for cover, the Fascists shooting at them every time they moved. By nightfall seven were dead, then the other five managed to creep away in the darkness.

And then, for many mornings to follow, the sound of the Anarchist attacks on the other side of Huesca. Always the same sound. Suddenly, at some time in the small hours, the opening crash of several score bombs bursting simultaneously—even from miles away a diabolical, rending crash—and then the unbroken roar of massed rifles and machine-guns, a heavy rolling sound curiously similar to the roll of drums. By degrees the firing would spread all round the lines that encircled Huesca, and we would stumble out into the trench to lean sleepily against the parapet while a ragged meaningless fire swept overhead.

In the daytime the guns thundered fitfully. *Torre Fabian*, now our cookhouse, was shelled and partially destroyed. It is curious that when you are watching artillery-fire from a safe distance you always want the gunner to hit his mark, even though the mark contains your dinner and some of your comrades. The Fascists were shooting well that morning; perhaps there were German gunners on the job. They bracketed neatly on *Torre Fabian*. One shell beyond it, one shell short of it, then whizz-BOOM' Burst rafters leaping upwards and a sheet of uralite skimming down the air like a nicked playing-card. The next shell took off a corner of a building as neatly as a giant might do it with a knife. But the cooks produced dinner on time—a memorable feat.

As the days went on the unseen but audible guns began each to assume a distinct personality. There were the two batteries of Russian 75-mm. guns which fired from close in our rear and which somehow evoked in my mind the picture of a fat man hitting a golf-ball. These were the first Russian guns I had seen—or heard, rather. They had a low trajectory and a very high velocity, so that you heard the cartridge explosion, the whizz, and the shell-burst almost simultaneously. Behind Monflorite were two very heavy guns which fired a few times a day, with a deep, muffled roar that was like the baying of distant chained-up monsters. Up at Mount Aragón, the medieval fortress which the Government troops had stormed last year (the first time in its history, it was said), and which guarded one of the approaches to Huesca, there was a heavy gun which must have dated well back into the nineteenth century. Its great shells whistled over so slowly that you felt certain you could run beside them and keep up with them. A shell from this gun sounded like nothing so much as a man riding along on a bicycle and whistling. The trench-mortars, small though they were, made the most evil sound of all. Their shells are really a kind of winged torpedo, shaped like the darts thrown in public-houses and about the size of a quart bottle; they go off with a devilish metallic crash, as of some monstrous globe of brittle steel being shattered on an anvil. Sometimes our aeroplanes flew over and let loose the aerial torpedoes whose tremendous echoing roar makes the earth tremble even at two miles' distance. The shell-bursts from the Fascist anti-aircraft guns dotted the sky like cloudlets in a bad water-colour, but I never saw them get within a thousand yards of an aeroplane. When an aeroplane swoops down and uses its machine-gun the sound, from below, is like the fluttering of wings.

On our part of the line not much was happening. Two hundred yards to the right of us, where the Fascists were on higher ground, their snipers picked off a few of our comrades. Two hundred yards to the left, at the bridge over the stream, a sort of duel was going on between the Fascist mortars and the men who were building a concrete barricade across the bridge. The evil little shells whizzed over, zwing-crash! zwing-crash!, making a doubly diabolical noise when they landed on the asphalt road. A hundred yards away you could stand in perfect safety and watch the columns of earth and black smoke leaping into the air like magic trees. The poor devils round the bridge spent much of the daytime cowering in the little manholes they had scooped in the side of the trench. But there were less casualties than might have been expected, and the barricade rose steadily, a wall of concrete two feet thick, with embrasures for two machine-guns and a small field gun. The concrete was being reinforced with old bedsteads, which apparently was the only iron that could be found for the purpose.

CHAPTER 7

One afternoon Benjamin told us that he wanted fifteen volunteers. The attack on the Fascist redoubt which had been called off on the previous occasion was to be carried out tonight. I oiled my ten Mexican cartridges, dirtied my bayonet (the things give your position away if they flash too much), and packed up a hunk of bread, three inches of red sausage, and a cigar which my wife had sent from Barcelona and which I had been hoarding for a long time. Bombs were served out, three to a man. The Spanish Government had at last succeeded in producing a decent bomb. It was on the principle of a Mills bomb, but with two pins instead of one. After you had pulled the pins out there was an interval of seven seconds before the bomb exploded. Its chief disadvantage was that one pin was very stiff and the other very loose, so that you had the choice of leaving both pins in place and being unable to pull the stiff one out in a moment of emergency, or pulling out the stiff one beforehand and being in a constant stew lest the thing should explode in your pocket. But it was a handy little bomb to throw.

A little before midnight Benjamin led the fifteen of us down to *Torre Fabian*. Ever since evening the rain had been pelting down. The irrigation ditches were brimming over, and every time you stumbled into one you were in water up to your waist. In the pitch darkness and sheeting rain in the farm-yard a dim mass of men was waiting. Kopp addressed us, first in Spanish, then in English, and explained the plan of attack. The Fascist line here made an L-bend and the parapet we were to attack lay on rising ground at the corner of the L. About thirty of us, half English, and half Spanish, under the command of Jorge Roca, our battalion commander (a battalion in the militia was about four hundred men), and Benjamin, were to creep up and cut the Fascist wire. Jorge would fling the first bomb as a signal, then the rest of us were to send in a rain of bombs, drive the Fascists out of the parapet, and seize it before they could rally. Simultaneously seventy Shock Troopers were to assault the next Fascist 'position', which lay two hundred yards to the right of the other, joined to it by a communication-trench. To prevent us from shooting each other in the darkness white armlets would be worn. At this moment a messenger arrived to say that there were no white armlets. Out of the darkness a plaintive voice suggested: 'Couldn't we arrange for the Fascists to wear white armlets instead?'

There was an hour or two to put in. The barn over the mule stable was so wrecked by shell-fire that you could not move about in it without a light. Half the floor had been torn away by a plunging shell and there was a twenty-foot drop on to the stones beneath. Someone found a pick and levered a burst plank out of the floor, and in a few minutes we had got a fire alight and our drenched clothes were steaming. Someone else produced a pack of cards. A rumour—one of those mysterious rumours that are endemic in war—flew round that hot coffee with brandy in it was about to be served out. We filed eagerly down the almost-collapsing staircase and wandered round the dark yard, inquiring where the coffee was to be found. Alas! there was no coffee. Instead, they called us together, ranged us into single file, and then Jorge and Benjamin set off rapidly into the darkness, the rest of us following.

It was still raining and intensely dark, but the wind had dropped. The mud was unspeakable. The paths through the beet-fields were simply a succession of lumps, as slippery as a greasy pole, with huge pools everywhere. Long before we got to the place where we were to leave our own parapet everyone had fallen several times and our rifles were coated with mud. At the parapet a small knot of men, our reserves, were waiting, and the doctor and a row of stretchers. We filed through the gap in the parapet and waded through another irrigation ditch. Splash-gurgle! Once again in water up to your waist, with the filthy, slimy mud oozing over your boot-tops. On the grass outside Jorge waited till we were all through. Then, bent almost double, he began creeping slowly forward. The Fascist parapet was about a hundred and fifty yards away. Our one chance of getting there was to move without noise.

I was in front with Jorge and Benjamin. Bent double, but with faces raised, we crept into the almost utter darkness at a pace that grew slower at every step. The rain beat lightly in our faces. When I glanced back I could see the men who were nearest to me, a bunch of humped shapes like huge black mushrooms gliding slowly forward. But every time I raised my head Benjamin, close beside me, whispered fiercely in my ear: 'To keep ze head down! To keep ze head down!' I could have told him that he needn't worry. I knew by experiment that on a dark night you can never see a man at twenty paces. It was far more important to go quietly. If they once heard us we were done for. They had only to spray the darkness with their machine-gun and there was nothing for it but to run or be massacred.

But on the sodden ground it was almost impossible to move quietly. Do what you would your feet stuck to the mud, and every step you took was slop-slop, slop-slop. And the devil of it was that the wind had dropped, and in spite of the rain it was a very quiet night. Sounds would carry a long way. There was a dreadful moment when I kicked against a tin and thought every Fascist within miles must have heard it. But no, not a sound, no answering shot, no movement in the Fascist lines. We crept onwards, always more slowly. I cannot convey to you the depth of my desire to get there. Just to get within bombing distance before they heard us! At such a time you have not even any fear, only a tremendous hopeless longing to get over the intervening ground. I have felt exactly the same thing when stalking a wild animal; the same agonized desire to get within range, the same dreamlike certainty that it is impossible. And how the distance stretched out! I knew the ground well, it was barely a hundred and fifty yards, and yet it seemed more like a mile. When you are creeping at that pace you are aware as an ant might be of the enormous variations in the ground; the splendid patch of smooth grass here, the evil patch of sticky mud there, the tall rustling reeds that have got to be avoided, the heap of stones that almost makes you give up hope because it seems impossible to get over it without noise.

We had been creeping forward for such an age that I began to think we had gone the wrong way. Then in the darkness thin parallel lines of something blacker were faintly visible. It was the outer wire (the Fascists had two lines of wire). Jorge knelt down, fumbled in his pocket. He had our only pair of wire-cutters. Snip, snip. The trailing stuff was lifted delicately aside. We waited for the men at the back to close up. They seemed to be making a frightful noise. It might be fifty yards to the Fascist parapet now. Still onwards, bent double. A stealthy step, lowering your foot as gently as a cat approaching a mousehole; then a pause to listen; then another step. Once I raised my head; in silence Benjamin put his hand behind my neck and pulled it violently down. I knew that the inner wire was barely twenty yards from the parapet. It seemed to me inconceivable that thirty men could get there unheard. Our breathing was enough to give us away. Yet somehow we did get there. The Fascist parapet was visible now, a dim black mound, looming high above us. Once again Jorge knelt and fumbled. Snip, snip. There was no way of cutting the stuff silently.

So that was the inner wire. We crawled through it on all fours and rather more rapidly. If we had time to deploy now all was well.

Jorge and Benjamin crawled across to the right. But the men behind, who were spread out, had to form into single file to get through the narrow gap in the wire, and just as this moment there was a flash and a bang from the Fascist parapet. The sentry had heard us at last. Jorge poised himself on one knee and swung his arm like a bowler. Crash! His bomb burst somewhere over the parapet. At once, far more promptly than one would have thought possible, a roar of fire, ten or twenty rifles, burst out from the Fascist parapet. They had been waiting for us after all. Momentarily you could see every sandbag in the lurid light. Men too far back were flinging their bombs and some of them were falling short of the parapet. Every loophole seemed to be spouting jets of flame. It is always hateful to be shot at in the dark—every rifle-flash seems to be pointed straight at yourself—but it was the bombs that were the worst. You cannot conceive the horror of these things till you have seen one burst close to you in darkness; in the daytime there is only the crash of the explosion, in the darkness there is the blinding red glare as well. I had flung myself down at the first volley. All this while I was lying on my side in the greasy mud, wrestling savagely with the pin of a bomb. The damned thing would not come out. Finally I realized that I was twisting it in the wrong direction. I got the pin out, rose to my knees, hurled the bomb, and threw myself down again. The bomb burst over to the right, outside the parapet; fright had spoiled my aim. Just at this moment another bomb burst right in front of me, so close that I could feel the heat of the explosion. I flattened myself out and dug my face into the mud so hard that I hurt my neck and thought that I was wounded. Through the din I heard an English voice behind me say quietly: 'I'm hit.' The bomb had, in fact, wounded several people round about me without touching myself. I rose to my knees and flung my second bomb. I forget where that one went.

The Fascists were firing, our people behind were firing, and I was very conscious of being in the middle. I felt the blast of a shot and realized that a man was firing from immediately behind me. I stood up and shouted at him: 'Don't shoot at me, you bloody fool!' At this moment I saw that Benjamin, ten or fifteen yards to my right, was motioning to me with his arm. I ran across to him. It meant crossing the line of spouting loop-holes, and as I went I clapped my left hand over my cheek; an idiotic gesture—as though one's hand could stop a bullet!—but I had a horror of being hit in the face. Benjamin was kneeling on one knee with a pleased, devilish sort of expression on his face and firing carefully at the rifle-flashes with his automatic pistol. Jorge had dropped wounded at the first volley and was somewhere out of sight. I knelt beside Benjamin, pulled the pin out of my third bomb and flung it. Ah! No doubt about it that time. The bomb crashed inside the parapet, at the corner, just by the machine-gun nest.

The Fascist fire seemed to have slackened very suddenly. Benjamin leapt to his feet and shouted: 'Forward! Charge!' We dashed up the short steep slope on which the parapet stood. I say 'dashed'; 'lumbered' would be a better word; the fact is that you can't move fast when you are sodden and mudded from head to foot and weighted down with a heavy rifle and bayonet and a hundred and fifty cartridges. I took it for granted that there would be a Fascist waiting for me at the top. If he fired at that range he could not miss me, and yet somehow I never expected him to fire, only to try for me with his bayonet. I seemed to feel in advance the sensation of our bayonets crossing, and I wondered whether his arm would be stronger than mine. However, there was no Fascist waiting. With a vague feeling of relief I found that it was a low parapet and the sandbags gave a good foothold. As a rule they are difficult to get over. Everything inside was smashed to pieces, beams flung all over the place, and great shards of uralite littered everywhere. Our bombs had wrecked all the huts and dug-outs. And still there was not a soul visible. I thought they would be lurking somewhere underground, and shouted in English (I could not think of any Spanish at the moment): 'Come on out of it! Surrender!' No answer. Then a man, a shadowy figure in the half-light, skipped over the roof of one of the ruined huts and dashed away to the left. I started after him, prodding my bayonet ineffectually into the darkness. As I rounded the comer of the hut I saw a man—I don't know whether or not it was the same man as I had seen before—fleeing up the communication-trench that led to the other Fascist position. I must have been very close to him, for I could see him clearly. He was bareheaded and seemed to have nothing on except a blanket which he was clutching round his shoulders. If I had fired I could have blown him to pieces. But for fear of shooting one another we had been ordered to use only bayonets once we were inside the parapet, and in any case I never even thought of firing. Instead, my mind leapt backwards twenty years, to our boxing instructor at school, showing me in vivid pantomime how he had bayoneted a Turk at the Dardanelles. I gripped my rifle by the small of the butt and lunged at the man's back. He was just out of my reach. Another lunge: still out of reach. And for a little distance we proceeded like this, he rushing up the trench and I after him on the ground above, prodding at his shoulder-blades and never quite getting there—a comic memory for me to look back upon, though I suppose it seemed less comic to him.

Of course, he knew the ground better than I and had soon slipped away from me. When I came back the position was full of shouting men. The noise of firing had lessened somewhat. The Fascists were still pouring a heavy fire at us from three sides, but it was coming from a greater distance.

We had driven them back for the time being. I remember saying in an oracular manner: 'We can hold this place for half an hour, not more.' I don't know why I picked on half an hour. Looking over the right-hand parapet you could see innumerable greenish rifle-flashes stabbing the darkness; but they were a long way back, a hundred or two hundred yards. Our job now was to search the position and loot anything that was worth looting. Benjamin and some others were already scrabbling among the ruins of a big hut or dug-out in the middle of the position. Benjamin staggered excitedly through the ruined roof, tugging at the rope handle of an ammunition box.

'Comrades! Ammunition! Plenty ammunition here!'

'We don't want ammunition,' said a voice, 'we want rifles.'

This was true. Half our rifles were jammed with mud and unusable. They could be cleaned, but it is dangerous to take the bolt out of a rifle in the darkness; you put it down somewhere and then you lose it. I had a tiny electric torch which my wife had managed to buy in Barcelona, otherwise we had no light of any description between us. A few men with good rifles began a desultory fire at the flashes in the distance. No one dared fire too rapidly; even the best of the rifles were liable to jam if they got too hot. There were about sixteen of us inside the parapet, including one or two who were wounded. A number of wounded, English and Spanish, were lying outside. Patrick O'Hara, a Belfast Irishman who had had some training in first-aid, went to and fro with packets of bandages, binding up the wounded men and, of course, being shot at every time he returned to the parapet, in spite of his indignant shouts of 'POUM!'

We began searching the position. There were several dead men lying about, but I did not stop to examine them. The thing I was after was the machine-gun. All the while when we were lying outside I had been wondering vaguely why the gun did not fire. I flashed my torch inside the machine-gun nest. A bitter disappointment! The gun was not there. Its tripod was there, and various boxes of ammunition and spare parts, but the gun was gone. They must have unscrewed it and carried it off at the first alarm. No doubt they were acting under orders, but it was a stupid and cowardly thing to do, for if they had kept the gun in place they could have slaughtered the whole lot of us. We were furious. We had set our hearts on capturing a machine-gun.

We poked here and there but did not find anything of much value. There were quantities of Fascist bombs lying about—a rather inferior type of bomb, which you touched off by pulling a string—and I put a couple of them in my pocket as souvenirs. It was impossible not to be struck by the bare misery of the Fascist dug-outs. The litter of spare clothes, books, food, petty personal belongings that you saw in our own dug-outs was completely absent; these poor unpaid conscripts seemed to own nothing except blankets and a few soggy hunks of bread. Up at the far end there was a small dug-out which was partly above ground and had a tiny window. We flashed the torch through the window and instantly raised a cheer. A cylindrical object in a leather case, four feet high and six inches in diameter, was leaning against the wall. Obviously the machine-gun barrel. We dashed round and got in at the doorway, to find that the thing in the leather case was not a machine-gun but something which, in our weapon-starved army, was even more precious. It was an enormous telescope, probably of at least sixty or seventy magnifications, with a folding tripod. Such telescopes simply did not exist on our side of the line and they were desperately needed. We brought it out in triumph and leaned it against the parapet, to be carried off after.

At this moment someone shouted that the Fascists were closing in. Certainly the din of firing had grown very much louder. But it was obvious that the Fascists would not counterattack from the right, which meant crossing no man's land and assaulting their own parapet. If they had any sense at all they would come at us from inside the line. I went round to the other side of the dug-outs. The position was roughly horseshoe-shaped, with the dug-outs in the middle, so that we had another parapet covering us on the left. A heavy fire was coming from that direction, but it did not matter greatly. The danger-spot was straight in front, where there was no protection at all. A stream of bullets was passing just overhead. They must be coming from the other Fascist position farther up the line; evidently the Shock Troopers had not captured it after all. But this time the noise was deafening. It was the unbroken, drum-like roar of massed rifles which I was used to hearing from a little distance; this was the first time I had been in the middle of it. And by now, of course, the firing had spread along the line for miles around. Douglas Thompson, with a wounded arm dangling useless at his side, was leaning against the parapet and firing one-handed at the flashes. Someone whose rifle had jammed was loading for him.

There were four or five of us round this side. It was obvious what we must do. We must drag the sand-bags from the front parapet and make a barricade across the unprotected side. And we had got to be quick. The fire was high at present, but they might lower it at any moment; by the flashes all round I could see that we had a hundred or two hundred men against us. We began wrenching the sand-bags loose, carrying them twenty yards forward and dumping them into a rough heap. It was a vile job. They were big sand-bags, weighing a hundredweight each and it took every ounce of your strength to prise them loose; and then the rotten sacking split and the damp earth cascaded all over you, down your neck and up your sleeves. I remember feeling a deep horror at everything: the chaos, the darkness, the frightful din, the slithering to and fro in the mud, the struggles with the bursting sand-bags—all the time encumbered with my rifle, which I dared not put down for fear of losing it. I even shouted to someone as we staggered along with a bag between us: 'This is war! Isn't it bloody?' Suddenly a succession of tall figures came leaping over the front parapet. As they came nearer we saw that they wore the uniform of the Shock Troopers, and we cheered, thinking they were reinforcements. However, there were only four of them, three Germans and a Spaniard. We heard afterwards what had happened to the Shock Troopers. They did not know the ground and in the darkness had been led to the wrong place, where they were caught on the Fascist wire and numbers of them were shot down. These were four who had got lost, luckily for themselves. The Germans did not speak a word of English, French, or Spanish. With difficulty and much gesticulation we explained what we were doing and got them to help us in building the barricade.

The Fascists had brought up a machine-gun now. You could see it spitting like a squib a hundred or two hundred yards away; the bullets came over us with a steady, frosty crackle. Before long we had flung enough sand-bags into place to make a low breastwork behind which the few men who were on this side of the position could lie down and fire. I was kneeling behind them. A mortar-shell whizzed over and crashed somewhere in no man's land. That was another danger, but it would take them some minutes to find our range. Now that we had finished wrestling with those beastly sand-bags it was not bad fun in a way; the noise, the darkness, the flashes approaching, our own men blazing back at the flashes. One even had time to think a little. I remember wondering whether I was frightened, and deciding that I was not. Outside, where I was probably in less danger, I had been half sick with fright. Suddenly there was another shout that the Fascists were closing in. There was no doubt about it this time, the rifle-flashes were much nearer. I saw a flash hardly twenty yards away. Obviously they were working their way up the communication-trench. At twenty yards they were within easy bombing range; there were eight or nine of us bunched together and a single well-placed bomb would blow us all to fragments. Bob Smillie, the blood running down his face from a small wound, sprang to his knee and flung a bomb. We cowered, waiting for the crash. The fuse fizzled red as it sailed through the air, but the bomb failed to explode. (At least a quarter of these bombs were duds). I had no bombs left except the Fascist ones and I was not certain how these worked. I shouted to the others to know if anyone had a bomb to spare. Douglas Moyle felt in his pocket and passed one across. I flung it and threw myself on my face. By one of those strokes of luck that happen about once in a year I had managed to drop the bomb almost exactly where the rifle had flashed. There was the roar of the explosion and then, instantly, a diabolical outcry of screams and groans. We had got one of them, anyway; I don't know whether he was killed, but certainly he was badly hurt. Poor wretch, poor wretch! I felt a vague sorrow as I heard him screaming. But at the same instant, in the dim light of the rifle-flashes, I saw or thought I saw a figure standing near the place where the rifle had flashed. I threw up my rifle and let fly. Another scream, but I think it was still the effect of the bomb. Several more bombs were thrown. The next rifle-flashes we saw were a long way off, a hundred yards or more. So we had driven them back, temporarily at least.

Everyone began cursing and saying why the hell didn't they send us some supports. With a sub-machine-gun or twenty men with clean rifles we could hold this place against a battalion. At this moment Paddy Donovan, who was second-in-command to Benjamin and had been sent back for orders, climbed over the front parapet.

'Hi! Come on out of it! All men to retire at once!'

'What?'

'Retire! Get out of it!'

'Why?'

'Orders. Back to our own lines double-quick.'

People were already climbing over the front parapet. Several of them were struggling with a heavy ammunition box. My mind flew to the telescope which I had left leaning against the parapet on the other side of the position. But at this moment I saw that the four Shock Troopers, acting I suppose on some mysterious orders they had received beforehand, had begun running up the communication-trench. It led to the other Fascist position and—if they got there—to certain death. They were disappearing into the darkness. I ran after them, trying to think of the Spanish for 'retire'; finally I shouted, '_Atrás! Atrás!_' which perhaps conveyed the right meaning. The Spaniard understood it and brought the others back. Paddy was waiting at the parapet.

'Come on, hurry up.'

'But the telescope!'

'Bugger the telescope! Benjamin's waiting outside.'

We climbed out. Paddy held the wire aside for me. As soon as we got away from the shelter of the Fascist parapet we were under a devilish fire that seemed to be coming at us from every direction. Part of it, I do not doubt, came from our own side, for everyone was firing all along the line. Whichever way we turned a fresh stream of bullets swept past; we were driven this way and that in the darkness like a flock of sheep. It did not make it any easier that we were dragging a captured box of ammunition—one of those boxes that hold 1750 rounds and weigh about a hundredweight—besides a box of bombs and several Fascist rifles. In a few minutes, although the distance from parapet to parapet was not two hundred yards and most of us knew the ground, we were completely lost. We found ourselves slithering about in a muddy field, knowing nothing except that bullets were coming from both sides. There was no moon to go by, but the sky was growing a little lighter. Our lines lay east of Huesca; I wanted to stay where we were till the first crack of dawn showed us which was east and which was west; but the others were against it. We slithered onwards, changing our direction several times and taking it in turns to haul at the ammunition-box. At last we saw the low flat line of a parapet looming in front of us. It might be ours or it might be the Fascists'; nobody had the dimmest idea which way we were going. Benjamin crawled on his belly through some tall whitish weed till he was about twenty yards from the parapet and tried a challenge. A shout of 'POUM!' answered him.

We jumped to our feet, found our way along the parapet, slopped once more through the irrigation ditch—splash-gurgle!—and were in safety.

Kopp was waiting inside the parapet with a few Spaniards. The doctor and the stretchers were gone. It appeared that all the wounded had been got in except Jorge and one of our own men, Hiddlestone by name, who were missing. Kopp was pacing up and down, very pale. Even the fat folds at the back of his neck were pale; he was paying no attention to the bullets that streamed over the low parapet and cracked close to his head. Most of us were squatting behind the parapet for cover. Kopp was muttering. '_Jorge! *Coño*! Jorge!_' And then in English. 'If Jorge is gone it is terreeble, terreeble!' Jorge was his personal friend and one of his best officers. Suddenly he turned to us and asked for five volunteers, two English and three Spanish, to go and look for the missing men. Moyle and I volunteered with three Spaniards.

As we got outside the Spaniards murmured that it was getting dangerously light. This was true enough; the sky was dimly blue. There was a tremendous noise of excited voices coming from the Fascist redoubt. Evidently they had re-occupied the place in much greater force than before. We were sixty or seventy yards from the parapet when they must have seen or heard us, for they sent over a heavy burst of fire which made us drop on our faces. One of them flung a bomb over the parapet—a sure sign of panic. We were lying in the grass, waiting for an opportunity to move on, when we heard or thought we heard—I have no doubt it was pure imagination, but it seemed real enough at the time—that the Fascist voices were much closer. They had left the parapet and were coming after us. 'Run!' I yelled to Moyle, and jumped to my feet. And heavens, how I ran! I had thought earlier in the night that you can't run when you are sodden from head to foot and weighted down with a rifle and cartridges; I learned now you can _always_ run when you think you have fifty or a hundred armed men after you. But if I could run fast, others could run faster. In my flight something that might have been a shower of meteors sped past me. It was the three Spaniards, who had been in front. They were back to our own parapet before they stopped and I could catch up with them. The truth was that our nerves were all to pieces. I knew, however, that in a half light one man is invisible where five are clearly visible, so I went back alone. I managed to get to the outer wire and searched the ground as well as I could, which was not very well, for I had to lie on my belly. There was no sign of Jorge or Hiddlestone, so I crept back. We learned afterwards that both Jorge and Hiddlestone had been taken to the dressing-station earlier. Jorge was lightly wounded through the shoulder. Hiddlestone had received a dreadful wound—a bullet which travelled right up his left arm, breaking the bone in several places; as he lay helpless on the ground a bomb had burst near him and torn various other parts of his body. He recovered, I am glad to say. Later he told me that he had worked his way some distance lying on his back, then had clutched hold of a wounded Spaniard and they had helped one another in.

It was getting light now. Along the line for miles around a ragged meaningless fire was thundering, like the rain that goes on raining after a storm. I remember the desolate look of everything, the morasses of mud, the weeping poplar trees, the yellow water in the trench-bottoms; and men's exhausted faces, unshaven, streaked with mud, and blackened to the eyes with smoke. When I got back to my dug-out the three men I shared it with were already fast sleep. They had flung themselves down with all their equipment on and their muddy rifles clutched against them. Everything was sodden, inside the dug-out as well as outside. By long searching I managed to collect enough chips of dry wood to make a tiny fire. Then I smoked the cigar which I had been hoarding and which, surprisingly enough, had not got broken during the night.

Afterwards we learned that the action had been a success, as such things go. It was merely a raid to make the Fascists divert troops from the other side of Huesca, where the Anarchists were attacking again. I had judged that the Fascists had thrown a hundred or two hundred men into the counterattack, but a deserter told us later on that it was six hundred. I dare say he was lying—deserters, for obvious reasons, often try to curry favour. It was a great pity about the telescope. The thought of losing that beautiful bit of loot worries me even now.

CHAPTER 8

The days grew hotter and even the nights grew tolerably warm. On a bullet-chipped tree in front of our parapet thick clusters of cherries were forming. Bathing in the river ceased to be an agony and became almost a pleasure. Wild roses with pink blooms the size of saucers straggled over the shell-holes round Torre Fabian. Behind the line you met peasants wearing wild roses over their ears. In the evenings they used to go out with green nets, hunting quails. You spread the net over the tops of the grasses and then lay down and made a noise like a female quail. Any male quail that was within hearing then came running towards you, and when he was underneath the net you threw a stone to scare him, whereupon he sprang into the air and was entangled in the net. Apparently only male quails were caught, which struck me as unfair.

There was a section of Andalusians next to us in the line now. I do not know quite how they got to this front. The current explanation was that they had run away from Málaga so fast that they had forgotten to stop at Valencia; but this, of course, came from the Catalans, who professed to look down on the Andalusians as a race of semi-savages. Certainly the Andalusians were very ignorant. Few if any of them could read, and they seemed not even to know the one thing that everybody knows in Spain—which political party they belonged to. They thought they were Anarchists, but were not quite certain; perhaps they were Communists. They were gnarled, rustic-looking men, shepherds or labourers from the olive groves, perhaps, with faces deeply stained by the ferocious suns of farther south. They were very useful to us, for they had an extraordinary dexterity at rolling the dried-up Spanish tobacco into cigarettes. The issue of cigarettes had ceased, but in Monflorite it was occasionally possible to buy packets of the cheapest kind of tobacco, which in appearance and texture was very like chopped chaff. Its flavour was not bad, but it was so dry that even when you had succeeded in making a cigarette the tobacco promptly fell out and left an empty cylinder. The Andalusians, however, could roll admirable cigarettes and had a special technique for tucking the ends in.

Two Englishmen were laid low by sunstroke. My salient memories of that time are the heat of the midday sun, and working half-naked with sand-bags punishing one's shoulders which were already flayed by the sun; and the lousiness of our clothes and boots, which were literally dropping to pieces; and the struggles with the mule which brought our rations and which did not mind rifle-fire but took to flight when shrapnel burst in the air; and the mosquitoes (just beginning to be active) and the rats, which were a public nuisance and would even devour leather belts and cartridge-pouches. Nothing was happening except an occasional casualty from a sniper's bullet and the sporadic artillery-fire and air-raids on Huesca. Now that the trees were in full leaf we had constructed snipers' platforms, like machans, in the poplar trees that fringed the line. On the other side of Huesca the attacks were petering out. The Anarchists had had heavy losses and had not succeeded in completely cutting the Jaca road. They had managed to establish themselves close enough on either side to bring the road itself under machine-gun fire and make it impassable for traffic; but the gap was a kilometre wide and the Fascists had constructed a sunken road, a sort of enormous trench, along which a certain number of lorries could come and go. Deserters reported that in Huesca there were plenty of munitions and very little food. But the town was evidently not going to fall. Probably it would have been impossible to take it with the fifteen thousand ill-armed men who were available. Later, in June, the Government brought troops from the Madrid front and concentrated thirty thousand men on Huesca, with an enormous quantity of aeroplanes, but still the town did not fall.

When we went on leave I had been a hundred and fifteen days in the line, and at the time this period seemed to me to have been one of the most futile of my whole life. I had joined the militia in order to fight against Fascism, and as yet I had scarcely fought at all, had merely existed as a sort of passive object, doing nothing in return for my rations except to suffer from cold and lack of sleep. Perhaps that is the fate of most soldiers in most wars. But now that I can see this period in perspective I do not altogether regret it. I wish, indeed, that I could have served the Spanish Government a little more effectively; but from a personal point of view—from the point of view of my own development—those first three or four months that I spent in the line were less futile than I then thought. They formed a kind of interregnum in my life, quite different from anything that had gone before and perhaps from anything that is to come, and they taught me things that I could not have learned in any other way.

The essential point is that all this time I had been isolated—for at the front one was almost completely isolated from the outside world: even of what was happening in Barcelona one had only a dim conception—among people who could roughly but not too inaccurately be described as revolutionaries. This was the result of the militia-system, which on the Aragón front was not radically altered till about June 1937. The workers' militias, based on the trade unions and each composed of people of approximately the same political opinions, had the effect of canalizing into one place all the most revolutionary sentiment in the country. I had dropped more or less by chance into the only community of any size in Western Europe where political consciousness and disbelief in capitalism were more normal than their opposites. Up here in Aragón one was among tens of thousands of people, mainly though not entirely of working-class origin, all living at the same level and mingling on terms of equality. In theory it was perfect equality, and even in practice it was not far from it. There is a sense in which it would be true to say that one was experiencing a foretaste of Socialism, by which I mean that the prevailing mental atmosphere was that of Socialism. Many of the normal motives of civilized life—snobbishness, money-grubbing, fear of the boss, etc.—had simply ceased to exist. The ordinary class-division of society had disappeared to an extent that is almost unthinkable in the money-tainted air of England; there was no one there except the peasants and ourselves, and no one owned anyone else as his master. Of course such a state of affairs could not last. It was simply a temporary and local phase in an enormous game that is being played over the whole surface of the earth. But it lasted long enough to have its effect upon anyone who experienced it. However much one cursed at the time, one realized afterwards that one had been in contact with something strange and valuable. One had been in a community where hope was more normal than apathy or cynicism, where the word 'comrade' stood for comradeship and not, as in most countries, for humbug. One had breathed the air of equality. I am well aware that it is now the fashion to deny that Socialism has anything to do with equality. In every country in the world a huge tribe of party-hacks and sleek little professors are busy 'proving' that Socialism means no more than a planned state-capitalism with the grab-motive left intact. But fortunately there also exists a vision of Socialism quite different from this. The thing that attracts ordinary men to Socialism and makes them willing to risk their skins for it, the 'mystique' of Socialism, is the idea of equality; to the vast majority of people Socialism means a classless society, or it means nothing at all. And it was here that those few months in the militia were valuable to me. For the Spanish militias, while they lasted, were a sort of microcosm of a classless society. In that community where no one was on the make, where there was a shortage of everything but no privilege and no boot-licking, one got, perhaps, a crude forecast of what the opening stages of Socialism might be like. And, after all, instead of disillusioning me it deeply attracted me. The effect was to make my desire to see Socialism established much more actual than it had been before. Partly, perhaps, this was due to the good luck of being among Spaniards, who, with their innate decency and their ever-present Anarchist tinge, would make even the opening stages of Socialism tolerable if they had the chance.

Of course at the time I was hardly conscious of the changes that were occurring in my own mind. Like everyone about me I was chiefly conscious of boredom, heat, cold, dirt, lice, privation, and occasional danger. It is quite different now. This period which then seemed so futile and eventless is now of great importance to me. It is so different from the rest of my life that already it has taken on the magic quality which, as a rule, belongs only to memories that are years old. It was beastly while it was happening, but it is a good patch for my mind to browse upon. I wish I could convey to you the atmosphere of that time. I hope I have done so, a little, in the earlier chapters of this book. It is all bound up in my mind with the winter cold, the ragged uniforms of militiamen, the oval Spanish faces, the morse-like tapping of machine-guns, the smells of urine and rotting bread, the tinny taste of bean-stews wolfed hurriedly out of unclean pannikins.

The whole period stays by me with curious vividness. In my memory I live over incidents that might seem too petty to be worth recalling. I am in the dug-out at Monte Pocero again, on the ledge of limestone that serves as a bed, and young Ramon is snoring with his nose flattened between my shoulder-blades. I am stumbling up the mucky trench, through the mist that swirls round me like cold steam. I am half-way up a crack in the mountain-side, struggling to keep my balance and to tug a root of wild rosemary out of the ground. High overhead some meaningless bullets are singing.

I am lying hidden among small fir-trees on the low ground west of Monte Oscuro, with Kopp and Bob Edwards and three Spaniards. Up the naked grey hill to the right of us a string of Fascists are climbing like ants. Close in front a bugle-call rings out from the Fascist lines. Kopp catches my eye and, with a schoolboy gesture, thumbs his nose at the sound.

I am in the mucky yard at *La Granja*, among the mob of men who are struggling with their tin pannikins round the cauldron of stew. The fat and harassed cook is warding them off with the ladle. At a table nearby a bearded man with a huge automatic pistol strapped to his belt is hewing loaves of bread into five pieces. Behind me a Cockney voice (Bill Chambers, with whom I quarrelled bitterly and who was afterwards killed outside Huesca) is singing:

> There are rats, rats,
> Rats as big as cats,
> In the...

A shell comes screaming over. Children of fifteen fling themselves on their faces. The cook dodges behind the cauldron. Everyone rises with a sheepish expression as the shell plunges and booms a hundred yards away.

I am walking up and down the line of sentries, under the dark boughs of the poplars. In the flooded ditch outside the rats are paddling about, making as much noise as otters. As the yellow dawn comes up behind us, the Andalusian sentry, muffled in his cloak, begins singing. Across no man's land, a hundred or two hundred yards away, you can hear the Fascist sentry also singing.

On 25 April, after the usual _*mañanas*_, another section relieved us and we handed over our rifles, packed our kits, and marched back to Monflorite. I was not sorry to leave the line. The lice were multiplying in my trousers far faster than I could massacre them, and for a month past I had had no socks and my boots had very little sole left, so that I was walking more or less barefoot. I wanted a hot bath, clean clothes, and a night between sheets more passionately than it is possible to want anything when one has been living a normal civilized life. We slept a few hours in a barn in Monflorite, jumped a lorry in the small hours, caught the five o'clock train at Barbastro, and—having the luck to connect with a fast train at Lérida—were in Barcelona by three o'clock in the afternoon of the 26th. And after that the trouble began.

CHAPTER 9

From Mandalay, in Upper Burma, you can travel by train to Maymyo, the principal hill-station of the province, on the edge of the Shan plateau. It is rather a queer experience. You start off in the typical atmosphere of an eastern city—the scorching sunlight, the dusty palms, the smells of fish and spices and garlic, the squashy tropical fruits, the swarming dark-faced human beings—and because you are so used to it you carry this atmosphere intact, so to speak, in your railway carriage. Mentally you are still in Mandalay when the train stops at Maymyo, four thousand feet above sea-level. But in stepping out of the carriage you step into a different hemisphere. Suddenly you are breathing cool sweet air that might be that of England, and all round you are green grass, bracken, fir-trees, and hill-women with pink cheeks selling baskets of strawberries.

Getting back to Barcelona, after three and a half months at the front, reminded me of this. There was the same abrupt and startling change of atmosphere. In the train, all the way to Barcelona, the atmosphere of the front persisted; the dirt, the noise, the discomfort, the ragged clothes, the feeling of privation, comradeship, and equality. The train, already full of militiamen when it left Barbastro, was invaded by more and more peasants at every station on the line; peasants with bundles of vegetables, with terrified fowls which they carried head-downwards, with sacks which looped and writhed all over the floor and were discovered to be full of live rabbits—finally with a quite considerable flock of sheep which were driven into the compartments and wedged into every empty space. The militiamen shouted revolutionary songs which drowned the rattle of the train and kissed their hands or waved red and black handkerchiefs to every pretty girl along the line. Bottles of wine and of anis, the filthy Aragónese liqueur, travelled from hand to hand. With the Spanish goat-skin water-bottles you can squirt a jet of wine right across a railway carriage into your friend's mouth, which saves a lot of trouble. Next to me a black-eyed boy of fifteen was recounting sensational and, I do not doubt, completely untrue stories of his own exploits at the front to two old leather-faced peasants who listened open-mouthed. Presently the peasants undid their bundles and gave us some sticky dark-red wine. Everyone was profoundly happy, more happy than I can convey. But when the train had rolled through Sabadell and into Barcelona, we stepped into an atmosphere that was scarcely less alien and hostile to us and our kind than if this had been Paris or London.

Everyone who has made two visits, at intervals of months, to Barcelona during the war has remarked upon the extraordinary changes that took place in it. And curiously enough, whether they went there first in August and again in January, or, like myself, first in December and again in April, the thing they said was always the same: that the revolutionary atmosphere had vanished. No doubt to anyone who had been there in August, when the blood was scarcely dry in the streets and militia were quartered in the smart hotels, Barcelona in December would have seemed bourgeois; to me, fresh from England, it was liker to a workers' city than anything I had conceived possible. Now the tide had rolled back. Once again it was an ordinary city, a little pinched and chipped by war, but with no outward sign of working-class predominance.

The change in the aspect of the crowds was startling. The militia uniform and the blue overalls had almost disappeared; everyone seemed to be wearing the smart summer suits in which Spanish tailors specialize. Fat prosperous men, elegant women, and sleek cars were everywhere. (It appeared that there were still no private cars; nevertheless, anyone who 'was anyone' seemed able to command a car.) The officers of the new Popular Army, a type that had scarcely existed when I left Barcelona, swarmed in surprising numbers. The Popular Army was officered at the rate of one officer to ten men. A certain number of these officers had served in the militia and been brought back from the front for technical instruction, but the majority were young men who had gone to the School of War in preference to joining the militia. Their relation to their men was not quite the same as in a bourgeois army, but there was a definite social difference, expressed by the difference of pay and uniform. The men wore a kind of coarse brown overalls, the officers wore an elegant khaki uniform with a tight waist, like a British Army officer's uniform, only a little more so. I do not suppose that more than one in twenty of them had yet been to the front, but all of them had automatic pistols strapped to their belts; we, at the front, could not get pistols for love or money. As we made our way up the street I noticed that people were staring at our dirty exteriors. Of course, like all men who have been several months in the line, we were a dreadful sight. I was conscious of looking like a scarecrow. My leather jacket was in tatters, my woollen cap had lost its shape and slid perpetually over one eye, my boots consisted of very little beyond splayed-out uppers. All of us were in more or less the same state, and in addition we were dirty and unshaven, so it was no wonder that the people stared. But it dismayed me a little, and brought it home to me that some queer things had been happening in the last three months.

During the next few days I discovered by innumerable signs that my first impression had not been wrong. A deep change had come over the town. There were two facts that were the keynote of all else. One was that the people—the civil population—had lost much of their interest in the war; the other was that the normal division of society into rich and poor, upper class and lower class, was reasserting itself.

The general indifference to the war was surprising and rather disgusting. It horrified people who came to Barcelona from Madrid or even from Valencia. Partly it was due to the remoteness of Barcelona from the actual fighting; I noticed the same thing a month later in Tarragona, where the ordinary life of a smart seaside town was continuing almost undisturbed. But it was significant that all over Spain voluntary enlistment had dwindled from about January onwards. In Catalonia, in February, there had been a wave of enthusiasm over the first big drive for the Popular Army, but it had not led to any great increase in recruiting. The war was only six months old or thereabouts when the Spanish Government had to resort to conscription, which would be natural in a foreign war, but seems anomalous in a civil war. Undoubtedly it was bound up with the disappointment of the revolutionary hopes with which the war had started. The trade union members who formed themselves into militias and chased the Fascists back to Zaragoza in the first few weeks of war had done so largely because they believed themselves to be fighting for working-class control; but it was becoming more and more obvious that working-class control was a lost cause, and the common people, especially the town proletariat, who have to fill the ranks in any war, civil or foreign, could not be blamed for a certain apathy. Nobody wanted to lose the war, but the majority were chiefly anxious for it to be over. You noticed this wherever you went. Everywhere you met with the same perfunctory remark: 'This war—terrible, isn't it? When is it going to end?' Politically conscious people were far more aware of the internecine struggle between Anarchist and Communist than of the fight against Franco. To the mass of the people the food shortage was the most important thing. 'The front' had come to be thought of as a mythical far-off place to which young men disappeared and either did not return or returned after three or four months with vast sums of money in their pockets.

(A militiaman usually received his back pay when he went on leave.) Wounded men, even when they were hopping about on crutches, did not receive any special consideration. To be in the militia was no longer fashionable. The shops, always the barometers of public taste, showed this clearly. When I first reached Barcelona the shops, poor and shabby though they were, had specialized in militiamen's equipment. Forage-caps, zipper jackets, Sam Browne belts, hunting-knives, water-bottles, revolver-holsters were displayed in every window. Now the shops were markedly smarter, but the war had been thrust into the background. As I discovered later, when buying my kit before going back to the front, certain things that one badly needed at the front were very difficult to procure.

Meanwhile there was going on a systematic propaganda against the party militias and in favour of the Popular Army. The position here was rather curious. Since February the entire armed forces had theoretically been incorporated in the Popular Army, and the militias were, on paper, reconstructed along Popular Army lines, with differential pay-rates, gazetted rank, etc., etc. The divisions were made up of 'mixed brigades', which were supposed to consist partly of Popular Army troops and partly of militia. But the only changes that had actually taken place were changes of name. The P.O.U.M. troops, for instance, previously called the Lenin Division, were now known as the 29th Division. Until June very few Popular Army troops reached the Aragón front, and in consequence the militias were able to retain their separate structure and their special character. But on every wall the Government agents had stencilled: 'We need a Popular Army', and over the radio and in the Communist Press there was a ceaseless and sometimes very malignant jibing against the militias, who were described as ill-trained, undisciplined, etc., etc.; the Popular Army was always described as 'heroic'. From much of this propaganda you would have derived the impression that there was something disgraceful in having gone to the front voluntarily and something praiseworthy in waiting to be conscripted. For the time being, however, the militias were holding the line while the Popular Army was training in the rear, and this fact had to be advertised as little as possible. Drafts of militia returning to the front were no longer marched through the streets with drums beating and flags flying. They were smuggled away by train or lorry at five o'clock in the morning. A few drafts of the Popular Army were now beginning to leave for the front, and these, as before, were marched ceremoniously through the streets; but even they, owing to the general waning of interest in the war, met with comparatively little enthusiasm. The fact that the militia troops were also, on paper. Popular Army troops, was skilfully used in the Press propaganda. Any credit that happened to be going was automatically handed to the Popular Army, while all blame was reserved for the militias. It sometimes happened that the same troops were praised in one capacity and blamed in the other.

But besides all this there was the startling change in the social atmosphere—a thing difficult to conceive unless you have actually experienced it. When I first reached Barcelona I had thought it a town where class distinctions and great differences of wealth hardly existed. Certainly that was what it looked like. 'Smart' clothes were an abnormality, nobody cringed or took tips, waiters and flower-women and bootblacks looked you in the eye and called you 'comrade'. I had not grasped that this was mainly a mixture of hope and camouflage. The working class believed in a revolution that had been begun but never consolidated, and the bourgeoisie were scared and temporarily disguising themselves as workers. In the first months of revolution there must have been many thousands of people who deliberately put on overalls and shouted revolutionary slogans as a way of saving their skins. Now things were returning to normal. The smart restaurants and hotels were full of rich people wolfing expensive meals, while for the working-class population food-prices had jumped enormously without any corresponding rise in wages. Apart from the expensiveness of everything, there were recurrent shortages of this and that, which, of course, always hit the poor rather than the rich. The restaurants and hotels seemed to have little difficulty in getting whatever they wanted, but in the working-class quarters the queues for bread, olive oil, and other necessaries were hundreds of yards long. Previously in Barcelona I had been struck by the absence of beggars; now there were quantities of them. Outside the delicatessen shop at the top of the *Ramblas* gangs of barefooted children were always waiting to swarm round anyone who came out and clamour for scraps of food. The 'revolutionary' forms of speech were dropping out of use. Strangers seldom addressed you as _tú_ and _camarada_ nowadays; it was usually _señor_ and _usted_. _Buenos días_ was beginning to replace _salud_. The waiters were back in their boiled shirts and the shop-walkers were cringing in the familiar manner. My wife and I went into a hosiery shop on the *Ramblas* to buy some stockings. The shopman bowed and rubbed his hands as they do not do even in England nowadays, though they used to do it twenty or thirty years ago. In a furtive indirect way the practice of tipping was coming back. The workers' patrols had been ordered to dissolve and the pre-war police forces were back on the streets. One result of this was that the cabaret show and high-class brothels, many of which had been closed by the workers' patrols, had promptly reopened.[9]

A small but significant instance of the way in which everything

---

[9] Orwell's footnote to the original edition read: "The workers' patrols are said to have closed 75 per cent of the brothels." An errata note found after his death says: "Remark should be modified. I have no good evidence that prostitution decreased 75 per cent in the early days of the war, and I believe the Anarchists went on the principle of 'collectivizing' the brothels, not suppressing them. But there was a drive against prostitution (posters, etc.) and it is a fact that the smart brothel and naked cabaret shows were shut in the early months of the war and open again when the war was about a year old."

was now orientated in favour of the wealthier classes could be seen in the tobacco shortage. For the mass of the people the shortage of tobacco was so desperate that cigarettes filled with sliced liquorice-root were being sold in the streets. I tried some of these once. (A lot of people tried them once.) Franco held the Canaries, where all the Spanish tobacco is grown; consequently the only stocks of tobacco left on the Government side were those that had been in existence before the war. These were running so low that the tobacconists' shops only opened once a week; after waiting for a couple of hours in a queue you might, if you were lucky, get a three-quarter-ounce packet of tobacco. Theoretically the Government would not allow tobacco to be purchased from abroad, because this meant reducing the gold-reserves, which had got to be kept for arms and other necessities. Actually there was a steady supply of smuggled foreign cigarettes of the more expensive kinds, Lucky Strikes and so forth, which gave a grand opportunity for profiteering. You could buy the smuggled cigarettes openly in the smart hotels and hardly less openly in the streets, provided that you could pay ten pesetas (a militiaman's daily wage) for a packet. The smuggling was for the benefit of wealthy people, and was therefore connived at. If you had enough money there was nothing that you could not get in any quantity, with the possible exception of bread, which was rationed fairly strictly. This open contrast of wealth and poverty would have been impossible a few months earlier, when the working class still were or seemed to be in control. But it would not be fair to attribute it solely to the shift of political power. Partly it was a result of the safety of life in Barcelona, where there was little to remind one of the war except an occasional air-raid. Everyone who had been in Madrid said that it was completely different there. In Madrid the common danger forced people of almost all kinds into some sense of comradeship. A fat man eating quails while children are begging for bread is a disgusting sight, but you are less likely to see it when you are within sound of the guns.

A day or two after the street-fighting I remember passing through one of the fashionable streets and coming upon a confectioner's shop with a window full of pastries and bonbons of the most elegant kinds, at staggering prices. It was the kind of shop you see in Bond Street or the *Rue de la Paix*. And I remember feeling a vague horror and amazement that money could still be wasted upon such things in a hungry war-stricken country. But God forbid that I should pretend to any personal superiority. After several months of discomfort I had a ravenous desire for decent food and wine, cocktails, American cigarettes, and so forth, and I admit to having wallowed in every luxury that I had money to buy. During that first week, before the street-fighting began, I had several preoccupations which interacted upon one another in a curious way. In the first place, as I have said, I was busy making myself as comfortable as I could. Secondly, thanks to over-eating and over-drinking, I was slightly out of health all that week. I would feel a little unwell, go to bed for half a day, get up and eat another excessive meal, and then feel ill again. At the same time I was making secret negotiations to buy a revolver. I badly wanted a revolver—in trench-fighting much more useful than a rifle—and they were very difficult to get hold of. The Government issued them to policemen and Popular Army officers, but refused to issue them to the militia; you had to buy them, illegally, from the secret stores of the Anarchists. After a lot of fuss and nuisance an Anarchist friend managed to procure me a tiny 26-mm. automatic pistol, a wretched weapon, useless at more than five yards but better than nothing. And besides all this I was making preliminary arrangements to leave the P.O.U.M. militia and enter some other unit that would ensure my being sent to the Madrid front.

I had told everyone for a long time past that I was going to leave the P.O.U.M. As far as my purely personal preferences went I would have liked to join the Anarchists. If one became a member of the

C.N.T. it was possible to enter the F.A.I. militia, but I was told that the F.A.I. were likelier to send me to Teruel than to Madrid. If I wanted to go to Madrid I must join the International Column, which meant getting a recommendation from a member of the Communist Party. I sought out a Communist friend, attached to the Spanish Medical Aid, and explained my case to him. He seemed very anxious to recruit me and asked me, if possible, to persuade some of the other I.L.P. Englishmen to come with me. If I had been in better health I should probably have agreed there and then. It is hard to say now what difference this would have made. Quite possibly I should have been sent to Albacete before the Barcelona fighting started; in which case, not having seen the fighting at close quarters, I might have accepted the official version of it as truthful. On the other hand, if I had been in Barcelona during the fighting, under Communist orders but still with a sense of personal loyalty to my comrades in the P.O.U.M., my position would have been impossible. But I had another week's leave due to me and I was very anxious to get my health back before returning to the line. Also—the kind of detail that is always deciding one's destiny—I had to wait while the boot-makers made me a new pair of marching boots. (The entire Spanish army had failed to produce a pair of boots big enough to fit me.) I told my Communist friend that I would make definite arrangements later. Meanwhile I wanted a rest. I even had a notion that we—my wife and I—might go to the seaside for two or three days. What an idea! The political atmosphere ought to have warned me that that was not the kind of thing one could do nowadays.

For under the surface-aspect of the town, under the luxury and growing poverty, under the seeming gaiety of the streets, with their flower-stalls, their many-coloured flags, their propaganda-posters, and thronging crowds, there was an unmistakable and horrible feeling of political rivalry and hatred. People of all shades of opinion were saying forebodingly: 'There's going to be trouble before long.'

The danger was quite simple and intelligible. It was the antagonism between those who wished the revolution to go forward and those who wished to check or prevent it—ultimately, between Anarchists and Communists. Politically there was now no power in Catalonia except the P.S.U.C. and their Liberal allies. But over against this there was the uncertain strength of the C.N.T., less well-armed and less sure of what they wanted than their adversaries, but powerful because of their numbers and their predominance in various key industries. Given this alignment of forces there was bound to be trouble. From the point of view of the P.S.U.C.-controlled Generalite, the first necessity, to make their position secure, was to get the weapons out of the C.N.T. workers' hands. As I have pointed out earlier, the move to break up the party militias was at bottom a manoeuvre towards this end. At the same time the pre-war armed police forces, Civil Guards, and so forth, had been brought back into use and were being heavily reinforced and armed. This could mean only one thing. The Civil Guards, in particular, were a gendarmerie of the ordinary continental type, who for nearly a century past had acted as the bodyguards of the possessing class. Meanwhile a decree had been issued that all arms held by private persons were to be surrendered. Naturally this order had not been obeyed; it was clear that the Anarchists' weapons could only be taken from them by force. Throughout this time there were rumours, always vague and contradictory owing to newspaper censorship, of minor clashes that were occurring all over Catalonia. In various places the armed police forces had made attacks on Anarchist strongholds. At Puigcerda, on the French frontier, a band of *Carabineros* were sent to seize the Customs Office, previously controlled by Anarchists and Antonio Martin, a well-known Anarchist, was killed.[10]

---

[10] Errata note found after Orwell's death: "I am told my reference to this incident is incorrect and misleading."

Similar incidents had occurred at Figueras and, I think, at Tarragona. In Barcelona there had been a series of more or less unofficial brawls in the working-class suburbs. C.N.T. and U.G.T. members had been murdering one another for some time past; on several occasions the murders were followed by huge, provocative funerals which were quite deliberately intended to stir up political hatred. A short time earlier a C.N.T. member had been murdered, and the C.N.T. had turned out in hundreds of thousands to follow the cortege. At the end of April, just after I got to Barcelona, Roldan, a prominent member of the U.G.T., was murdered, presumably by someone in the C.N.T. The Government ordered all shops to close and staged an enormous funeral procession, largely of Popular Army troops, which took two hours to pass a given point. From the hotel window I watched it without enthusiasm. It was obvious that the so-called funeral was merely a display of strength; a little more of this kind of thing and there might be bloodshed. The same night my wife and I were woken by a fusillade of shots from the *Plaza de Cataluña*, a hundred or two hundred yards away. We learned next day that it was a man being bumped off, presumably by someone in the U.G.T. It was of course distinctly possible that all these murders were committed by _agents provocateurs_. One can gauge the attitude of the foreign capitalist Press towards the Communist-Anarchist feud by the fact that Roldan's murder was given wide publicity, while the answering murder was carefully unmentioned.

The 1st of May was approaching, and there was talk of a monster demonstration in which both the C.N.T. and the U.G.T. were to take part. The C.N.T. leaders, more moderate than many of their followers, had long been working for a reconciliation with the U.G.T.; indeed the keynote of their policy was to try and form the two blocks of unions into one huge coalition. The idea was that the C.N.T.and U.G.T. should march together and display their solidarity. But at the last moment the demonstration was called off.

It was perfectly clear that it would only lead to rioting. So nothing happened on 1 May. It was a queer state of affairs. Barcelona, the so-called revolutionary city, was probably the only city in non-Fascist Europe that had no celebrations that day. But I admit I was rather relieved. The I.L.P. contingent was expected to march in the P.O.U.M. section of the procession, and everyone expected trouble. The last thing I wished for was to be mixed up in some meaningless street-fight. To be marching up the street behind red flags inscribed with elevating slogans, and then to be bumped off from an upper window by some total stranger with a sub-machine-gun—that is not my idea of a useful way to die.

CHAPTER 10

About midday on 3 May a friend crossing the lounge of the hotel said casually: 'There's been some kind of trouble at the Telephone Exchange, I hear.' For some reason I paid no attention to it at the time.

That afternoon, between three and four, I was half-way down the Ramblas when I heard several rifle-shots behind me. I turned round and saw some youths, with rifles in their hands and the red and black handkerchiefs of the Anarchists round their throats, edging up a side-street that ran off the *Ramblas* northward. They were evidently exchanging shots with someone in a tall octagonal tower—a church, I think—that commanded the side-street. I thought instantly: 'It's started!' But I thought it without any very great feeling of surprise—for days past everyone had been expecting 'it' to start at any moment. I realized that I must get back to the hotel at once and see if my wife was all right. But the knot of Anarchists round the opening of the side-street were motioning the people back and shouting to them not to cross the line of fire. More shots rang out. The bullets from the tower were flying across the street and a crowd of panic-stricken people was rushing down the *Ramblas*, away from the firing; up and down the street you could hear snap-snap-snap as the shopkeepers slammed the steel shutters over their windows. I saw two Popular Army officers retreating cautiously from tree to tree with their hands on their revolvers. In front of me the crowd was surging into the Metro station in the middle of the *Ramblas* to take cover. I immediately decided not to follow them. It might mean being trapped underground for hours.

At this moment an American doctor who had been with us at the front ran up to me and grabbed me by the arm. He was greatly excited.

'Come on, we must get down to the Hotel Falcon.' (The Hotel Falcon was a sort of boarding-house maintained by the P.O.U.M. and used chiefly by militiamen on leave.) 'The P.O.U.M. chaps will be meeting there. The trouble's starting. We must hang together.'

'But what the devil is it all about?' I said.

The doctor was hauling me along by the arm. He was too excited to give a very clear statement. It appeared that he had been in the Plaza de Cataluña when several lorry-loads of armed Civil Guards[11] had driven up to the Telephone Exchange, which was operated mainly by C.N.T. workers, and made a sudden assault upon it. Then some Anarchists had arrived and there had been a general affray. I gathered that the 'trouble' earlier in the day had been a demand by the Government to hand over the Telephone Exchange, which, of course, was refused.

As we moved down the street a lorry raced past us from the opposite direction. It was full of Anarchists with rifles in their hands. In front a ragged youth was lying on a pile of mattresses behind a light machine-gun. When we got to the Hotel Falcon, which was at the bottom of the *Ramblas*, a crowd of people was seething in the entrance-hall; there was a great confusion, nobody seemed to know what we were expected to do, and nobody was armed except the

---

11 Errata note found after Orwell's death: 'All through these chapters are constant references to 'Civil Guards.' Should be 'Assault Guards' all the way through. I was misled because the Assault Guards in Catalonia wore a different uniform from those afterwards sent from Valenica, and by the Spaniards' referring to all these formations as '_la guardia._' The undoubted fact that civil guards often joined Franco when able to do so makes no reflection on the Assault Guards who were a formation raised since the Second Republic. But the general reference to popular hostility to '_la guardia_' and this having played its part in the Barcelona business should stand.

handful of Shock Troopers who usually acted as guards for the building. I went across to the Comite Local of the P.O.U.M., which was almost opposite. Upstairs, in the room where militiamen normally went to draw their pay, another crowd was seething. A tall, pale, rather handsome man of about thirty, in civilian clothes, was trying to restore order and handing out belts and cartridge-boxes from a pile in the corner. There seemed to be no rifles as yet. The doctor had disappeared—I believe there had already been casualties and a call for doctors—but another Englishman had arrived. Presently, from an inner office, the tall man and some others began bringing out armfuls of rifles and handing them round. The other Englishman and myself, as foreigners, were slightly under suspicion and at first nobody would give us a rifle. Then a militiaman whom I had known at the front arrived and recognized me, after which we were given rifles and a few clips of cartridges, somewhat grudgingly.

There was a sound of firing in the distance and the streets were completely empty of people. Everyone said that it was impossible to go up the Ramblas. The Civil Guards had seized buildings in commanding positions and were letting fly at everyone who passed. I would have risked it and gone back to the hotel, but there was a vague idea floating round that the *Comite Local* was likely to be attacked at any moment and we had better stand by. All over the building, on the stairs, and on the pavement outside, small knots of people were standing and talking excitedly. No one seemed to have a very clear idea of what was happening. All I could gather was that the Civil Guards had attacked the Telephone Exchange and seized various strategic spots that commanded other buildings belonging to the workers. There was a general impression that the Civil Guards were 'after' the C.N.T. and the working class generally. It was noticeable that, at this stage, no one seemed to put the blame on the Government. The poorer classes in Barcelona looked upon the Civil Guards as something rather resembling the Black and

Tans, and it seemed to be taken for granted that they had started this attack on their own initiative. Once I heard how things stood I felt easier in my mind. The issue was clear enough. On one side the C.N.T., on the other side the police. I have no particular love for the idealized 'worker' as he appears in the bourgeois Communist's mind, but when I see an actual flesh-and-blood worker in conflict with his natural enemy, the policeman, I do not have to ask myself which side I am on.

A long time passed and nothing seemed to be happening at our end of the town. It did not occur to me that I could ring up the hotel and find out whether my wife was all right; I took it for granted that the Telephone Exchange would have stopped working—though, as a matter of fact, it was only out of action for a couple of hours. There seemed to be about three hundred people in the two buildings. Predominantly they were people of the poorest class, from the back-streets down by the quays; there was a number of women among them, some of them carrying babies, and a crowd of little ragged boys. I fancy that many of them had no notion what was happening and had simply fled into the P.O.U.M. buildings for protection. There was also a number of militiamen on leave, and a sprinkling of foreigners. As far as I could estimate, there were only about sixty rifles between the lot of us. The office upstairs was ceaselessly besieged by a crowd of people who were demanding rifles and being told that there were none left. The younger militia boys, who seemed to regard the whole affair as a kind of picnic, were prowling round and trying to wheedle or steal rifles from anyone who had them. It was not long before one of them got my rifle away from me by a clever dodge and immediately made himself scarce. So I was unarmed again, except for my tiny automatic pistol, for which I had only one clip of cartridges.

It grew dark, I was getting hungry, and seemingly there was no food in the Falcon. My friend and I slipped out to his hotel, which was not far away, to get some dinner. The streets were utterly dark and silent, not a soul stirring, steel shutters drawn over all the shop windows, but no barricades built yet. There was a great fuss before they would let us into the hotel, which was locked and barred. When we got back I learned that the Telephone Exchange was working and went to the telephone in the office upstairs to ring up my wife. Characteristically, there was no telephone directory in the building, and I did not know the number of the Hotel Continental; after a searching from room to room for about an hour I came upon a guide-book which gave me the number. I could not make contact with my wife, but I managed to get hold of John McNair, the I.L.P. representative in Barcelona. He told me that all was well, nobody had been shot, and asked me if we were all right at the *Comite Local*. I said that we should be all right if we had some cigarettes. I only meant this as a joke; nevertheless half an hour later McNair appeared with two packets of Lucky Strikes. He had braved the pitch-dark streets, roamed by Anarchist patrols who had twice stopped him at the pistol's point and examined his papers. I shall not forget this small act of heroism. We were very glad of the cigarettes.

They had placed armed guards at most of the windows, and in the street below a little group of Shock Troopers were stopping and questioning the few passers-by. An Anarchist patrol car drove up, bristling with weapons. Beside the driver a beautiful dark-haired girl of about eighteen was nursing a sub-machine-gun across her knees. I spent a long time wandering about the building, a great rambling place of which it was impossible to learn the geography. Everywhere was the usual litter, the broken furniture and torn paper that seem to be the inevitable products of revolution. All over the place people were sleeping; on a broken sofa in a passage two poor women from the quayside were peacefully snoring. The place had been a cabaret-theatre before the P.O.U.M. took it over. There were raised stages in several of the rooms; on one of them was a desolate grand piano. Finally I discovered what I was looking for—the armoury. I did not know how this affair was going to turn out, and I badly wanted a weapon. I had heard it said so often that all the rival parties, P.S.U.C., P.O.U.M., and C.N.T.-F.A.I. alike, were hoarding arms in Barcelona, that I could not believe that two of the principal P.O.U.M. buildings contained only the fifty or sixty rifles that I had seen. The room which acted as an armoury was unguarded and had a flimsy door; another Englishman and myself had no difficulty in prizing it open. When we got inside we found that what they had told us was true—there _were_ no more weapons. All we found there were about two dozen small-bore rifles of an obsolete pattern and a few shot-guns, with no cartridges for any of them. I went up to the office and asked if they had any spare pistol ammunition; they had none. There were a few boxes of bombs, however, which one of the Anarchist patrol cars had brought us. I put a couple in one of my cartridge-boxes. They were a crude type of bomb, ignited by rubbing a sort of match at the top and very liable to go off of their own accord.

People were sprawling asleep all over the floor. In one room a baby was crying, crying ceaselessly. Though this was May the night was getting cold. On one of the cabaret-stages the curtains were still up, so I ripped a curtain down with my knife, rolled myself up in it, and had a few hours' sleep. My sleep was disturbed, I remember, by the thought of those beastly bombs, which might blow me into the air if I rolled on them too vigorously. At three in the morning the tall handsome man who seemed to be in command woke me up, gave me a rifle, and put me on guard at one of the windows. He told me that Salas, the Chief of Police responsible for the attack on the Telephone Exchange, had been placed under arrest. (Actually, as we learned later, he had only been deprived of his post. Nevertheless the news confirmed the general impression that the Civil Guards had acted without orders.) As soon as it was dawn the people downstairs began building two barricades, one outside the *Comite Local* and the other outside the Hotel Falcon. The Barcelona streets are paved with square cobbles, easily built up into a wall, and under the cobbles is a kind of shingle that is good for filling sand-bags. The building of those barricades was a strange and wonderful sight; I would have given something to be able to photograph it. With the kind of passionate energy that Spaniards display when they have definitely decided to begin upon any job of work, long lines of men, women, and quite small children were tearing up the cobblestones, hauling them along in a hand-cart that had been found somewhere, and staggering to and fro under heavy sacks of sand. In the doorway of the *Comite Local* a German-Jewish girl, in a pair of militiaman's trousers whose knee-buttons just reached her ankles, was watching with a smile. In a couple of hours the barricades were head-high, with riflemen posted at the loopholes, and behind one barricade a fire was burning and men were frying eggs.

They had taken my rifle away again, and there seemed to be nothing that one could usefully do. Another Englishman and myself decided to go back to the Hotel Continental. There was a lot of firing in the distance, but seemingly none in the *Ramblas*. On the way up we looked in at the food-market. A very few stalls had opened; they were besieged by a crowd of people from the working-class quarters south of the *Ramblas*. Just as we got there, there was a heavy crash of rifle-fire outside, some panes of glass in the roof were shivered, and the crowd went flying for the back exits. A few stalls remained open, however; we managed to get a cup of coffee each and buy a wedge of goat's-milk cheese which I tucked in beside my bombs. A few days later I was very glad of that cheese.

At the street-corner where I had seen the Anarchists begin firing the day before a barricade was now standing. The man behind it (I was on the other side of the street) shouted to me to be careful. The Civil Guards in the church tower were firing indiscriminately at everyone who passed. I paused and then crossed the opening at a run; sure enough, a bullet cracked past me, uncomfortably close. When I neared the P.O.U.M. Executive Building, still on the other side of the road, there were fresh shouts of warning from some Shock Troopers standing in the doorway—shouts which, at the moment, I did not understand. There were trees and a newspaper kiosk between myself and the building (streets of this type in Spain have a broad walk running down the middle), and I could not see what they were pointing at. I went up to the Continental, made sure that all was well, washed my face, and then went back to the P.O.U.M. Executive Building (it was about a hundred yards down the street) to ask for orders. By this time the roar of rifle and machine-gun fire from various directions was almost comparable to the din of a battle. I had just found Kopp and was asking him what we were supposed to do when there was a series of appalling crashes down below. The din was so loud that I made sure someone must be firing at us with a field-gun. Actually it was only hand-grenades, which make double their usual noise when they burst among stone buildings.

Kopp glanced out of the window, cocked his stick behind his back, said: 'Let us investigate,' and strolled down the stairs in his usual unconcerned manner, I following. Just inside the doorway a group of Shock Troopers were bowling bombs down the pavement as though playing skittles. The bombs were bursting twenty yards away with a frightful, ear-splitting crash which was mixed up with the banging of rifles. Half across the street, from behind the newspaper kiosk, a head—it was the head of an American militiaman whom I knew well—was sticking up, for all the world like a coconut at a fair. It was only afterwards that I grasped what was really happening. Next door to the P.O.U.M. building there was a *café* with a hotel above it, called the *Café Moka*. The day before twenty or thirty armed Civil Guards had entered the *café* and then, when the fighting started, had suddenly seized the building and barricaded themselves in. Presumably they had been ordered to seize the café as a preliminary to attacking the P.O.U.M. offices later. Early in the morning they had attempted to come out, shots had been exchanged, and one Shock Trooper was badly wounded and a Civil Guard killed. The Civil Guards had fled back into the *café*, but when the American came down the street they had opened fire on him, though he was not armed. The American had flung himself behind the kiosk for cover, and the Shock Troopers were flinging bombs at the Civil Guards to drive them indoors again.

Kopp took in the scene at a glance, pushed his way forward and hauled back a red-haired German Shock Trooper who was just drawing the pin out of a bomb with his teeth. He shouted to everyone to stand back from the doorway, and told us in several languages that we had got to avoid bloodshed. Then he stepped out on to the pavement and, in sight of the Civil Guards, ostentatiously took off his pistol and laid it on the ground. Two Spanish militia officers did the same, and the three of them walked slowly up to the doorway where the Civil Guards were huddling. It was a thing I would not have done for twenty pounds. They were walking, unarmed, up to men who were frightened out of their wits and had loaded guns in their hands. A Civil Guard, in shirt-sleeves and livid with fright, came out of the door to parley with Kopp. He kept pointing in an agitated manner at two unexploded bombs that were lying on the pavement. Kopp came back and told us we had better touch the bombs off. Lying there, they were a danger to anyone who passed. A Shock Trooper fired his rifle at one of the bombs and burst it, then fired at the other and missed. I asked him to give me his rifle, knelt down and let fly at the second bomb. I also missed it, I am sorry to say. This was the only shot I fired during the disturbances. The pavement was covered with broken glass from the sign over the *Café Moka*, and two cars that were parked outside, one of them Kopp's official car, had been riddled with bullets and their windscreens smashed by bursting bombs.

Kopp took me upstairs again and explained the situation. We had got to defend the P.O.U.M. buildings if they were attacked, but the P.O.U.M. leaders had sent instructions that we were to stand on the defensive and not open fire if we could possibly avoid it. Immediately opposite there was a cinematograph, called the Poliorama, with a museum above it, and at the top, high above the general level of the roofs, a small observatory with twin domes. The domes commanded the street, and a few men posted up there with rifles could prevent any attack on the P.O.U.M. buildings. The caretakers at the cinema were C.N.T. members and would let us come and go. As for the Civil Guards in the *Café Moka*, there would be no trouble with them; they did not want to fight and would be only too glad to live and let live. Kopp repeated that our orders were not to fire unless we were fired on ourselves or our buildings attacked. I gathered, though he did not say so, that the P.O.U.M. leaders were furious at being dragged into this affair, but felt that they had got to stand by the C.N.T.

They had already placed guards in the observatory. The next three days and nights I spent continuously on the roof of the Poliorama, except for brief intervals when I slipped across to the hotel for meals. I was in no danger, I suffered from nothing worse than hunger and boredom, yet it was one of the most unbearable periods of my whole life. I think few experiences could be more sickening, more disillusioning, or, finally, more nerve-racking than those evil days of street warfare.

I used to sit on the roof marvelling at the folly of it all. From the little windows in the observatory you could see for miles around—vista after vista of tall slender buildings, glass domes, and fantastic curly roofs with brilliant green and copper tiles; over to eastward the glittering pale blue sea—the first glimpse of the sea that I had had since coming to Spain. And the whole huge town of a million people was locked in a sort of violent inertia, a nightmare of noise without movement. The sunlit streets were quite empty. Nothing was happening except the streaming of bullets from barricades and sand-bagged windows. Not a vehicle was stirring in the streets; here and there along the *Ramblas* the trams stood motionless where their drivers had jumped out of them when the fighting started. And all the while the devilish noise, echoing from thousands of stone buildings, went on and on and on, like a tropical rainstorm. Crack-crack, rattle-rattle, roar—sometimes it died away to a few shots, sometimes it quickened to a deafening fusillade, but it never stopped while daylight lasted, and punctually next dawn it started again.

What the devil was happening, who was fighting whom, and who was winning, was at first very difficult to discover. The people of Barcelona are so used to street-fighting and so familiar with the local geography that they knew by a kind of instinct which political party will hold which streets and which buildings. A foreigner is at a hopeless disadvantage. Looking out from the observatory, I could grasp that the *Ramblas*, which is one of the principal streets of the town, formed a dividing line. To the right of the *Ramblas* the working-class quarters were solidly Anarchist; to the left a confused fight was going on among the tortuous by-streets, but on that side the P.S.U.C. and the Civil Guards were more or less in control. Up at our end of the *Ramblas*, round the *Plaza de Cataluña*, the position was so complicated that it would have been quite unintelligible if every building had not flown a party flag. The principal landmark here was the *Hotel Colon*, the headquarters of the P.S.U.C., dominating the *Plaza de Cataluña*. In a window near the last O but one in the huge '*Hotel Colon*' that sprawled across its face they had a machine-gun that could sweep the square with deadly effect. A hundred yards to the right of us, down the *Ramblas*, the J.S.U., the youth league of the P.S.U.C. (corresponding to the Young Communist League in England), were holding a big department store whose sandbagged side-windows fronted our observatory. They had hauled down their red flag and hoisted the Catalan national flag. On the Telephone Exchange, the starting-point of all the trouble, the Catalan national flag and the Anarchist flag were flying side by side. Some kind of temporary compromise had been arrived at there, the exchange was working uninterruptedly and there was no firing from the building.

In our position it was strangely peaceful. The Civil Guards in the *Café Moka* had drawn down the steel curtains and piled up the café furniture to make a barricade. Later half a dozen of them came on to the roof, opposite to ourselves, and built another barricade of mattresses, over which they hung a Catalan national flag. But it was obvious that they had no wish to start a fight. Kopp had made a definite agreement with them: if they did not fire at us we would not fire at them. He had grown quite friendly with the Civil Guards by this time, and had been to visit them several times in the *Café Moka*. Naturally they had looted everything drinkable the *café* possessed, and they made Kopp a present of fifteen bottles of beer. In return Kopp had actually given them one of our rifles to make up for one they had somehow lost on the previous day. Nevertheless, it was a queer feeling sitting on that roof. Sometimes I was merely bored with the whole affair, paid no attention to the hellish noise, and spent hours reading a succession of Penguin Library books which, luckily, I had bought a few days earlier; sometimes I was very conscious of the armed men watching me fifty yards away. It was a little like being in the trenches again; several times I caught myself, from force of habit, speaking of the Civil Guards as 'the Fascists'. There were generally about six of us up there. We placed a man on guard in each of the observatory towers, and the rest of us sat on the lead roof below, where there was no cover except a stone palisade. I was well aware that at any moment the Civil Guards might receive telephone orders to open fire. They had agreed to give us warning before doing so, but there was no certainty that they would keep to their agreement. Only once, however, did trouble look like starting. One of the Civil Guards opposite knelt down and began firing across the barricade. I was on guard in the observatory at the time. I trained my rifle on him and shouted across:

'Hi! Don't you shoot at us!'

'What?'

'Don't you fire at us or we'll fire back!'

'No, no! I wasn't firing at you. Look—down there!'

He motioned with his rifle towards the side-street that ran past the bottom of our building. Sure enough, a youth in blue overalls, with a rifle in his hand, was dodging round the corner. Evidently he had just taken a shot at the Civil Guards on the roof.

'I was firing at him. He fired first.' (I believe this was true.) 'We don't want to shoot you. We're only workers, the same as you are.'

He made the anti-Fascist salute, which I returned. I shouted across:

'Have you got any more beer left?'

'No, it's all gone.'

The same day, for no apparent reason, a man in the J.S.U. building farther down the street suddenly raised his rifle and let fly at me when I was leaning out of the window. Perhaps I made a tempting mark. I did not fire back. Though he was only a hundred yards away the bullet went so wide that it did not even hit the roof of the observatory. As usual, Spanish standards of marksmanship had saved me. I was fired at several times from this building.

The devilish racket of firing went on and on. But so far as I could see, and from all I heard, the fighting was defensive on both sides. People simply remained in their buildings or behind their barricades and blazed away at the people opposite. About half a mile away from us there was a street where some of the main offices of the C.N.T. and the U.G.T. were almost exactly facing one another; from that direction the volume of noise was terrific. I passed down that street the day after the fighting was over and the panes of the shop-windows were like sieves. (Most of the shopkeepers in Barcelona had their windows criss-crossed with strips of paper, so that when a bullet hit a pane it did not shiver to pieces.) Sometimes the rattle of rifle and machine-gun fire was punctuated by the crash of hand-grenades. And at long intervals, perhaps a dozen times in all, there were tremendously heavy explosions which at the time I could not account for; they sounded like aerial bombs, but that was impossible, for there were no aeroplanes about. I was told afterwards—quite possibly it was true—that _agents provocateurs_ were touching off masses of explosive in order to increase the general noise and panic. There was, however, no artillery-fire. I was listening for this, for if the guns began to fire it would mean that the affair was becoming serious (artillery is the determining factor in street warfare). Afterwards there were wild tales in the newspapers about batteries of guns firing in the streets, but no one was able to point to a building that had been hit by a shell. In any case the sound of gunfire is unmistakable if one is used to it.

Almost from the start food was running short. With difficulty and under cover of darkness (for the Civil Guards were constantly sniping into the *Ramblas*) food was brought from the *Hotel Falcon* for the fifteen or twenty militiamen who were in the P.O.U.M. Executive Building, but there was barely enough to go round, and as many of us as possible went to the *Hotel Continental* for our meals. The *Continental* had been 'collectivized' by the *Generalite* and not, like most of the hotels, by the C.N.T. or U.G.T., and it was regarded as neutral ground. No sooner had the fighting started than the hotel filled to the brim with a most extraordinary collection of people. There were foreign journalists, political suspects of every shade, an American airman in the service of the Government, various Communist agents, including a fat, sinister-looking Russian, said to be an agent of the Ogpu, who was nicknamed Charlie Chan and wore attached to his waist-band a revolver and a neat little bomb, some families of well-to-do Spaniards who looked like Fascist sympathizers, two or three wounded men from the International Column, a gang of lorry drivers from some huge French lorries which had been carrying a load of oranges back to France and had been held up by the fighting, and a number of Popular Army officers. The Popular Army, as a body, remained neutral throughout the fighting, though a few soldiers slipped away from the barracks and took part as individuals; on the Tuesday morning I had seen a couple of them at the P.O.U.M. barricades. At the beginning, before the food-shortage became acute and the newspapers began stirring up hatred, there was a tendency to regard the whole affair as a joke. This was the kind of thing that happened every year in Barcelona, people were saying. George Tioli, an Italian journalist, a great friend of ours, came in with his trousers drenched with blood. He had gone out to see what was happening and had been binding up a wounded man on the pavement when someone playfully tossed a hand-grenade at him, fortunately not wounding him seriously. I remember his remarking that the Barcelona paving-stones ought to be numbered; it would save such a lot of trouble in building and demolishing barricades. And I remember a couple of men from the International Column sitting in my room at the hotel when I came in tired, hungry, and dirty after a night on guard. Their attitude was completely neutral. If they had been good party-men they would, I suppose, have urged me to change sides, or even have pinioned me and taken away the bombs of which my pockets were full; instead they merely commiserated with me for having to spend my leave in doing guard-duty on a roof. The general attitude was: 'This is only a dust-up between the Anarchists and the police—it doesn't mean anything.' In spite of the extent of the fighting and the number of casualties I believe this was nearer the truth than the official version which represented the affair as a planned rising.

It was about Wednesday (5 May) that a change seemed to come over things. The shuttered streets looked ghastly. A very few pedestrians, forced abroad for one reason or another, crept to and fro, flourishing white handkerchiefs, and at a spot in the middle of the *Ramblas* that was safe from bullets some men were crying newspapers to the empty street. On Tuesday _Solidaridad Obrera_, the Anarchist paper, had described the attack on the Telephone Exchange as a 'monstrous provocation' (or words to that effect), but on Wednesday it changed its tune and began imploring everyone to go back to work. The Anarchist leaders were broadcasting the same message. The office of _La Batalla_, the P.O.U.M. paper, which was not defended, had been raided and seized by the Civil Guards at about the same time as the Telephone Exchange, but the paper was being printed, and a few copies distributed, from another address. I urged everyone to remain at the barricades. People were divided in their minds and wondering uneasily how the devil this was going to end. I doubt whether anyone left the barricades as yet, but everyone was sick of the meaningless fighting, which could obviously lead to no real decision, because no one wanted this to develop into a full-sized civil war which might mean losing the war against Franco. I heard this fear expressed on all sides. So far as one could gather from what people were saying at the time the C.N.T. rank and file wanted, and had wanted from the beginning, only two things: the handing back of the Telephone Exchange and the disarming of the hated Civil Guards. If the *Generalite* had promised to do these two things, and also promised to put an end to the food profiteering, there is little doubt that the barricades would have been down in two hours. But it was obvious that the Generalite was not going to give in. Ugly rumours were flying round. It was said that the Valencia Government was sending six thousand men to occupy Barcelona, and that five thousand Anarchist and P.O.U.M. troops had left the Aragón front to oppose them. Only the first of these rumours was true. Watching from the observatory tower we saw the low grey shapes of warships closing in upon the harbour. Douglas Moyle, who had been a sailor, said that they looked like British destroyers. As a matter of fact they _were_ British destroyers, though we did not learn this till afterwards.

That evening we heard that on the *Plaza de España* four hundred Civil Guards had surrendered and handed their arms to the Anarchists; also the news was vaguely filtering through that in the suburbs (mainly working-class quarters) the C.N.T. were in control. It looked as though we were winning. But the same evening Kopp sent for me and, with a grave face, told me that according to information he had just received the Government was about to outlaw the P.O.U.M. and declare a state of war upon it. The news gave me a shock. It was the first glimpse I had had of the interpretation that was likely to be put upon this affair later on. I dimly foresaw that when the fighting ended the entire blame would be laid upon the P.O.U.M., which was the weakest party and therefore the most suitable scapegoat. And meanwhile our local neutrality was at an end. If the Government declared war upon us we had no choice but to defend ourselves, and here at the Executive building we could be certain that the Civil Guards next door would get orders to attack us. Our only chance was to attack them first. Kopp was waiting for orders on the telephone; if we heard definitely that the P.O.U.M. was outlawed we must make preparations at once to seize the *Café Moka*.

I remember the long, nightmarish evening that we spent in fortifying the building. We locked the steel curtains across the front entrance and behind them built a barricade of slabs of stone left behind by the workmen who had been making some alterations. We went over our stock of weapons. Counting the six rifles that were on the roof of the *Poliorama* opposite, we had twenty-one rifles, one of them defective, about fifty rounds of ammunition for each rifle, and a few dozen bombs; otherwise nothing except a few pistols and revolvers. About a dozen men, mostly Germans, had volunteered for the attack on the *Café Moka*, if it came off. We should attack from the roof, of course, some time in the small hours, and take them by surprise; they were more numerous, but our morale was better, and no doubt we could storm the place, though people were bound to be killed in doing so. We had no food in the building except a few slabs of chocolate, and the rumour had gone round that 'they' were going to cut off the water supply. (Nobody knew who 'they' were. It might be the Government that controlled the waterworks, or it might be the C.N.T.—nobody knew.) We spent a long time filling up every basin in the lavatories, every bucket we could lay hands on, and, finally, the fifteen beer bottles, now empty, which the Civil Guards had given to Kopp.

I was in a ghastly frame of mind and dog-tired after about sixty hours without much sleep. It was now late into the night. People were sleeping all over the floor behind the barricade downstairs. Upstairs there was a small room, with a sofa in it, which we intended to use as a dressing-station, though, needless to say, we discovered that there was neither iodine nor bandages in the building. My wife had come down from the hotel in case a nurse should be needed. I lay down on the sofa, feeling that I would like half an hour's rest before the attack on the *Moka*, in which I should presumably be killed. I remember the intolerable discomfort caused by my pistol, which was strapped to my belt and sticking into the small of my back. And the next thing I remember is waking up with a jerk to find my wife standing beside me. It was broad daylight, nothing had happened, the Government had not declared war on the P.O.U.M., the water had not been cut off, and except for the sporadic firing in the streets everything was normal. My wife said that she had not had the heart to wake me and had slept in an arm-chair in one of the front rooms.

That afternoon there was a kind of armistice. The firing died away and with surprising suddenness the streets filled with people.

A few shops began to pull up their shutters, and the market was packed with a huge crowd clamouring for food, though the stalls were almost empty. It was noticeable, however, that the trams did not start running. The Civil Guards were still behind their barricades in the *Moka*; on neither side were the fortified buildings evacuated. Everyone was rushing round and trying to buy food. And on every side you heard the same anxious questions: 'Do you think it's stopped? Do you think it's going to start again?' 'It'—the fighting—was now thought of as some kind of natural calamity, like a hurricane or an earthquake, which was happening to us all alike and which we had no power of stopping. And sure enough, almost immediately—I suppose there must really have been several hours' truce, but they seemed more like minutes than hours—a sudden crash of rifle-fire, like a June cloud-burst, sent everyone scurrying; the steel shutters snapped into place, the streets emptied like magic, the barricades were manned, and 'it' had started again.

I went back to my post on the roof with a feeling of concentrated disgust and fury. When you are taking part in events like these you are, I suppose, in a small way, making history, and you ought by rights to feel like a historical character. But you never do, because at such times the physical details always outweigh everything else. Throughout the fighting I never made the correct 'analysis' of the situation that was so glibly made by journalists hundreds of miles away. What I was chiefly thinking about was not the rights and wrongs of this miserable internecine scrap, but simply the discomfort and boredom of sitting day and night on that intolerable roof, and the hunger which was growing worse and worse—for none of us had had a proper meal since Monday. It was in my mind all the while that I should have to go back to the front as soon as this business was over. It was infuriating. I had been a hundred and fifteen days in the line and had come back to Barcelona ravenous for a bit of rest and comfort; and instead I had to spend my time sitting on a roof opposite Civil Guards as bored as myself, who periodically waved to me and assured me that they were 'workers' (meaning that they hoped I would not shoot them), but who would certainly open fire if they got the order to do so. If this was history it did not feel like it. It was more like a bad period at the front, when men were short and we had to do abnormal hours of guard-duty; instead of being heroic one just had to stay at one's post, bored, dropping with sleep, and completely uninterested as to what it was all about.

Inside the hotel, among the heterogeneous mob who for the most part had not dared to put their noses out of doors, a horrible atmosphere of suspicion had grown up. Various people were infected with spy mania and were creeping round whispering that everyone else was a spy of the Communists, or the Trotskyists, or the Anarchists, or what-not. The fat Russian agent was cornering all the foreign refugees in turn and explaining plausibly that this whole affair was an Anarchist plot. I watched him with some interest, for it was the first time that I had seen a person whose profession was telling lies—unless one counts journalists. There was something repulsive in the parody of smart hotel life that was still going on behind shuttered windows amid the rattle of rifle-fire. The front dining-room had been abandoned after a bullet came through the window and chipped a pillar, and the guests were crowded into a darkish room at the back, where there were never quite enough tables to go round. The waiters were reduced in numbers—some of them were C.N.T. members and had joined in the general strike—and had dropped their boiled shirts for the time being, but meals were still being served with a pretence of ceremony. There was, however, practically nothing to eat. On that Thursday night the principal dish at dinner was one sardine each. The hotel had had no bread for days, and even the wine was running so low that we were drinking older and older wines at higher and higher prices. This shortage of food went on for several days after the fighting was over.

Three days running, I remember, my wife and I breakfasted off a little piece of goat's-milk cheese with no bread and nothing to drink. The only thing that was plentiful was oranges. The French lorry drivers brought quantities of their oranges into the hotel. They were a tough-looking bunch; they had with them some flashy Spanish girls and a huge porter in a black blouse. At any other time the little snob of a hotel manager would have done his best to make them uncomfortable, in fact would have refused to have them on the premises, but at present they were popular because, unlike the rest of us, they had a private store of bread which everyone was trying to cadge from them.

I spent that final night on the roof, and the next day it did really look as though the fighting was coming to an end. I do not think there was much firing that day—the Friday. No one seemed to know for certain whether the troops from Valencia were really coming; they arrived that evening, as a matter of fact. The Government was broadcasting half-soothing, half-threatening messages, asking everyone to go home and saying that after a certain hour anyone found carrying arms would be arrested. Not much attention was paid to the Government's broadcasts, but everywhere the people were fading away from the barricades. I have no doubt that it was mainly the food shortage that was responsible. From every side you heard the same remark: 'We have no more food, we must go back to work.' On the other hand the Civil Guards, who could count on getting their rations so long as there was any food in the town, were able to stay at their posts. By the afternoon the streets were almost normal, though the deserted barricades were still standing; the *Ramblas* were thronged with people, the shops nearly all open, and—most reassuring of all—the trams that had stood so long in frozen blocks jerked into motion and began running. The Civil Guards were still holding the *Café Moka* and had not taken down their barricades, but some of them brought chairs out and sat on the pavement with their rifles across their knees. I winked at one of them as I went past and got a not unfriendly grin; he recognized me, of course. Over the Telephone Exchange the Anarchist flag had been hauled down and only the Catalan flag was flying. That meant that the workers were definitely beaten; I realized—though, owing to my political ignorance, not so clearly as I ought to have done—that when the Government felt more sure of itself there would be reprisals. But at the time I was not interested in that aspect of things. All I felt was a profound relief that the devilish din of firing was over, and that one could buy some food and have a bit of rest and peace before going back to the front.

It must have been late that evening that the troops from Valencia first appeared in the streets. They were the Assault Guards, another formation similar to the Civil Guards and the *Carabineros* (i.e. a formation intended primarily for police work), and the picked troops of the Republic. Quite suddenly they seemed to spring up out of the ground; you saw them everywhere patrolling the streets in groups of ten—tall men in grey or blue uniforms, with long rifles slung over their shoulders, and a sub-machine-gun to each group. Meanwhile there was a delicate job to be done. The six rifles which we had used for the guard in the observatory towers were still lying there, and by hook or by crook we had got to get them back to the P.O.U.M. building. It was only a question of getting them across the street. They were part of the regular armoury of the building, but to bring them into the street was to contravene the Government's order, and if we were caught with them in our hands we should certainly be arrested—worse, the rifles would be confiscated. With only twenty-one rifles in the building we could not afford to lose six of them. After a lot of discussion as to the best method, a red-haired Spanish boy and myself began to smuggle them out. It was easy enough to dodge the Assault Guard patrols; the danger was the Civil Guards in the *Moka*, who were well aware that we had rifles in the observatory and might give the show away if they saw us carrying them across. Each of us partially undressed and slung a rifle over the left shoulder, the butt under the armpit, the barrel down the trouser-leg. It was unfortunate that they were long Mausers. Even a man as tall as I am cannot wear a long Mauser down his trouser-leg without discomfort. It was an intolerable job getting down the corkscrew staircase of the observatory with a completely rigid left leg. Once in the street, we found that the only way to move was with extreme slowness, so slowly that you did not have to bend your knees. Outside the picture-house I saw a group of people staring at me with great interest as I crept along at tortoise-speed. I have often wondered what they thought was the matter with me. Wounded in the war, perhaps. However, all the rifles were smuggled across without incident.

Next day the Assault Guards were everywhere, walking the streets like conquerors. There was no doubt that the Government was simply making a display of force in order to overawe a population which it already knew would not resist; if there had been any real fear of further outbreaks the Assault Guards would have been kept in barracks and not scattered through the streets in small bands. They were splendid troops, much the best I had seen in Spain, and, though I suppose they were in a sense 'the enemy', I could not help liking the look of them. But it was with a sort of amazement that I watched them strolling to and fro. I was used to the ragged, scarcely-armed militia on the Aragón front, and I had not known that the Republic possessed troops like these. It was not only that they were picked men physically, it was their weapons that most astonished me. All of them were armed with brand-new rifles of the type known as 'the Russian rifle' (these rifles were sent to Spain by the U.S.S.R., but were, I believe, manufactured in America). I examined one of them. It was a far from perfect rifle, but vastly better than the dreadful old blunderbusses we had at the front. The

Assault Guards had one submachine-gun between ten men and an automatic pistol each; we at the front had approximately one machine-gun between fifty men, and as for pistols and revolvers, you could only procure them illegally. As a matter of fact, though I had not noticed it till now, it was the same everywhere. The Civil Guards and *Carabineros*, who were not intended for the front at all, were better armed and far better clad than ourselves. I suspect it is the same in all wars—always the same contrast between the sleek police in the rear and the ragged soldiers in the line. On the whole the Assault Guards got on very well with the population after the first day or two. On the first day there was a certain amount of trouble because some of the Assault Guards—acting on instructions, I suppose—began behaving in a provocative manner. Bands of them boarded trams, searched the passengers, and, if they had C.N.T. membership cards in their pockets, tore them up and stamped on them. This led to scuffles with armed Anarchists, and one or two people were killed. Very soon, however, the Assault Guards dropped their conquering air and relations became more friendly. It was noticeable that most of them had picked up a girl after a day or two.

The Barcelona fighting had given the Valencia Government the long-wanted excuse to assume fuller control of Catalonia. The workers' militias were to be broken up and redistributed among the Popular Army. The Spanish Republican flag was flying all over Barcelona—the first time I had seen it, I think, except over a Fascist trench. In the working-class quarters the barricades were being pulled down, rather fragmentarily, for it is a lot easier to build a barricade than to put the stones back. Outside the P.S.U.C. buildings the barricades were allowed to remain standing, and indeed many were standing as late as June. The Civil Guards were still occupying strategic points. Huge seizures of arms were being made from C.N.T. strongholds, though I have no doubt a good many escaped seizure. _*La Batalla*_ was still appearing, but it was censored until the front page was almost completely blank. The P.S.U.C. papers were uncensored and were publishing inflammatory articles demanding the suppression of the P.O.U.M. The P.O.U.M. was declared to be a disguised Fascist organization, and a cartoon representing the P.O.U.M. as a figure slipping off a mask marked with the hammer and sickle and revealing a hideous, maniacal face marked with the swastika, was being circulated all over the town by P.S.U.C. agents. Evidently the official version of the Barcelona fighting was already fixed upon: it was to be represented as a 'fifth column' Fascist rising engineered solely by the P.O.U.M.

In the hotel the horrible atmosphere of suspicion and hostility had grown worse now that the fighting was over. In the face of the accusations that were being flung about it was impossible to remain neutral. The posts were working again, the foreign Communist papers were beginning to arrive, and their accounts of the fighting were not only violently partisan but, of course, wildly inaccurate as to facts. I think some of the Communists on the spot, who had seen what was actually happening, were dismayed by the interpretation that was being put upon events, but naturally they had to stick to their own side. Our Communist friend approached me once again and asked me whether I would not transfer into the International Column.

I was rather surprised. 'Your papers are saying I'm a Fascist,' I said. 'Surely I should be politically suspect, coming from the P.O.U.M.'

'Oh, that doesn't matter. After all, you were only acting under orders.'

I had to tell him that after this affair I could not join any Communist-controlled unit. Sooner or later it might mean being used against the Spanish working class. One could not tell when this kind of thing would break out again, and if I had to use my rifle at all in such an affair I would use it on the side of the working class and not against them. He was very decent about it. But from now on the whole atmosphere was changed. You could not, as before, 'agree to differ' and have drinks with a man who was supposedly your political opponent. There were some ugly wrangles in the hotel lounge. Meanwhile the jails were already full and overflowing. After the fighting was over the Anarchists had, of course, released their prisoners, but the Civil Guards had not released theirs, and most of them were thrown into prison and kept there without trial, in many cases for months on end. As usual, completely innocent people were being arrested owing to police bungling. I mentioned earlier that Douglas Thompson was wounded about the beginning of April. Afterwards we had lost touch with him, as usually happened when a man was wounded, for wounded men were frequently moved from one hospital to another. Actually he was at Tarragona hospital and was sent back to Barcelona about the time when the fighting started. On the Tuesday morning I met him in the street, considerably bewildered by the firing that was going on all round. He asked the question everyone was asking:

'What the devil is this all about?'

I explained as well as I could. Thompson said promptly:

'I'm going to keep out of this. My arm's still bad. I shall go back to my hotel and stay there.'

He went back to his hotel, but unfortunately (how important it is in street-fighting to understand the local geography!) it was a hotel in a part of the town controlled by the Civil Guards. The place was raided and Thompson was arrested, flung into jail, and kept for eight days in a cell so full of people that nobody had room to lie down. There were many similar cases. Numerous foreigners with doubtful political records were on the run, with the police on their track and in constant fear of denunciation. It was worst for the Italians and Germans, who had no passports and were generally wanted by the secret police in their own countries. If they were arrested they were liable to be deported to France, which might mean being sent back to Italy or Germany, where God knew what horrors were awaiting them. One or two foreign women hurriedly regularized their position by 'marrying' Spaniards. A German girl who had no papers at all dodged the police by posing for several days as a man's mistress. I remember the look of shame and misery on the poor girl's face when I accidentally bumped into her coming out of the man's bedroom. Of course she was not his mistress, but no doubt she thought I thought she was. You had all the while a hateful feeling that someone hitherto your friend might be denouncing you to the secret police. The long nightmare of the fighting, the noise, the lack of food and sleep, the mingled strain and boredom of sitting on the roof and wondering whether in another minute I should be shot myself or be obliged to shoot somebody else had put my nerves on edge. I had got to the point when every time a door banged I grabbed for my pistol. On the Saturday morning there was an uproar of shots outside and everyone cried out: 'It's starting again!' I ran into the street to find that it was only some Assault Guards shooting a mad dog. No one who was in Barcelona then, or for months later, will forget the horrible atmosphere produced by fear, suspicion, hatred, censored newspapers, crammed jails, enormous food queues, and prowling gangs of armed men.

I have tried to give some idea of what it felt like to be in the middle of the Barcelona fighting; yet I do not suppose I have succeeded in conveying much of the strangeness of that time. One of the things that stick in my mind when I look back is the casual contacts one made at the time, the sudden glimpses of non-combatants to whom the whole thing was simply a meaningless uproar. I remember the fashionably-dressed woman I saw strolling down the *Ramblas*, with a shopping-basket over her arm and leading a white poodle, while the rifles cracked and roared a street or two away. It is conceivable that she was deaf. And the man I saw rushing across the completely empty *Plaza de Cataluña*, brandishing a white handkerchief in each hand. And the large party of people all dressed in black who kept trying for about an hour to cross the *Plaza de Cataluña* and always failing. Every time they emerged from the side-street at the corner the P.S.U.C. machine-gunners in the *Hotel Colon* opened fire and drove them back—I don't know why, for they were obviously unarmed. I have since thought that they may have been a funeral party. And the little man who acted as caretaker at the museum over the *Poliorama* and who seemed to regard the whole affair as a social occasion. He was so pleased to have the English visiting him—the English were so _*simpático*_, he said. He hoped we would all come and see him again when the trouble was over; as a matter of fact I did go and see him. And the other little man, sheltering in a doorway, who jerked his head in a pleased manner towards the hell of firing on the *Plaza de Cataluña* and said (as though remarking that it was a fine morning): 'So we've got the nineteenth of July back again!' And the people in the shoe-shop who were making my marching-boots. I went there before the fighting, after it was over, and, for a very few minutes, during the brief armistice on 5 May. It was an expensive shop, and the shop-people were U.G.T. and may have been P.S.U.C. members—at any rate they were politically on the other side and they knew that I was serving with the P.O.U.M. Yet their attitude was completely indifferent. 'Such a pity, this kind of thing, isn't it? And so bad for business. What a pity it doesn't stop! As though there wasn't enough of that kind of thing at the front!' etc., etc. There must have been quantities of people, perhaps a majority of the inhabitants of Barcelona, who regarded the whole affair without a flicker of interest, or with no more interest than they would have felt in an air-raid.

In this chapter I have described only my personal experiences. In the next chapter I must discuss as best I can the larger issues—what actually happened and with what results, what were the rights and wrongs of the affair, and who if anyone was responsible. So much political capital has been made out of the Barcelona fighting that it is important to try and get a balanced view of it. An immense amount, enough to fill many books, has already been written on the subject, and I do not suppose I should exaggerate if I said that nine-tenths of it is untruthful. Nearly all the newspaper accounts published at the time were manufactured by journalists at a distance, and were not only inaccurate in their facts but intentionally misleading. As usual, only one side of the question has been allowed to get to the wider public. Like everyone who was in Barcelona at the time. I saw only what was happening in my immediate neighbourhood, but I saw and heard quite enough to be able to contradict many of the lies that have been circulated. As before, if you are not interested in political controversy and the mob of parties and sub-parties with their confusing names (rather like the names of the generals in a Chinese war), please skip. It is a horrible thing to have to enter into the details of inter-party polemics; it is like diving into a cesspool. But it is necessary to try and establish the truth, so far as it is possible. This squalid brawl in a distant city is more important than might appear at first sight.

CHAPTER 11

It will never be possible to get a completely accurate and unbiased account of the Barcelona fighting, because the necessary records do not exist. Future historians will have nothing to go upon except a mass of accusations and party propaganda. I myself have little data beyond what I saw with my own eyes and what I have learned from other eyewitnesses whom I believe to be reliable. I can, however, contradict some of the more flagrant lies and help to get the affair into some kind of perspective.

First of all, what actually happened?

For some time past there had been tension throughout Catalonia. In earlier chapters of this book I have given some account of the struggle between Communists and Anarchists. By May 1937 things had reached a point at which some kind of violent outbreak could be regarded as inevitable. The immediate cause of friction was the Government's order to surrender all private weapons, coinciding with the decision to build up a heavily-armed 'non-political' police-force from which trade union members were to be excluded. The meaning of this was obvious to everyone; and it was also obvious that the next move would be the taking over of some of the key industries controlled by the C.N.T. In addition there was a certain amount of resentment among the working classes because of the growing contrast of wealth and poverty and a general vague feeling that the revolution had been sabotaged. Many people were agreeably surprised when there was no rioting on 1 May. On 3 May the Government decided to take over the Telephone Exchange, which had been operated since the beginning of the war mainly by C.N.T. workers; it was alleged that it was badly run and that official calls were being tapped. Salas, the Chief of Police (who may or may not have been exceeding his orders), sent three lorry-loads of armed Civil Guards to seize the building, while the streets outside were cleared by armed police in civilian clothes. At about the same time bands of Civil Guards seized various other buildings in strategic spots. Whatever the real intention may have been, there was a widespread belief that this was the signal for a general attack on the C.N.T. by the Civil Guards and the P.S.U.C. (Communists and Socialists). The word flew round the town that the workers' buildings were being attacked, armed Anarchists appeared on the streets, work ceased, and fighting broke out immediately. That night and the next morning barricades were built all over the town, and there was no break in the fighting until the morning of 6 May. The fighting was, however, mainly defensive on both sides. Buildings were besieged, but, so far as I know, none were stormed, and there was no use of artillery. Roughly speaking, the C.N.T.-F.A.I.-P.O.U.M. forces held the working-class suburbs, and the armed police-forces and the P.S.U.C. held the central and official portion of the town. On 6 May there was an armistice, but fighting soon broke out again, probably because of premature attempts by Civil Guards to disarm C.N.T. workers. Next morning, however, the people began to leave the barricades of their own accord. Up till, roughly, the night of 5 May the C.N.T. had had the better of it, and large numbers of Civil Guards had surrendered. But there was no generally accepted leadership and no fixed plan—indeed, so far as one could judge, no plan at all except a vague determination to resist the Civil Guards. The official leaders of the C.N.T. had joined with those of the U.G.T. in imploring everyone to go back to work; above all, food was running short. In such circumstances nobody was sure enough of the issue to go on fighting. By the afternoon of 7 May conditions were almost normal. That evening six thousand Assault Guards, sent by sea from Valencia, arrived and took control of the town. The Government issued an order for the surrender of all arms except those held by the regular forces, and during the next few days large numbers of arms were seized. The casualties during the fighting were officially given out as four hundred killed and about a thousand wounded. Four hundred killed is possibly an exaggeration, but as there is no way of verifying this we must accept it as accurate.

Secondly, as to the after-effects of the fighting. Obviously it is impossible to say with any certainty what these were. There is no evidence that the outbreak had any direct effect upon the course of the war, though obviously it must have had if it continued even a few days longer. It was made the excuse for bringing Catalonia under the direct control of Valencia, for hastening the break-up of the militias, and for the suppression of the P.O.U.M., and no doubt it also had its share in bringing down the *Caballero* Government. But we may take it as certain that these things would have happened in any case. The real question is whether the C.N.T. workers who came into the street gained or lost by showing fight on this occasion. It is pure guess-work, but my own opinion is that they gained more than they lost. The seizure of the Barcelona Telephone Exchange was simply one incident in a long process. Since the previous year direct power had been gradually manoeuvred out of the hands of the syndicates, and the general movement was away from working-class control and towards centralized control, leading on to State capitalism or, possibly, towards the reintroduction of private capitalism. The fact that at this point there was resistance probably slowed the process down. A year after the outbreak of war the Catalan workers had lost much of their power, but their position was still comparatively favourable. It might have been much less so if they had made it clear that they would lie down under no matter what provocation. There are occasions when it pays better to fight and be beaten than not to fight at all.

Thirdly, what purpose, if any, lay behind the outbreak? Was it any kind of _coup d'état_ or revolutionary attempt? Did it definitely aim at overthrowing the Government? Was it preconcerted at all?

My own opinion is that the fighting was only preconcerted in the sense that everyone expected it. There were no signs of any very definite plan on either side. On the Anarchist side the action was almost certainly spontaneous, for it was an affair mainly of the rank and file. The people came into the streets and their political leaders followed reluctantly, or did not follow at all. The only people who even talked in a revolutionary strain were the Friends of Durruti, a small extremist group within the F.A.I., and the P.O.U.M. But once again they were following and not leading. The Friends of Durruti distributed some kind of revolutionary leaflet, but this did not appear until 5 May and cannot be said to have started the fighting, which had started of its own accord two days earlier. The official leaders of the C.N.T. disowned the whole affair from the start. There were a number of reasons for this. To begin with, the fact that the C.N.T. was still represented in the Government and the Generalite ensured that its leaders would be more conservative than their followers. Secondly, the main object of the C.N.T. leaders was to form an alliance with the U.G.T., and the fighting was bound to widen the split between C.N.T. and U.G.T., at any rate for the time being. Thirdly—though this was not generally known at the time—the Anarchist leaders feared that if things went beyond a certain point and the workers took possession of the town, as they were perhaps in a position to do on 5 May, there would be foreign intervention. A British cruiser and two British destroyers had closed in upon the harbour, and no doubt there were other warships not far away. The English newspapers gave it out that these ships were proceeding to Barcelona 'to protect British interests', but in fact they made no move to do so; that is, they did not land any men or take off any refugees. There can be no certainty about this, but it was at least inherently likely that the British Government, which had not raised a finger to save the Spanish Government from Franco, would intervene quickly enough to save it from its own working class.

The P.O.U.M. leaders did not disown the affair, in fact they encouraged their followers to remain at the barricades and even gave their approval (in _La Batalla_, 6 May) to the extremist leaflet issued by the Friends of Durruti. (There is great uncertainty about this leaflet, of which no one now seems able to produce a copy.) In some of the foreign papers it was described as an 'inflammatory poster' which was 'plastered' all over the town. There was certainly no such poster. From comparison of various reports I should say that the leaflet called for (i) The formation of a revolutionary council (*junta*), (ii) The shooting of those responsible for the attack on the Telephone Exchange, (iii) The disarming of the Civil Guards. There is also some uncertainty as to how far _La Batalla_ expressed agreement with the leaflet. I myself did not see the leaflet or _La Batalla_ of that date. The only handbill I saw during the fighting was one issued by the tiny group of Trotskyists ('Bolshevik-Leninists') on 4 May. This merely said: 'Everyone to the barricades—general strike of all industries except war industries.' (In other words, it merely demanded what was happening already.) But in reality the attitude of the P.O.U.M. leaders was hesitating. They had never been in favour of insurrection until the war against Franco was won; on the other hand the workers had come into the streets, and the P.O.U.M. leaders took the rather pedantic Marxist line that when the workers are on the streets it is the duty of the revolutionary parties to be with them. Hence, in spite of uttering revolutionary slogans about the 'reawakening of the spirit of 19 July', and so forth, they did their best to limit the workers' action to the defensive. They never, for instance, ordered an attack on any building; they merely ordered their followers to remain on guard and, as I mentioned in the last chapter, not to fire when it could be avoided. _La Batalla_ also issued instructions that no troops were to leave the front.[12]

As far as one can estimate it, I should say that the responsibility of the P.O.U.M. amounts to having urged everyone to remain at the barricades, and probably to having persuaded a certain number to remain there longer than they would otherwise have done. Those who were in personal touch with the P.O.U.M. leaders at the time (I myself was not) have told me that they were in reality dismayed by the whole business, but felt that they had got to associate themselves with it. Afterwards, of course, political capital was made out of it in the usual manner. Gorkin, one of the P.O.U.M. leaders, even spoke later of 'the glorious days of May'.From the propaganda point of view this may have been the right line; certainly the P.O.U.M. rose somewhat in numbers during the brief period before its suppression. Tactically it was probably a mistake to give countenance to the leaflet of the Friends of Durruti, which was a very small organization and normally hostile to the P.O.U.M. Considering the general excitement and the things that were being said on both sides, the leaflet did not in effect mean much more than 'Stay at the barricades', but by seeming to approve of it while _*Solidaridad Obrera*_, the Anarchist paper, repudiated it, the P.O.U.M. leaders made it easy for the Communist press to say afterwards that the fighting was a kind of insurrection engineered solely by the P.O.U.M. However, we may be certain that the Communist press would have said this in any case. It was nothing compared with the accusations that were made both before and afterwards on less evidence. The C.N.T. leaders did not gain much by their more cautious attitude; they were praised for their loyalty but were levered out of both the Government and the *Generalite* as soon as the opportunity arose.

---

[12] A recent number of _Inprecor_ states the exact opposite—that _*La Batalla*_ ordered the P.O.U.M. troops to leave the front! The point can easily be settled by referring to _*La Batalla*_ of the date named.

So far as one could judge from what people were saying at the time, there was no real revolutionary intention anywhere. The people behind the barricades were ordinary C.N.T. workers, probably with a sprinkling of U.G.T. workers among them, and what they were attempting was not to overthrow the Government but to resist what they regarded, rightly or wrongly, as an attack by the police. Their action was essentially defensive, and I doubt whether it should be described, as it was in nearly all the foreign newspapers, as a 'rising'. A rising implies aggressive action and a definite plan. More exactly it was a riot—a very bloody riot, because both sides had firearms in their hands and were willing to use them.

But what about the intentions on the other side? If it was not an Anarchist _coup d'état_, was it perhaps a Communist _coup d'état_—a planned effort to smash the power of the C.N.T. at one blow?

I do not believe it was, though certain things might lead one to suspect it. It is significant that something very similar (seizure of the Telephone Exchange by armed police acting under orders from Barcelona) happened in Tarragona two days later. And in Barcelona the raid on the Telephone Exchange was not an isolated act. In various parts of the town bands of Civil Guards and P.S.U.C. adherents seized buildings in strategic spots, if not actually before the fighting started, at any rate with surprising promptitude. But what one has got to remember is that these things were happening in Spain and not in England. Barcelona is a town with a long history of street-fighting. In such places things happen quickly, the factions are ready-made, everyone knows the local geography, and when the guns begin to shoot people take their places almost as in a fire-drill. Presumably those responsible for the seizure of the Telephone Exchange expected trouble—though not on the scale that actually happened—and had made ready to meet it. But it does not follow that they were planning a general attack on the C.N.T. There are two reasons why I do not believe that either side had made preparations for large-scale fighting:

(i) Neither side had brought troops to Barcelona beforehand. The fighting was only between those who were in Barcelona already, mainly civilians and police.

(ii) The food ran short almost immediately. Anyone who has served in Spain knows that the one operation of war that Spaniards really perform really well is that of feeding their troops. It is most unlikely that if either side had contemplated a week or two of street-fighting and a general strike they would not have stored food beforehand.

Finally, as to the rights and wrongs of the affair.

A tremendous dust was kicked up in the foreign anti-Fascist press, but, as usual, only one side of the case has had anything like a hearing. As a result the Barcelona fighting has been represented as an insurrection by disloyal Anarchists and Trotskyists who were 'stabbing the Spanish Government in the back', and so forth. The issue was not quite so simple as that. Undoubtedly when you are at war with a deadly enemy it is better not to begin fighting among yourselves; but it is worth remembering that it takes two to make a quarrel and that people do not begin building barricades unless they have received something that they regard as a provocation.

The trouble sprang naturally out of the Government's order to the Anarchists to surrender their arms. In the English press this was translated into English terms and took this form: that arms were desperately needed on the Aragón front and could not be sent there because the unpatriotic Anarchists were holding them back. To put it like this is to ignore the conditions actually existing in Spain. Everyone knew that both the Anarchists and the P.S.U.C. were hoarding arms, and when the fighting broke out in Barcelona this was made clearer still; both sides produced arms in abundance. The Anarchists were well aware that even if they surrendered their arms, the P.S.U.C., politically the main power in Catalonia, would still retain theirs; and this in fact was what happened after the fighting was over. Meanwhile actually visible on the streets, there were quantities of arms which would have been very welcome at the front, but which were being retained for the 'non-political' police forces in the rear. And underneath this there was the irreconcilable difference between Communists and Anarchists, which was bound to lead to some kind of struggle sooner or later. Since the beginning of the war the Spanish Communist Party had grown enormously in numbers and captured most of the political power, and there had come into Spain thousands of foreign Communists, many of whom were openly expressing their intention of 'liquidating' Anarchism as soon as the war against Franco was won. In the circumstances one could hardly expect the Anarchists to hand over the weapons which they had got possession of in the summer of 1936.

The seizure of the Telephone Exchange was simply the match that fired an already existing bomb. It is perhaps just conceivable that those responsible imagined that it would not lead to trouble. Companys, the Catalan President, is said to have declared laughingly a few days earlier that the Anarchists would put up with anything.[13] But certainly it was not a wise action. For months past there had been a long series of armed clashes between Communists and Anarchists in various parts of Spain. Catalonia and especially Barcelona was in a state of tension that had already led to street affrays, assassinations, and so forth. Suddenly the news ran round the city that armed men were attacking the buildings that the workers had captured in the July fighting and to which they attached great sentimental importance. One must remember that the Civil Guards were not loved by the working-class population. For generations past _*la guardia*_ had been simply an appendage of the landlord and the boss, and the Civil

[13] _New Statesman_ (14 May).

Guards were doubly hated because they were suspected, quite justly, of being of very doubtful loyalty against the Fascists.[14]

It is probable that the emotion that brought people into the streets in the first few hours was much the same emotion as had led them to resist the rebel generals at the beginning of the war. Of course it is arguable that the C.N.T. workers ought to have handed over the Telephone Exchange without protest. One's opinion here will be governed by one's attitude on the question of centralized government and working-class control. More relevantly it may be said: 'Yes, very likely the C.N.T. had a case. But, after all, there was a war on, and they had no business to start a fight behind the lines.' Here I agree entirely. Any internal disorder was likely to aid Franco. But what actually precipitated the fighting? The Government may or may not have had the right to seize the Telephone Exchange; the point is that in the actual circumstances it was bound to lead to a fight. It was a provocative action, a gesture which said in effect, and presumably was meant to say: 'Your power is at an end—we are taking over.' It was not common sense to expect anything but resistance. If one keeps a sense of proportion one must realize that the fault was not—could not be, in a matter of this kind—entirely on one side. The reason why a one-sided version has been accepted is simply that the Spanish revolutionary parties have no footing in the foreign press. In the English press, in particular, you would have to search for a long time before finding any favourable reference, at any period of the war, to the Spanish Anarchists. They have been systematically denigrated, and, as I know by my own experience, it is almost impossible to get anyone to print anything in their defence.

I have tried to write objectively about the Barcelona fighting,

---

[14] At the outbreak of war the Civil Guards had everywhere sided with the stronger party. On several occasions later in the war, e.g. at Santander, the local Civil Guards went over to the Fascists in a body.

though, obviously, no one can be completely objective on a question of this kind. One is practically obliged to take sides, and it must be clear enough which side I am on. Again, I must inevitably have made mistakes of fact, not only here but in other parts of this narrative. It is very difficult to write accurately about the Spanish war, because of the lack of non-propagandist documents. I warn everyone against my bias, and I warn everyone against my mistakes. Still, I have done my best to be honest. But it will be seen that the account I have given is completely different from that which appeared in the foreign and especially the Communist press. It is necessary to examine the Communist version, because it was published all over the world, has been supplemented at short intervals ever since, and is probably the most widely accepted one.

In the Communist and pro-Communist press the entire blame for the Barcelona fighting was laid upon the P.O.U.M. The affair was represented not as a spontaneous outbreak, but as a deliberate, planned insurrection against the Government, engineered solely by the P.O.U.M. with the aid of a few misguided 'uncontrollables'. More than this, it was definitely a Fascist plot, carried out under Fascist orders with the idea of starting civil war in the rear and thus paralysing the Government. The P.O.U.M. was 'Franco's Fifth Column'—a 'Trotskyist' organization working in league with the Fascists. According to the _Daily Worker_ (11 May):

The German and Italian agents, who poured into Barcelona ostensibly to 'prepare' the notorious 'Congress of the Fourth International', had one big task. It was this:

They were—in cooperation with the local Trotskyists—to prepare a situation of disorder and bloodshed, in which it would be possible for the Germans and Italians to declare that they were 'unable to exercise naval control of the Catalan coasts effectively because of the disorder prevailing in Barcelona' and were, therefore, 'unable to do otherwise than land forces in Barcelona'.

In other words, what was being prepared was a situation in which the German and Italian Governments could land troops or marines quite openly on the Catalan coasts, declaring that they were doing so 'in order to preserve order'…

The instrument for all this lay ready to hand for the Germans and Italians in the shape of the Trotskyist organization known as the P.O.U.M.

The P.O.U.M., acting in cooperation with well-known criminal elements, and with certain other deluded persons in the Anarchist organizations planned, organized, and led the attack in the rear-guard, accurately timed to coincide with the attack on the front at Bilbao, etc., etc.

Later in the article the Barcelona fighting becomes 'the P.O.U.M. attack', and in another article in the same issue it is stated that there is 'no doubt that it is at the door of the P.O.U.M. that the responsibility for the bloodshed in Catalonia must be laid'. _Inprecor_ (29 May) states that those who erected the barricades in Barcelona were 'only members of the P.O.U.M. organized from that party for this purpose'.

I could quote a great deal more, but this is clear enough. The P.O.U.M. was wholly responsible and the P.O.U.M. was acting under Fascist orders. In a moment I will give some more extracts from the accounts that appeared in the Communist press; it will be seen that they are so self-contradictory as to be completely worthless. But before doing so it is worth pointing to several _a priori_ reasons why this version of the May fighting as a Fascist rising engineered by the P.O.U.M. is next door to incredible.

(i) The P.O.U.M. had not the numbers or influence to provoke disorders of this magnitude. Still less had it the power to call a general strike. It was a political organization with no very definite footing in the trade unions, and it would have been hardly more capable of producing a strike throughout Barcelona than (say) the

English Communist Party would be of producing a general strike throughout Glasgow. As I said earlier, the attitude of the P.O.U.M. leaders may have helped to prolong the fighting to some extent; but they could not have originated it even if they had wanted to.

(ii) The alleged Fascist plot rests on bare assertion and all the evidence points in the other direction. We are told that the plan was for the German and Italian Governments to land troops in Catalonia; but no German or Italian troopships approached the coast. As to the 'Congress of the Fourth International' and the 'German and Italian agents', they are pure myth. So far as I know there had not even been any talk of a Congress of the Fourth International. There were vague plans for a Congress of the P.O.U.M. and its brother-parties (English I.L.P., German S.A.P., etc., etc.); this had been tentatively fixed for some time in July—two months later—and not a single delegate had yet arrived. The 'German and Italian agents' have no existence outside the pages of the _Daily Worker_. Anyone who crossed the frontier at that time knows that it was not so easy to 'pour' into Spain, or out of it, for that matter.

(iii) Nothing happened either at Lérida, the chief stronghold of the P.O.U.M., or at the front. It is obvious that if the P.O.U.M. leaders had wanted to aid the Fascists they would have ordered their militia to walk out of the line and let the Fascists through. But nothing of the kind was done or suggested. Nor were any extra men brought out of the line beforehand, though it would have been easy enough to smuggle, say, a thousand or two thousand men back to Barcelona on various pretexts. And there was no attempt even at indirect sabotage of the front. The transport of food, munitions, and so forth continued as usual; I verified this by inquiry afterwards. Above all, a planned rising of the kind suggested would have needed months of preparation, subversive propaganda among the militia, and so forth. But there was no sign or rumour of any such thing. The fact that the militia at the front played no part in the 'rising' should be conclusive. If the P.O.U.M. were really planning a _coup d'état_ it is inconceivable that they would not have used the ten thousand or so armed men who were the only striking force they had.

It will be clear enough from this that the Communist thesis of a P.O.U.M. 'rising' under Fascist orders rests on less than no evidence. I will add a few more extracts from the Communist press. The Communist accounts of the opening incident, the raid on the Telephone Exchange, are illuminating; they agree in nothing except in putting the blame on the other side. It is noticeable that in the English Communist papers the blame is put first upon the Anarchists and only later upon the P.O.U.M. There is a fairly obvious reason for this. Not everyone in England has heard of 'Trotskyism', whereas every English-speaking person shudders at the name of 'Anarchist'. Let it once be known that 'Anarchists' are implicated, and the right atmosphere of prejudice is established; after that the blame can safely be transferred to the 'Trotskyists'. The _Daily Worker_ begins thus (6 May):

A minority gang of Anarchists on Monday and Tuesday seized and attempted to hold the telephone and telegram buildings, and started firing into the street.

There is nothing like starting off with a reversal of roles. The Civil Guards attack a building held by the C.N.T.; so the C.N.T. are represented as attacking their own building—attacking themselves, in fact. On the other hand, the _Daily Worker_ of 11 May states:

The Left Catalan Minister of Public Security, Aiguade, and the United Socialist General Commissar of Public Order, Rodrigue Salas, sent the armed republican police into the Telefonica building to disarm the employees there, most of them members of C.N.T. unions.

This does not seem to agree very well with the first statement; nevertheless the _Daily Worker_ contains no admission that the first statement was wrong. The _Daily Worker_ of 11 May states that the leaflets of the Friends of Durruti, which were disowned by the C.N.T., appeared on 4 May and 5 May, during the fighting. _Inprecor_ (22 May) states that they appeared on 3 May, _before_ the fighting, and adds that 'in view of these facts' (the appearance of various leaflets):

The police, led by the Prefect of Police in person, occupied the central telephone exchange in the afternoon of 3 May. The police were shot at while discharging their duty. This was the signal for the provocateurs to begin shooting affrays all over the city.

And here is _Inprecor_ for 29 May:

At three o'clock in the afternoon the Commissar for Public Security, Comrade Salas, went to the Telephone Exchange, which on the previous night had been occupied by 50 members of the P.O.U.M. and various uncontrollable elements.

This seems rather curious. The occupation of the Telephone Exchange by 50 P.O.U.M. members is what one might call a picturesque circumstance, and one would have expected somebody to notice it at the time. Yet it appears that it was discovered only three or four weeks later. In another issue of _Inprecor_ the 50 P.O.U.M. members become 50 P.O.U.M. militiamen. It would be difficult to pack together more contradictions than are contained in these few short passages. At one moment the C.N.T. are attacking the Telephone Exchange, the next they are being attacked there; a leaflet appears before the seizure of the Telephone Exchange and is the cause of it, or, alternatively, appears afterwards and is the result of it; the people in the Telephone Exchange are alternatively C.N.T. members and P.O.U.M. members—and so on. And in a still later issue of the _Daily Worker_ (3 June) Mr J. R. Campbell informs us that the Government only seized the Telephone Exchange because the barricades were already erected!

For reasons of space I have taken only the reports of one incident, but the same discrepancies run all through the accounts in the

Communist press. In addition there are various statements which are obviously pure fabrication. Here for instance is something quoted by the _Daily Worker_ (7 May) and said to have been issued by the Spanish Embassy in Paris:

A significant feature of the uprising has been that the old monarchist flag was flown from the balcony of various houses in Barcelona, doubtless in the belief that those who took part in the rising had become masters of the situation.

The _Daily Worker_ very probably reprinted this statement in good faith, but those responsible for it at the Spanish Embassy must have been quite deliberately lying. Any Spaniard would understand the internal situation better than that. A monarchist flag in Barcelona! It was the one thing that could have united the warring factions in a moment. Even the Communists on the spot were obliged to smile when they read about it. It is the same with the reports in the various Communist papers upon the arms supposed to have been used by the P.O.U.M. during the 'rising'. They would be credible only if one knew nothing whatever of the facts. In the _Daily Worker_ of 17 May Mr Frank Pitcairn states:

There were actually all sorts of arms used by them in the outrage. There were the arms which they have been stealing for months past, and hidden, and there were arms such as tanks, which they stole from the barracks just at the beginning of the rising. It is clear that scores of machine-guns and several thousand rifles are still in their possession.

Inprecor (29 May) also states:

On 3 May the P.O.U.M. had at its disposal some dozens of machine-guns and several thousand rifles...On the *Plaza de España* the Trotskyists brought into action batteries of '75' guns which were destined for the front in Aragón and which the militia had carefully concealed on their premises.

Mr Pitcairn does not tell us how and when it became clear that the P.O.U.M. possessed scores of machine-guns and several thousand rifles. I have given an estimate of the arms which were at three of the principal P.O.U.M. buildings—about eighty rifles, a few bombs, and no machine-guns; i.e. about sufficient for the armed guards which, at that time, all the political parties placed on their buildings. It seems strange that afterwards, when the P.O.U.M. was suppressed and all its buildings seized, these thousands of weapons never came to light; especially the tanks and field-guns, which are not the kind of thing that can be hidden up the chimney. But what is revealing in the two statements above is the complete ignorance they display of the local circumstances. According to Mr Pitcairn the P.O.U.M. stole tanks 'from the barracks'. He does not tell us which barracks. The P.O.U.M. militiamen who were in Barcelona (now comparatively few, as direct recruitment to the party militias had ceased) shared the Lenin Barracks with a considerably larger number of Popular Army troops. Mr Pitcairn is asking us to believe, therefore, that the P.O.U.M. stole tanks with the connivance of the Popular Army. It is the same with the 'premises' on which the 75-mm. guns were concealed. There is no mention of where these 'premises' were. Those batteries of guns, firing on the *Plaza de España*, appeared in many newspaper reports, but I think we can say with certainty that they never existed. As I mentioned earlier, I heard no artillery-fire during the fighting, though the *Plaza de España* was only a mile or so away. A few days later I examined the *Plaza de España* and could find no buildings that showed marks of shell-fire. And an eye-witness who was in that neighbourhood throughout the fighting declares that no guns ever appeared there. (Incidentally, the tale of the stolen guns may have originated with Antonov-Ovseenko, the Russian Consul-General. He, at any rate, communicated it to a well-known English journalist, who afterwards repeated it in good faith in a weekly paper. Antonov-Ovseenko has since been 'purged'. How this would affect his credibility I do not know.) The truth is, of course, that these tales about tanks, field-guns, and so forth have only been invented because otherwise it is difficult to reconcile the scale of the Barcelona fighting with the P.O.U.M.'s small numbers. It was necessary to claim that the P.O.U.M. was wholly responsible for the fighting; it was also necessary to claim that it was an insignificant party with no following and 'numbered only a few thousand members', according to _Inprecor_. The only hope of making both statements credible was to pretend that the P.O.U.M. had all the weapons of a modern mechanized army.

It is impossible to read through the reports in the Communist Press without realizing that they are consciously aimed at a public ignorant of the facts and have no other purpose than to work up prejudice. Hence, for instance, such statements as Mr Pitcairn's in the _Daily Worker_ of 11 May that the 'rising' was suppressed by the Popular Army. The idea here is to give outsiders the impression that all Catalonia was solid against the 'Trotskyists'. But the Popular Army remained neutral throughout the fighting; everyone in Barcelona knew this, and it is difficult to believe that Mr Pitcairn did not know it too. Or again, the juggling in the Communist Press with the figures for killed and wounded, with the object of exaggerating the scale of the disorders. Diaz, General Secretary of the Spanish Communist Party, widely quoted in the Communist Press, gave the numbers as 900 dead and 2500 wounded. The Catalan Minister of Propaganda, who was hardly likely to underestimate, gave the numbers as 400 killed and 1000 wounded. The Communist Party doubles the bid and adds a few more hundreds for luck.

The foreign capitalist newspapers, in general, laid the blame for the fighting upon the Anarchists, but there were a few that followed the Communist line. One of these was the English _News Chronicle_, whose correspondent, Mr John Langdon-Davies, was in Barcelona at the time. I quote portions of his article here:

A Trotskyist revolt

...This has not been an Anarchist uprising. It is a frustrated _putsch_ of the 'Trotskyist' P.O.U.M., working through their controlled organizations, 'Friends of Durruti' and Libertarian Youth... The tragedy began on Monday afternoon when the Government sent armed police into the Telephone Building, to disarm the workers there, mostly C.N.T. men. Grave irregularities in the service had been a scandal for some time. A large crowd gathered in the *Plaza de Cataluña* outside, while the C.N.T. men resisted, retreating floor by floor to the top of the building...The incident was very obscure, but word went round that the Government was out against the Anarchists. The streets filled with armed men...By nightfall every workers'centre and Government building was barricaded, and at ten o'clock the first volleys were fired and the first ambulances began ringing their way through the streets. By dawn all Barcelona was under fire...As the day wore on and the dead mounted to over a hundred, one could make a guess at what was happening. The Anarchist C.N.T. and Socialist U.G.T. were not technically 'out in the street'. So long as they remained behind the barricades they were merely watchfully waiting, an attitude which included the right to shoot at anything armed in the open street...(the) general bursts were invariably aggravated by *_pacos_*—hidden solitary men, usually Fascists, shooting from roof-tops at nothing in particular, but doing all they could to add to the general panic...By Wednesday evening, however, it began to be clear who was behind the revolt. All the walls had been plastered with an inflammatory poster calling for an immediate revolution and for the shooting of Republican and Socialist leaders. It was signed by the 'Friends of Durruti'. On Thursday morning the Anarchists daily denied all knowledge or sympathy with it, but *_La Batalla_*, the P.O.U.M. paper, reprinted the document with the highest praise. Barcelona, the first city of Spain, was plunged into bloodshed by _agents provocateurs_ using this subversive organization.

This does not agree very completely with the Communist versions I have quoted above, but it will be seen that even as it stands it is self-contradictory. First the affair is described as 'a Trotskyist revolt', then it is shown to have resulted from a raid on the Telephone building and the general belief that the Government was 'out against' the Anarchists. The city is barricaded and both C.N.T. and U.G.T. are behind the barricades; two days afterwards the inflammatory poster (actually a leaflet) appears, and this is declared by implication to have started the whole business—effect preceding cause. But there is a piece of very serious misrepresentation here. Mr Langdon-Davies describes the Friends of Durruti and Libertarian Youth as 'controlled organizations' of the P.O.U.M. Both were Anarchist organizations and had no connexion with the P.O.U.M. The Libertarian Youth was the youth league of the Anarchists, corresponding to the J.S.U. of the P.S.U.C., etc. The Friends of Durruti was a small organization within the F.A.I., and was in general bitterly hostile to the P.O.U.M. So far as I can discover, there was no one who was a member of both. It would be about equally true to say that the Socialist League is a 'controlled organization' of the English Liberal Party. Was Mr Langdon-Davies unaware of this? If he was, he should have written with more caution about this very complex subject.

I am not attacking Mr Langdon-Davies's good faith; but admittedly he left Barcelona as soon as the fighting was over, i.e. at the moment when he could have begun serious inquiries, and throughout his report there are clear signs that he has accepted the official version of a 'Trotskyist revolt' without sufficient verification. This is obvious even in the extract I have quoted. 'By nightfall' the barricades are built, and 'at ten o'clock' the first volleys are fired. These are not the words of an eye-witness. From this you would gather that it is usual to wait for your enemy to build a barricade before beginning to shoot at him. The impression given is that some hours elapsed between the building of the barricades and the firing of the first volleys; whereas—naturally—it was the other way about. I and many others saw the first volleys fired early in the afternoon. Again, there are the solitary men, 'usually Fascists', who are shooting from the roof-tops. Mr Langdon-Davies does not explain how he knew that these men were Fascists. Presumably he did not climb on to the roofs and ask them. He is simply repeating what he has been told and, as it fits in with the official version, is not questioning it. As a matter of fact, he indicates one probable source of much of his information by an incautious reference to the Minister of Propaganda at the beginning of his article. Foreign journalists in Spain were hopelessly at the mercy of the Ministry of Propaganda, though one would think that the very name of this ministry would be a sufficient warning. The Minister of Propaganda was, of course, about as likely to give an objective account of the Barcelona trouble as (say) the late Lord Carson would have been to give an objective account of the Dublin rising of 1916.

I have given reasons for thinking that the Communist version of the Barcelona fighting cannot be taken seriously. In addition I must say something about the general charge that the P.O.U.M. was a secret Fascist organization in the pay of Franco and Hitler.

This charge was repeated over and over in the Communist Press, especially from the beginning of 1937 onwards. It was part of the world-wide drive of the official Communist Party against 'Trotskyism', of which the P.O.U.M. was supposed to be representative in Spain.'Trotskyism', according to _Frente Rojo_ (the Valencia Communist paper) 'is not a political doctrine. Trotskyism is an official capitalist organization, a Fascist terrorist band occupied in crime and sabotage against the people.' The P.O.U.M. was a 'Trotskyist' organization in league with the Fascists and part of 'Franco's Fifth Column'. What was noticeable from the start was that no evidence was produced in support of this accusation; the thing was simply asserted with an air of authority. And the attack was made with the maximum of personal libel and with complete irresponsibility as to any effects it might have upon the war. Compared with the job of libelling the P.O.U.M., many Communist writers appear to have considered the betrayal of military secrets unimportant. In a February number of the _Daily Worker_, for instance, a writer (Winifred Bates) is allowed to state that the P.O.U.M. had only half as many troops on its section of the front as it pretended. This was not true, but presumably the writer believed it to be true. She and the _Daily Worker_ were perfectly willing, therefore, to hand to the enemy one of the most important pieces of information that can be handed through the columns of a newspaper. In the _New Republic_ Mr Ralph Bates stated that the P.O.U.M. troops were 'playing football with the Fascists in no man's land' at a time when, as a matter of fact, the P.O.U.M. troops were suffering heavy casualties and a number of my personal friends were killed and wounded. Again, there was the malignant cartoon which was widely circulated, first in Madrid and later in Barcelona, representing the P.O.U.M. as slipping off a mask marked with the hammer and sickle and revealing a face marked with the swastika. Had the Government not been virtually under Communist control it would never have permitted a thing of this kind to be circulated in wartime. It was a deliberate blow at the morale not only of the P.O.U.M. militia, but of any others who happened to be near them; for it is not encouraging to be told that the troops next to you in the line are traitors. As a matter of fact, I doubt whether the abuse that was heaped upon them from the rear actually had the effect of demoralizing the P.O.U.M. militia. But certainly it was calculated to do so, and those responsible for it must be held to have put political spite before anti-Fascist unity.

The accusation against the P.O.U.M. amounted to this: that a body of some scores of thousands of people, almost entirely working class, besides numerous foreign helpers and sympathizers, mostly refugees from Fascist countries, and thousands of militia, was simply a vast spying organization in Fascist pay. The thing was opposed to common sense, and the past history of the P.O.U.M. was enough to make it incredible. All the P.O.U.M. leaders had revolutionary histories behind them. Some of them had been mixed up in the 1934 revolt, and most of them had been imprisoned for Socialist activities under the Lerroux Government or the monarchy. In 1936 its then leader, Joaquin Maurin, was one of the deputies who gave warning in the *Cortes* of Franco's impending revolt. Some time after the outbreak of war he was taken prisoner by the Fascists while trying to organize resistance in Franco's rear. When the revolt broke out the P.O.U.M. played a conspicuous part in resisting it, and in Madrid, in particular, many of its members were killed in the street-fighting. It was one of the first bodies to form columns of militia in Catalonia and Madrid. It seems almost impossible to explain these as the actions of a party in Fascist pay. A party in Fascist pay would simply have joined in on the other side.

Nor was there any sign of pro-Fascist activities during the war. It was arguable—though finally I do not agree—that by pressing for a more revolutionary policy the P.O.U.M. divided the Government forces and thus aided the Fascists. I think any Government of reformist type would be justified in regarding a party like the P.O.U.M. as a nuisance. But this is a very different matter from direct treachery. There is no way of explaining why, if the P.O.U.M. was really a Fascist body, its militia remained loyal. Here were eight or ten thousand men holding important parts of the line during the intolerable conditions of the winter of 1936-7. Many of them were in the trenches four or five months at a stretch. It is difficult to see why they did not simply walk out of the line or go over to the enemy. It was always in their power to do so, and at times the effect might have been decisive. Yet they continued to fight, and it was shortly after the P.O.U.M. was suppressed as a political party, when the event was fresh in everyone's mind, that the militia—not yet redistributed among the Popular Army—took part in the murderous attack to the east of Huesca when several thousand men were killed in one or two days. At the very least one would have expected fraternization with the enemy and a constant trickle of deserters. But, as I have pointed out earlier, the number of desertions was exceptionally small. Again, one would have expected pro-Fascist propaganda, 'defeatism', and so forth. Yet there was no sign of any such thing. Obviously there must have been Fascist spies and _agents provocateurs_ in the P.O.U.M.; they exist in all Left-wing parties; but there is no evidence that there were more of them there than elsewhere.

It is true that some of the attacks in the Communist Press said, rather grudgingly, that only the P.O.U.M. leaders were in Fascist pay, and not the rank and file. But this was merely an attempt to detach the rank and file from their leaders. The nature of the accusation implied that ordinary members, militiamen, and so forth, were all in the plot together; for it was obvious that if Nin, Gorkin, and the others were really in Fascist pay, it was more likely to be known to their followers, who were in contact with them, than to journalists in London, Paris, and New York. And in any case, when the P.O.U.M. was suppressed the Communist-controlled secret police acted on the assumption that all were guilty alike, and arrested everyone connected with the P.O.U.M. whom they could lay hands on, including even wounded men, hospital nurses, wives of P.O.U.M. members, and in some cases, even children.

Finally, on 15-16 June, the P.O.U.M. was suppressed and declared an illegal organization. This was one of the first acts of the Negrin Government which came into office in May. When the Executive Committee of the P.O.U.M. had been thrown into jail, the Communist Press produced what purported to be the discovery of an enormous Fascist plot. For a while the Communist Press of the whole world was flaming with this kind of thing (_Daily Worker_, 21 June, summarizing various Spanish Communist papers):

Spanish Trotskyists plot with Franco

Following the arrest of a large number of leading Trotskyists in Barcelona and elsewhere…there became known, over the weekend, details of one of the most ghastly pieces of espionage ever known in wartime, and the ugliest revelation of Trotskyist treachery to date… Documents in the possession of the police, together with the full confession of no less than 200 persons under arrest, prove, etc. etc.

What these revelations 'proved' was that the P.O.U.M. leaders were transmitting military secrets to General Franco by radio, were in touch with Berlin, and were acting in collaboration with the secret Fascist organization in Madrid. In addition there were sensational details about secret messages in invisible ink, a mysterious document signed with the letter N. (standing for Nin), and so on and so forth.

But the final upshot was this: six months after the event, as I write, most of the P.O.U.M. leaders are still in jail, but they have never been brought to trial, and the charges of communicating with Franco by radio, etc., have never even been formulated. Had they really been guilty of espionage they would have been tried and shot in a week, as so many Fascist spies had been previously. But not a scrap of evidence was ever produced except the unsupported statements in the Communist Press. As for the two hundred 'full confessions', which, if they had existed, would have been enough to convict anybody, they have never been heard of again. They were, in fact, two hundred efforts of somebody's imagination.

More than this, most of the members of the Spanish Government have disclaimed all belief in the charges against the

P.O.U.M. Recently the cabinet decided by five to two in favour of releasing anti-Fascist political prisoners; the two dissentients being the Communist ministers. In August an international delegation headed by James Maxton M.P., went to Spain to inquire into the charges against the P.O.U.M. and the disappearance of Andres Nin. Prieto, the Minister of National Defence, Irujo, the Minister of Justice, Zugazagoitia, Minister of the Interior, Ortega y Gasset, the Procureur-General, Prat Garcia, and others all repudiated any belief in the P.O.U.M. leaders being guilty of espionage. Irujo added that he had been through the dossier of the case, that none of the so-called pieces of evidence would bear examination, and that the document supposed to have been signed by Nin was 'valueless'—i.e. a forgery. Prieto considered the P.O.U.M. leaders to be responsible for the May fighting in Barcelona, but dismissed the idea of their being Fascist spies. 'What is most grave,' he added, 'is that the arrest of the P.O.U.M. leaders was not decided upon by the Government, and the police carried out these arrests on their own authority. Those responsible are not the heads of the police, but their entourage, which has been infiltrated by the Communists according to their usual custom.' He cited other cases of illegal arrests by the police. Irujo likewise declared that the police had become 'quasi-independent' and were in reality under the control of foreign Communist elements. Prieto hinted fairly broadly to the delegation that the Government could not afford to offend the Communist Party while the Russians were supplying arms. When another delegation, headed by John McGovern M.P., went to Spain in December, they got much the same answers as before, and Zugazagoitia, the Minister of the Interior, repeated Prieto's hint in even plainer terms. 'We have received aid from Russia and have had to permit certain actions which we did not like.' As an illustration of the autonomy of the police, it is interesting to learn that even with a signed order from the Director of Prisons and the Minister of Justice, McGovern and the others could not obtain admission to one of the 'secret prisons' maintained by the Communist Party in Barcelona.[15]

I think this should be enough to make the matter clear. The accusation of espionage against the P.O.U.M. rested solely upon articles in the Communist press and the activities of the Communist-controlled secret police. The P.O.U.M. leaders, and hundreds or thousands of their followers, are still in prison, and for six months past the Communist press has continued to clamour for the execution of the 'traitors.' But Negrin and the others have kept their heads and refused to stage a wholesale massacre of 'Trotskyists'. Considering the pressure that has been put upon them, it is greatly to their credit that they have done so. Meanwhile, in face of what I have quoted above, it becomes very difficult to believe that the P.O.U.M. was really a Fascist spying organization, unless one also believes that Maxton, McGovern, Prieto, Irujo, Zugazagoitia, and the rest are all in Fascist pay together.

Finally, as to the charge that the P.O.U.M. was 'Trotskyist'. This word is now flung about with greater and greater freedom, and it is used in a way that is extremely misleading and is often intended to mislead. It is worth stopping to define it. The word Trotskyist is used to mean three distinct things:

(i) One who, like Trotsky, advocates 'world revolution' as against 'Socialism in a single country'. More loosely, a revolutionary extremist.

(ii) A member of the actual organization of which Trotsky is head.

(iii) A disguised Fascist posing as a revolutionary who acts especially by sabotage in the U.S.S.R., but, in general, by splitting and

[15] For reports on the two delegations see _*Le Populaire*_ (7 September),_ *La Flèche*_ (18 September), report on the Maxton Delegation published by _Independent News_ (219 *Rue Saint-Denis*, Paris), and McGovern's pamphlet _*Terror in Spain*_.

undermining the Left-wing forces.

In sense (i) the P.O.U.M. could probably be described as Trotskyist. So can the English I.L.P., the German S.A.P., the Left Socialists in France, and so on. But the P.O.U.M. had no connexion with Trotsky or the Trotskyist ('Bolshevik-Leninist') organization. When the war broke out the foreign Trotskyists who came to Spain (fifteen or twenty in number) worked at first for the P.O.U.M., as the party nearest to their own viewpoint, but without becoming party-members; later Trotsky ordered his followers to attack the P.O.U.M. policy, and the Trotskyists were purged from the party offices, though a few remained in the militia. Nin, the P.O.U.M. leader after Maurin's capture by the Fascists, was at one time Trotsky's secretary, but had left him some years earlier and formed the P.O.U.M. by the amalgamation of various Opposition Communists with an earlier party, the Workers' and Peasants' Bloc. Nin's one-time association with Trotsky has been used in the Communist press to show that the P.O.U.M. was really Trotskyist. By the same line of argument it could be shown that the English Communist Party is really a Fascist organization, because of Mr John Strachey's one-time association with Sir Oswald Mosley.

In sense (ii), the only exactly defined sense of the word, the P.O.U.M. was certainly not Trotskyist. It is important to make this distinction, because it is taken for granted by the majority of Communists that a Trotskyist in sense (ii) is invariably a Trotskyist in sense (iii)—i.e. that the whole Trotskyist organization is simply a Fascist spying-machine. 'Trotskyism' only came into public notice in the time of the Russian sabotage trials, and to call a man a Trotskyist is practically equivalent to calling him a murderer, agent provocateur, etc. But at the same time anyone who criticizes Communist policy from a Left-wing standpoint is liable to be denounced as a Trotskyist. Is it then asserted that everyone professing revolutionary extremism is in Fascist pay?

In practice it is or is not, according to local convenience. When Maxton went to Spain with the delegation I have mentioned above, _Verdad_, _Frente Rojo_, and other Spanish Communist papers instantly denounced him as a 'Trotsky-Fascist', spy of the Gestapo, and so forth. Yet the English Communists were careful not to repeat this accusation. In the English Communist press Maxton becomes merely a 'reactionary enemy of the working class', which is conveniently vague. The reason, of course, is simply that several sharp lessons have given the English Communist press a wholesome dread of the law of libel. The fact that the accusation was not repeated in a country where it might have to be proved is sufficient confession that it is a lie.

It may seem that I have discussed the accusations against the P.O.U.M. at greater length than was necessary. Compared with the huge miseries of a civil war, this kind of internecine squabble between parties, with its inevitable injustices and false accusations, may appear trivial. It is not really so. I believe that libels and press-campaigns of this kind, and the habits of mind they indicate, are capable of doing the most deadly damage to the anti-Fascist cause.

Anyone who has given the subject a glance knows that the Communist tactic of dealing with political opponents by means of trumped-up accusations is nothing new. Today the key-word is 'Trotsky-Fascist'; yesterday it was 'Social-Fascist'. It is only six or seven years since the Russian State trials 'proved' that the leaders of the Second International, including, for instance, Leon Blum and prominent members of the British Labour Party, were hatching a huge plot for the military invasion of the U.S.S.R. Yet today the French Communists are glad enough to accept Blum as a leader, and the English Communists are raising heaven and earth to get inside the Labour Party. I doubt whether this kind of thing pays, even from a sectarian point of view. And meanwhile there is no possible doubt about the hatred and dissension that the 'Trotsky-Fascist' accusation is causing. Rank-and-file Communists everywhere are led away on a senseless witch-hunt after 'Trotskyists', and parties of the type of the P.O.U.M. are driven back into the terribly sterile position of being mere anti-Communist parties. There is already the beginning of a dangerous split in the world working-class movement. A few more libels against life-long Socialists, a few more frame-ups like the charges against the P.O.U.M., and the split may become irreconcilable. The only hope is to keep political controversy on a plane where exhaustive discussion is possible. Between the Communists and those who stand or claim to stand to the Left of them there is a real difference. The Communists hold that Fascism can be beaten by alliance with sections of the capitalist class (the Popular Front); their opponents hold that this manoeuvre simply gives Fascism new breeding-grounds. The question has got to be settled; to make the wrong decision may be to land ourselves in for centuries of semi-slavery. But so long as no argument is produced except a scream of 'Trotsky-Fascist!' the discussion cannot even begin. It would be impossible for me, for instance, to debate the rights and wrongs of the Barcelona fighting with a Communist Party member, because no Communist—that is to say, no 'good' Communist—could admit that I have given a truthful account of the facts. If he followed his party line dutifully he would have to declare that I am lying or, at best, that I am hopelessly misled and that anyone who glanced at the _Daily Worker_ headlines a thousand miles from the scene of events knows more of what was happening in Barcelona than I do. In such circumstances there can be no argument; the necessary minimum of agreement cannot be reached. What purpose is served by saying that men like Maxton are in Fascist pay? Only the purpose of making serious discussion impossible. It is as though in the middle of a chess tournament one competitor should suddenly begin screaming that the other is guilty of arson or bigamy. The point that is really at issue remains untouched. Libel settles nothing.

CHAPTER 12

It must have been three days after the Barcelona fighting ended that we returned to the front. After the fighting—more particularly after the slanging-match in the newspapers—it was difficult to think about this war in quite the same naively idealistic manner as before. I suppose there is no one who spent more than a few weeks in Spain without being in some degree disillusioned. My mind went back to the newspaper correspondent whom I had met my first day in Barcelona, and who said to me: 'This war is a racket the same as any other.' The remark had shocked me deeply, and at that time (December) I do not believe it was true; it was not true even now, in May; but it was becoming truer. The fact is that every war suffers a kind of progressive degradation with every month that it continues, because such things as individual liberty and a truthful press are simply not compatible with military efficiency.

One could begin now to make some kind of guess at what was likely to happen. It was easy to see that the *Caballero* Government would fall and be replaced by a more Right-wing Government with a stronger Communist influence (this happened a week or two later), which would set itself to break the power of the trade unions once and for all. And afterwards, when Franco was beaten—and putting aside the huge problems raised by the reorganization of Spain—the prospect was not rosy. As for the newspaper talk about this being a 'war for democracy', it was plain eyewash. No one in his senses supposed that there was any hope of democracy, even as we understand it in England or France, in a country so divided and exhausted as Spain would be when the war was over. It would have to be a dictatorship, and it was clear that the chance of a working-class dictatorship had passed. That meant that the general movement would be in the direction of some kind of Fascism. Fascism called, no doubt, by some politer name, and—because this was Spain—more human and less efficient than the German or Italian varieties. The only alternatives were an infinitely worse dictatorship by Franco, or (always a possibility) that the war would end with Spain divided up, either by actual frontiers or into economic zones.

Whichever way you took it it was a depressing outlook. But it did not follow that the Government was not worth fighting for as against the more naked and developed Fascism of Franco and Hitler. Whatever faults the post-war Government might have, Franco's regime would certainly be worse. To the workers—the town proletariat—it might in the end make very little difference who won, but Spain is primarily an agricultural country and the peasants would almost certainly benefit by a Government victory. Some at least of the seized lands would remain in their possession, in which case there would also be a distribution of land in the territory that had been Franco's, and the virtual serfdom that had existed in some parts of Spain was not likely to be restored. The Government in control at the end of the war would at any rate be anti-clerical and anti-feudal. It would keep the Church in check, at least for the time being, and would modernize the country—build roads, for instance, and promote education and public health; a certain amount had been done in this direction even during the war. Franco, on the other hand, in so far as he was not merely the puppet of Italy and Germany, was tied to the big feudal landlords and stood for a stuffy clerico-military reaction. The Popular Front might be a swindle, but Franco was an anachronism. Only millionaires or romantics could want him to win.

Moreover, there was the question of the international prestige of Fascism, which for a year or two past had been haunting me like a nightmare. Since 1930 the Fascists had won all the victories; it was time they got a beating, it hardly mattered from whom. If we could drive Franco and his foreign mercenaries into the sea it might make an immense improvement in the world situation, even if Spain itself emerged with a stifling dictatorship and all its best men in jail. For that alone the war would have been worth winning.

This was how I saw things at the time. I may say that I now think much more highly of the Negrin Government than I did when it came into office. It has kept up the difficult fight with splendid courage, and it has shown more political tolerance than anyone expected. But I still believe that—unless Spain splits up, with unpredictable consequences—the tendency of the post-war Government is bound to be Fascistic. Once again I let this opinion stand, and take the chance that time will do to me what it does to most prophets.

We had just reached the front when we heard that Bob Smillie, on his way back to England, had been arrested at the frontier, taken down to Valencia, and thrown into jail. Smillie had been in Spain since the previous October. He had worked for several months at the P.O.U.M. office and had then joined the militia when the other I.L.P. members arrived, on the understanding that he was to do three months at the front before going back to England to take part in a propaganda tour. It was some time before we could discover what he had been arrested for. He was being kept _*incommunicado*_, so that not even a lawyer could see him. In Spain there is—at any rate in practice—no _*habeas corpus*_, and you can be kept in jail for months at a stretch without even being charged, let alone tried. Finally we learned from a released prisoner that Smillie had been arrested for 'carrying arms'. The 'arms', as I happened to know, were two hand-grenades of the primitive type used at the beginning of the war, which he had been taking home to show off at his lectures, along with shell splinters and other souvenirs. The charges and fuses had been removed from them—they were mere cylinders of steel and completely harmless. It was obvious that this was only a pretext and that he had been arrested because of his known connexion with the P.O.U.M. The Barcelona fighting had only just ended and the authorities were, at that moment, extremely anxious not to let anyone out of Spain who was in a position to contradict the official version. As a result people were liable to be arrested at the frontier on more or less frivolous pretexts. Very possibly the intention, at the beginning, was only to detain Smillie for a few days. But the trouble is that, in Spain, once you are in jail you generally stay there, with or without trial.

We were still at Huesca, but they had placed us further to the right, opposite the Fascist redoubt which we had temporarily captured a few weeks earlier. I was now acting as _teniente_—corresponding to second-lieutenant in the British Army, I suppose—in command of about thirty men, English and Spanish. They had sent my name in for a regular commission; whether I should get it was uncertain. Previously the militia officers had refused to accept regular commissions, which meant extra pay and conflicted with the equalitarian ideas of the militia, but they were now obliged to do so. Benjamin had already been gazetted captain and Kopp was in process of being gazetted major. The Government could not, of course, dispense with the militia officers, but it was not confirming any of them in a higher rank than major, presumably in order to keep the higher commands for Regular Army officers and the new officers from the School of War. As a result, in our division, the 29th, and no doubt in many others, you had the queer temporary situation of the divisional commander, the brigade commanders, and the battalion commanders all being majors.

There was not much happening at the front. The battle round the Jaca road had died away and did not begin again till mid June. In our position the chief trouble was the snipers. The Fascist trenches were more than a hundred and fifty yards away, but they were on higher ground and were on two sides of us, our line forming a right-angle salient. The corner of the salient was a dangerous spot; there had always been a toll of sniper casualties there. From time to time the Fascists let fly at us with a rifle-grenade or some similar weapon. It made a ghastly crash—unnerving, because you could not hear it coming in time to dodge—but was not really dangerous; the hole it blew in the ground was no bigger than a wash-tub. The nights were pleasantly warm, the days blazing hot, the mosquitoes were becoming a nuisance, and in spite of the clean clothes we had brought from Barcelona we were almost immediately lousy. Out in the deserted orchards in no man's land the cherries were whitening on the trees. For two days there were torrential rains, the dug-outs flooded, and the parapet sank a foot; after that there were more days of digging out the sticky clay with the wretched Spanish spades which have no handles and bend like tin spoons.

They had promised us a trench-mortar for the company; I was looking forward to it greatly. At nights we patrolled as usual—more dangerous than it used to be, because the Fascist trenches were better manned and they had grown more alert; they had scattered tin cans just outside their wire and used to open up with the machine-guns when they heard a clank. In the daytime we sniped from no man's land. By crawling a hundred yards you could get to a ditch, hidden by tall grasses, which commanded a gap in the Fascist parapet. We had set up a rifle-rest in the ditch. If you waited long enough you generally saw a khaki-clad figure slip hurriedly across the gap. I had several shots. I don't know whether I hit anyone—it is most unlikely; I am a very poor shot with a rifle. But it was rather fun, the Fascists did not know where the shots were coming from, and I made sure I would get one of them sooner or later. However, the dog it was that died—a Fascist sniper got me instead. I had been about ten days at the front when it happened. The whole experience of being hit by a bullet is very interesting and I think it is worth describing in detail.

It was at the corner of the parapet, at five o'clock in the morning. This was always a dangerous time, because we had the dawn at our backs, and if you stuck your head above the parapet it was clearly outlined against the sky. I was talking to the sentries preparatory to changing the guard. Suddenly, in the very middle of saying something, I felt—it is very hard to describe what I felt, though I remember it with the utmost vividness.

Roughly speaking it was the sensation of being _at the centre_ of an explosion. There seemed to be a loud bang and a blinding flash of light all round me, and I felt a tremendous shock—no pain, only a violent shock, such as you get from an electric terminal; with it a sense of utter weakness, a feeling of being stricken and shrivelled up to nothing. The sand-bags in front of me receded into immense distance. I fancy you would feel much the same if you were struck by lightning. I knew immediately that I was hit, but because of the seeming bang and flash I thought it was a rifle near-by that had gone off accidentally and shot me. All this happened in a space of time much less than a second. The next moment my knees crumpled up and I was falling, my head hitting the ground with a violent bang which, to my relief, did not hurt. I had a numb, dazed feeling, a consciousness of being very badly hurt, but no pain in the ordinary sense.

The American sentry I had been talking to had started forward. 'Gosh! Are you hit?' People gathered round. There was the usual fuss—'Lift him up! Where's he hit? Get his shirt open!'etc., etc. The American called for a knife to cut my shirt open. I knew that there was one in my pocket and tried to get it out, but discovered that my right arm was paralysed. Not being in pain, I felt a vague satisfaction. This ought to please my wife, I thought; she had always wanted me to be wounded, which would save me from being killed when the great battle came. It was only now that it occurred to me to wonder where I was hit, and how badly; I could feel nothing, but I was conscious that the bullet had struck me somewhere in the front of the body. When I tried to speak I found that I had no voice, only a faint squeak, but at the second attempt I managed to ask where I was hit. In the throat, they said. Harry Webb, our stretcher-bearer, had brought a bandage and one of the little bottles of alcohol they gave us for field-dressings. As they lifted me up a lot of blood poured out of my mouth, and I heard a Spaniard behind me say that the bullet had gone clean through my neck. I felt the alcohol, which at ordinary times would sting like the devil, splash on to the wound as a pleasant coolness.

They laid me down again while somebody fetched a stretcher. As soon as I knew that the bullet had gone clean through my neck I took it for granted that I was done for. I had never heard of a man or an animal getting a bullet through the middle of the neck and surviving it. The blood was dribbling out of the corner of my mouth. 'The artery's gone,' I thought. I wondered how long you last when your carotid artery is cut; not many minutes, presumably. Everything was very blurry. There must have been about two minutes during which I assumed that I was killed. And that too was interesting—I mean it is interesting to know what your thoughts would be at such a time. My first thought, conventionally enough, was for my wife. My second was a violent resentment at having to leave this world which, when all is said and done, suits me so well. I had time to feel this very vividly. The stupid mischance infuriated me. The meaninglessness of it! To be bumped off, not even in battle, but in this stale corner of the trenches, thanks to a moment's carelessness! I thought, too, of the man who had shot me—wondered what he was like, whether he was a Spaniard or a foreigner, whether he knew he had got me, and so forth. I could not feel any resentment against him. I reflected that as he was a Fascist I would have killed him if

I could, but that if he had been taken prisoner and brought before me at this moment I would merely have congratulated him on his good shooting. It may be, though, that if you were really dying your thoughts would be quite different.

They had just got me on to the stretcher when my paralysed right arm came to life and began hurting damnably. At the time I imagined that I must have broken it in falling; but the pain reassured me, for I knew that your sensations do not become more acute when you are dying. I began to feel more normal and to be sorry for the four poor devils who were sweating and slithering with the stretcher on their shoulders. It was a mile and a half to the ambulance, and vile going, over lumpy, slippery tracks. I knew what a sweat it was, having helped to carry a wounded man down a day or two earlier. The leaves of the silver poplars which, in places, fringed our trenches brushed against my face; I thought what a good thing it was to be alive in a world where silver poplars grow. But all the while the pain in my arm was diabolical, making me swear and then try not to swear, because every time I breathed too hard the blood bubbled out of my mouth.

The doctor re-bandaged the wound, gave me a shot of morphia, and sent me off to Sietamo. The hospitals at Sietamo were hurriedly constructed wooden huts where the wounded were, as a rule, only kept for a few hours before being sent on to Barbastro or Lérida. I was dopey from morphia but still in great pain, practically unable to move and swallowing blood constantly. It was typical of Spanish hospital methods that while I was in this state the untrained nurse tried to force the regulation hospital meal—a huge meal of soup, eggs, greasy stew, and so forth—down my throat and seemed surprised when I would not take it. I asked for a cigarette, but this was one of the periods of tobacco famine and there was not a cigarette in the place. Presently two comrades who had got permission to leave the line for a few hours appeared at my bedside.

'Hullo! You're alive, are you? Good. We want your watch and your revolver and your electric torch. And your knife, if you've got one.'

They made off with all my portable possessions. This always happened when a man was wounded—everything he possessed was promptly divided up; quite rightly, for watches, revolvers, and so forth were precious at the front and if they went down the line in a wounded man's kit they were certain to be stolen somewhere on the way.

By the evening enough sick and wounded had trickled in to make up a few ambulance-loads, and they sent us on to Barbastro. What a journey! It used to be said that in this war you got well if you were wounded in the extremities, but always died of a wound in the abdomen. I now realized why. No one who was liable to bleed internally could have survived those miles of jolting over metal roads that had been smashed to pieces by heavy lorries and never repaired since the war began. Bang, bump, wallop! It took me back to my early childhood and a dreadful thing called the Wiggle-Woggle at the White City Exhibition. They had forgotten to tie us into the stretchers. I had enough strength in my left arm to hang on, but one poor wretch was spilt on to the floor and suffered God knows what agonies. Another, a walking case who was sitting in the corner of the ambulance, vomited all over the place. The hospital in Barbastro was very crowded, the beds so close together that they were almost touching. Next morning they loaded a number of us on to the hospital train and sent us down to Lérida.

I was five or six days in Lérida. It was a big hospital, with sick, wounded, and ordinary civilian patients more or less jumbled up together. Some of the men in my ward had frightful wounds. In the next bed to me there was a youth with black hair who was suffering from some disease or other and was being given medicine that made his urine as green as emerald. His bed-bottle was one of the sights of the ward. An English-speaking Dutch Communist, having heard that there was an Englishman in the hospital, befriended me and brought me English newspapers. He had been terribly wounded in the October fighting, and had somehow managed to settle down at Lérida hospital and had married one of the nurses. Thanks to his wound, one of his legs had shrivelled till it was no thicker than my arm. Two militiamen on leave, whom I had met my first week at the front, came in to see a wounded friend and recognized me. They were kids of about eighteen. They stood awkwardly beside my bed, trying to think of something to say, and then, as a way of demonstrating that they were sorry I was wounded, suddenly took all the tobacco out of their pockets, gave it to me, and fled before I could give it back. How typically Spanish! I discovered afterwards that you could not buy tobacco anywhere in the town and what they had given me was a week's ration.

After a few days I was able to get up and walk about with my arm in a sling. For some reason it hurt much more when it hung down. I also had, for the time being, a good deal of internal pain from the damage I had done myself in falling, and my voice had disappeared almost completely, but I never had a moment's pain from the bullet wound itself. It seems this is usually the case. The tremendous shock of a bullet prevents sensation locally; a splinter of shell or bomb, which is jagged and usually hits you less hard, would probably hurt like the devil. There was a pleasant garden in the hospital grounds, and in it was a pool with gold-fishes and some small dark grey fish—bleak, I think. I used to sit watching them for hours. The way things were done at Lérida gave me an insight into the hospital system on the Aragón front—whether it was the same on other fronts I do not know. In some ways the hospitals were very good. The doctors were able men and there seemed to be no shortage of drugs and equipment. But there were two bad faults on account of which, I have no doubt, hundreds or thousands of men have died who might have been saved.

One was the fact that all the hospitals anywhere near the front line were used more or less as casualty clearing-stations. The result was that you got no treatment there unless you were too badly wounded to be moved. In theory most of the wounded were sent straight to Barcelona or Tarragona, but owing to the lack of transport they were often a week or ten days in getting there. They were kept hanging about at Sietamo, Barbastro, Monzon, Lérida, and other places, and meanwhile they were getting no treatment except an occasional clean bandage, sometimes not even that. Men with dreadful shell wounds, smashed bones, and so forth, were swathed in a sort of casing made of bandages and plaster of Paris; a description of the wound was written in pencil on the outside, and as a rule the casing was not removed till the man reached Barcelona or Tarragona ten days later. It was almost impossible to get one's wound examined on the way; the few doctors could not cope with the work, and they simply walked hurriedly past your bed, saying: 'Yes, yes, they'll attend to you at Barcelona.' There were always rumours that the hospital train was leaving for Barcelona _*mañana*_. The other fault was the lack of competent nurses. Apparently there was no supply of trained nurses in Spain, perhaps because before the war this work was done chiefly by nuns. I have no complaint against the Spanish nurses, they always treated me with the greatest kindness, but there is no doubt that they were terribly ignorant. All of them knew how to take a temperature, and some of them knew how to tie a bandage, but that was about all. The result was that men who were too ill to fend for themselves were often shamefully neglected. The nurses would let a man remain constipated for a week on end, and they seldom washed those who were too weak to wash themselves. I remember one poor devil with a smashed arm telling me that he had been three weeks without having his face washed. Even beds were left unmade for days together. The food in all the hospitals was very good—too good, indeed. Even more in Spain than elsewhere it seemed to be the tradition to stuff sick people with heavy food. At Lérida the meals were terrific. Breakfast, at about six in the morning, consisted of soup, an omelette, stew, bread, white wine, and coffee, and lunch was even larger—this at a time when most of the civil population was seriously underfed. Spaniards seem not to recognize such a thing as a light diet. They give the same food to sick people as to well ones—always the same rich, greasy cookery, with everything sodden in olive oil.

One morning it was announced that the men in my ward were to be sent down to Barcelona today. I managed to send a wire to my wife, telling her that I was coming, and presently they packed us into buses and took us down to the station. It was only when the train was actually starting that the hospital orderly who travelled with us casually let fall that we were not going to Barcelona after all, but to Tarragona. I suppose the engine-driver had changed his mind. 'Just like Spain!' I thought. But it was very Spanish, too, that they agreed to hold up the train while I sent another wire, and more Spanish still that the wire never got there.

They had put us into ordinary third-class carriages with wooden seats, and many of the men were badly wounded and had only got out of bed for the first time that morning. Before long, what with the heat and the jolting, half of them were in a state of collapse and several vomited on the floor. The hospital orderly threaded his way among the corpse-like forms that sprawled everywhere, carrying a large goatskin bottle full of water which he squirted into this mouth or that. It was beastly water; I remember the taste of it still. We got into Tarragona as the sun was getting low. The line runs along the shore a stone's throw from the sea. As our train drew into the station a troop-train full of men from the International Column was drawing out, and a knot of people on the bridge were waving to them. It was a very long train, packed to bursting-point with men, with field-guns lashed on the open trucks and more men clustering round the guns. I remember with peculiar vividness the spectacle of that train passing in the yellow evening light; window after window full of dark, smiling faces, the long tilted barrels of the guns, the scarlet scarves fluttering—all this gliding slowly past us against a turquoise-coloured sea.

'_*Extranjeros*_—foreigners,' said someone. 'They're Italians.'

Obviously they were Italians. No other people could have grouped themselves so picturesquely or returned the salutes of the crowd with so much grace—a grace that was none the less because about half the men on the train were drinking out of up-ended wine bottles. We heard afterwards that these were some of the troops who won the great victory at Guadalajara in March; they had been on leave and were being transferred to the Aragón front. Most of them, I am afraid, were killed at Huesca only a few weeks later. The men who were well enough to stand had moved across the carriage to cheer the Italians as they went past. A crutch waved out of the window; bandaged forearms made the Red *Salute*. It was like an allegorical picture of war; the trainload of fresh men gliding proudly up the line, the maimed men sliding slowly down, and all the while the guns on the open trucks making one's heart leap as guns always do, and reviving that pernicious feeling, so difficult to get rid of, that war is glorious after all.

The hospital at Tarragona was a very big one and full of wounded from all fronts. What wounds one saw there! They had a way of treating certain wounds which I suppose was in accordance with the latest medical practice, but which was peculiarly horrible to look at. This was to leave the wound completely open and unbandaged, but protected from flies by a net of butter-muslin, stretched over wires. Under the muslin you would see the red jelly of a half-healed wound. There was one man wounded in the face and throat who had his head inside a sort of spherical helmet of butter-muslin; his mouth was closed up and he breathed through a little tube that was fixed between his lips. Poor devil, he looked so lonely, wandering to and fro, looking at you through his muslin cage and unable to speak. I was three or four days at Tarragona. My strength was coming back, and one day, by going slowly, I managed to walk down as far as the beach. It was queer to see the seaside life going on almost as usual; the smart cafés along the promenade and the plump local bourgeoisie bathing and sunning themselves in deck-chairs as though there had not been a war within a thousand miles. Nevertheless, as it happened, I saw a bather drowned, which one would have thought impossible in that shallow and tepid sea.

Finally, eight or nine days after leaving the front, I had my wound examined. In the surgery where newly-arrived cases were examined, doctors with huge pairs of shears were hacking away the breast-plates of plaster in which men with smashed ribs, collar-bones, and so forth had been cased at the dressing-stations behind the line; out of the neck-hole of the huge clumsy breastplate you would see protruding an anxious, dirty face, scrubby with a week's beard. The doctor, a brisk, handsome man of about thirty, sat me down in a chair, grasped my tongue with a piece of rough gauze, pulled it out as far as it would go, thrust a dentist's mirror down my throat, and told me to say 'Eh!' After doing this till my tongue was bleeding and my eyes running with water, he told me that one vocal cord was paralysed.

'When shall I get my voice back?' I said.

'Your voice? Oh, you'll never get your voice back,' he said cheerfully.

However, he was wrong, as it turned out. For about two months I could not speak much above a whisper, but after that my voice became normal rather suddenly, the other vocal cord having 'compensated'. The pain in my arm was due to the bullet having pierced a bunch of nerves at the back of the neck. It was a shooting pain like neuralgia, and it went on hurting continuously for about a month, especially at night, so that I did not get much sleep. The fingers of my right hand were also semi-paralysed. Even now, five months afterwards, my forefinger is still numb—a queer effect for a neck wound to have.

The wound was a curiosity in a small way and various doctors examined it with much clicking of tongues and ‘_Qué suerte! Qué suerte!_’ One of them told me with an air of authority that the bullet had missed the artery by ‘about a millimetre’. I don’t know how he knew. No one I met at this time—doctors, nurses, _practicantes_, or fellow-patients—failed to assure me that a man who is hit through the neck and survives it is the luckiest creature alive. I could not help thinking that it would be even luckier not to be hit at all.

CHAPTER 13

In Barcelona, during all those last weeks I spent there, there was a peculiar evil feeling in the air—an atmosphere of suspicion, fear, uncertainty, and veiled hatred. The May fighting had left ineradicable after-effects behind it. With the fall of the *Caballero* Government the Communists had come definitely into power, the charge of internal order had been handed over to Communist ministers, and no one doubted that they would smash their political rivals as soon as they got a quarter of a chance. Nothing was happening as yet, I myself had not even any mental picture of what was going to happen; and yet there was a perpetual vague sense of danger, a consciousness of some evil thing that was impending. However little you were actually conspiring, the atmosphere forced you to feel like a conspirator. You seemed to spend all your time holding whispered conversations in corners of cafés and wondering whether that person at the next table was a police spy.

Sinister rumours of all kinds were flying round, thanks to the Press censorship. One was that the Negrin-Prieto Government was planning to compromise the war. At the time I was inclined to believe this, for the Fascists were closing in on Bilbao and the Government was visibly doing nothing to save it. Basque flags were displayed all over the town, girls rattled collecting-boxes in the *cafés*, and there were the usual broadcasts about 'heroic defenders', but the Basques were getting no real assistance. It was tempting to believe that the Government was playing a double game. Later events have proved that I was quite wrong here, but it seems probable that Bilbao could have been saved if a little more energy had been shown. An offensive on the Aragón front, even an unsuccessful one, would have forced Franco to divert part of his army; as it was the Government did not begin any offensive action till it was far too late—indeed, till about the time when Bilbao fell. The C.N.T. was distributing in huge numbers a leaflet saying: 'Be on your guard!' and hinting that 'a certain Party' (meaning the Communists) was plotting a _coup d'état_. There was also a widespread fear that Catalonia was going to be invaded. Earlier, when we went back to the front, I had seen the powerful defences that were being constructed scores of miles behind the front line, and fresh bomb-proof shelters were being dug all over Barcelona. There were frequent scares of air-raids and sea-raids; more often than not these were false alarms, but every time the sirens blew the lights all over the town blacked out for hours on end and timid people dived for the cellars. Police spies were everywhere. The jails were still crammed with prisoners left over from the May fighting, and others—always, of course, Anarchist and P.O.U.M. adherents—were disappearing into jail by ones and twos. So far as one could discover, no one was ever tried or even charged—not even charged with anything so definite as 'Trotskyism'; you were simply flung into jail and kept there, usually _incommunicado_. Bob Smillie was still in jail in Valencia. We could discover nothing except that neither the I.L.P. representative on the spot nor the lawyer who had been engaged, was permitted to see him. Foreigners from the International Column and other militias were getting into jail in larger and larger numbers. Usually they were arrested as deserters. It was typical of the general situation that nobody now knew for certain whether a militiaman was a volunteer or a regular soldier. A few months earlier anyone enlisting in the militia had been told that he was a volunteer and could, if he wished, get his discharge papers at any time when he was due for leave. Now it appeared that the Government had changed its mind, a militiaman was a regular soldier and counted as a deserter if he tried to go home. But even about this no one seemed certain. At some parts of the front the authorities were still issuing discharges. At the frontier these were sometimes recognized, sometimes not; if not, you were promptly thrown into jail. Later the number of foreign 'deserters' in jail swelled into hundreds, but most of them were repatriated when a fuss was made in their own countries.

Bands of armed Assault Guards roamed everywhere in the streets, the Civil Guards were still holding cafés and other buildings in strategic spots, and many of the P.S.U.C. buildings were still sandbagged and barricaded. At various points in the town there were posts manned by Civil Guards of Carabineros who stopped passers-by and demanded their papers. Everyone warned me not to show my P.O.U.M. militiaman's card but merely to show my passport and my hospital ticket. Even to be known to have served in the P.O.U.M. militia was vaguely dangerous. P.O.U.M. militiamen who were wounded or on leave were penalized in petty ways—it was made difficult for them to draw their pay, for instance. _*La Batalla*_ was still appearing, but it was censored almost out of existence, and _*Solidaridad*_ and the other Anarchist papers were also heavily censored. There was a new rule that censored portions of a newspaper must not be left blank but filled up with other matter; as a result it was often impossible to tell when something had been cut out.

The food shortage, which had fluctuated throughout the War, was in one of its bad stages. Bread was scarce and the cheaper sorts were being adulterated with rice; the bread the soldiers were getting in the barracks was dreadful stuff like putty. Milk and sugar were very scarce and tobacco almost non-existent, except for the expensive smuggled cigarettes. There was an acute shortage of olive oil, which Spaniards use for half a dozen different purposes. The queues of women waiting to buy olive oil were controlled by mounted Civil Guards who sometimes amused themselves by backing their horses into the queue and trying to make them tread on the women's toes. A minor annoyance of the time was the lack of small change. The silver had been withdrawn and as yet no new coinage had been issued, so that there was nothing between the ten-centime piece and the note for two and a half pesetas, and all notes below ten *pesetas* were very scarce.*[16] For the poorest people this meant an aggravation of the food shortage. A woman with only a ten-*peseta* note in her possession might wait for hours in a queue outside the grocery and then be unable to buy anything after all because the grocer had no change and she could not afford to spend the whole note.

It is not easy to convey the nightmare atmosphere of that time—the peculiar uneasiness produced by rumours that were always changing, by censored newspapers, and the constant presence of armed men. It is not easy to convey it because, at the moment, the thing essential to such an atmosphere does not exist in England. In England political intolerance is not yet taken for granted. There is political persecution in a petty way; if I were a coal-miner I would not care to be known to the boss as a Communist; but the 'good party man', the gangster-gramophone of continental politics, is still a rarity, and the notion of 'liquidating' or 'eliminating' everyone who happens to disagree with you does not yet seem natural. It seemed only too natural in Barcelona. The 'Stalinists' were in the saddle, and therefore it was a matter of course that every 'Trotskyist' was in danger. The thing everyone feared was a thing which, after all, did not happen—a fresh outbreak of street-fighting, which, as before, would be blamed on the P.O.U.M. and the Anarchists. There were times when I caught my ears listening for the first shots. It was as though some huge evil intelligence were brooding over the town. Everyone noticed it and remarked upon it. And it was queer how everyone expressed it in almost the same words: 'The atmosphere of this place—it's horrible.

[16] The purchasing value of the peseta was about fourpence.

Like being in a lunatic asylum.' But perhaps I ought not to say _everyone_. Some of the English visitors who flitted briefly through Spain, from hotel to hotel, seem not to have noticed that there was anything wrong with the general atmosphere. The Duchess of Atholl writes, I notice (_Sunday Express_, 17 October 1937):

I was in Valencia, Madrid, and Barcelona…perfect order prevailed in all three towns without any display of force. All the hotels in which I stayed were not only 'normal' and 'decent', but extremely comfortable, in spite of the shortage of butter and coffee.

It is a peculiarity of English travellers that they do not really believe in the existence of anything outside the smart hotels. I hope they found some butter for the Duchess of Atholl.

I was at the *Sanatorium Maurin*, one of the sanatoria run by the P.O.U.M. It was in the suburbs near Tibidabo, the queer-shaped mountain that rises abruptly behind Barcelona and is traditionally supposed to have been the hill from which Satan showed Jesus the countries of the earth (hence its name). The house had previously belonged to some wealthy bourgeois and had been seized at the time of the revolution. Most of the men there had either been invalided out of the line or had some wound that had permanently disabled them—amputated limbs, and so forth. There were several other Englishmen there: Williams, with a damaged leg, and Stafford Cottman, a boy of eighteen, who had been sent back from the trenches with suspected tuberculosis, and Arthur Clinton, whose smashed left arm was still strapped on to one of those huge wire contraptions, nicknamed *aeroplanes*, which the Spanish hospitals were using. My wife was still staying at the Hotel Continental, and I generally came into Barcelona in the daytime. In the morning I used to attend the General Hospital for electrical treatment of my arm. It was a queer business—a series of prickly electric shocks that made the various sets of muscles jerk up and down—but it seemed to do some good; the use of my fingers came back and the pain grew somewhat less. Both of us had decided that the best thing we could do was to go back to England as soon as possible. I was extremely weak, my voice was gone, seemingly for good, and the doctors told me that at best it would be several months before I was fit to fight. I had got to start earning some money sooner or later, and there did not seem much sense in staying in Spain and eating food that was needed for other people. But my motives were mainly selfish. I had an overwhelming desire to get away from it all; away from the horrible atmosphere of political suspicion and hatred, from streets thronged by armed men, from air-raids, trenches, machine-guns, screaming trams, milkless tea, oil cookery, and shortage of cigarettes—from almost everything that I had learnt to associate with Spain.

The doctors at the General Hospital had certified me medically unfit, but to get my discharge I had to see a medical board at one of the hospitals near the front and then go to Sietamo to get my papers stamped at the P.O.U.M. militia headquarters. Kopp had just come back from the front, full of jubilation. He had just been in action and said that Huesca was going to be taken at last. The Government had brought troops from the Madrid front and were concentrating thirty thousand men, with aeroplanes in huge numbers. The Italians I had seen going up the line from Tarragona had attacked on the Jaca road but had had heavy casualties and lost two tanks. However, the town was bound to fall, Kopp said. (Alas! It didn't. The attack was a frightful mess-up and led to nothing except an orgy of lying in the newspapers.) Meanwhile Kopp had to go down to Valencia for an interview at the Ministry of War. He had a letter from General Pozas, now commanding the Army of the East—the usual letter, describing Kopp as a 'person of all confidence' and recommending him for a special appointment in the engineering section (Kopp had been an engineer in civil life). He left for Valencia the same day as I left for Sietamo—15 June.

It was five days before I got back to Barcelona. A lorry-load of us reached Sietamo about midnight, and as soon as we got to the P.O.U.M. headquarters they lined us up and began handling out rifles and cartridges, before even taking our names. It seemed that the attack was beginning and they were likely to call for reserves at any moment. I had my hospital ticket in my pocket, but I could not very well refuse to go with the others. I kipped down on the ground, with a cartridge-box for a pillow, in a mood of deep dismay. Being wounded had spoiled my nerve for the time being—I believe this usually happens—and the prospect of being under fire frightened me horribly. However, there was a bit of _*mañana*_, as usual, we were not called out after all, and next morning I produced my hospital ticket and went in search of my discharge. It meant a series of confused, tiresome journeys. As usual they bandied one to and fro from hospital to hospital—Sietamo, Barbastro, Monzon, then back to Sietamo to get my discharge stamped, then down the line again via Barbastro and Lérida—and the convergence of troops on Huesca had monopolized all the transport and disorganized everything. I remember sleeping in queer places—once in a hospital bed, but once in a ditch, once on a very narrow bench which I fell off in the middle of the night, and once in a sort of municipal lodging-house in Barbastro. As soon as you got away from the railroad there was no way of travelling except by jumping chance lorries. You had to wait by the roadside for hours, sometimes three or four hours at a stretch, with knots of disconsolate peasants who carried bundles full of ducks and rabbits, waving to lorry after lorry. When finally you struck a lorry that was not chock full of men, loaves of bread, or ammunition-boxes the bumping over the vile roads wallowed you to pulp. No horse has ever thrown me so high as those lorries used to throw me. The only way of travelling was to crowd all together and cling to one another. To my humiliation I found that I was still too weak to climb on to a lorry without being helped.

I slept a night at Monzón Hospital, where I went to see my medical board. In the next bed to me there was an Assault Guard, wounded over the left eye. He was friendly and gave me cigarettes. I said: 'In Barcelona we should have been shooting one another,' and we laughed over this. It was queer how the general spirit seemed to change when you got anywhere near the front line. All or nearly all of the vicious hatred of the political parties evaporated. During all the time I was at the front I never once remember any P.S.U.C. adherent showing me hostility because I was P.O.U.M. That kind of thing belonged in Barcelona or in places even remoter from the war. There were a lot of Assault Guards in Sietamo. They had been sent on from Barcelona to take part in the attack on Huesca. The Assault Guards were a corps not intended primarily for the front, and many of them had not been under fire before. Down in Barcelona they were lords of the street, but up here they were *_quintos_* (rookies) and palled up with militia children of fifteen who had been in the line for months.

At Monzón Hospital the doctor did the usual tongue-pulling and mirror-thrusting business, assured me in the same cheerful manner as the others that I should never have a voice again, and signed my certificate. While I waited to be examined there was going on inside the surgery some dreadful operation without anaesthetics—why without anaesthetics I do not know. It went on and on, scream after scream, and when I went in there were chairs flung about and on the floor were pools of blood and urine.

The details of that final journey stand out in my mind with strange clarity. I was in a different mood, a more observing mood, than I had been in for months past. I had got my discharge, stamped with the seal of the 29th Division, and the doctor's certificate in which I was 'declared useless'. I was free to go back to England; consequently I felt able, almost for the first time, to look at Spain. I had a day to put in to Barbastro, for there was only one train a day.

Previously I had seen Barbastro in brief glimpses, and it had seemed to me simply a part of the war—a grey, muddy, cold place, full of roaring lorries and shabby troops. It seemed queerly different now. Wandering through it I became aware of pleasant tortuous streets, old stone bridges, wine shops with great oozy barrels as tall as a man, and intriguing semi-subterranean shops where men were making cartwheels, daggers, wooden spoons, and goatskin water-bottles. I watched a man making a skin bottle and discovered with great interest, what I had never known before, that they are made with the fur inside and the fur is not removed, so that you are really drinking distilled goat's hair. I had drunk out of them for months without knowing this. And at the back of the town there was a shallow jade-green river, and rising out of it a perpendicular cliff of rock, with houses built into the rock, so that from your bedroom window you could spit straight into the water a hundred feet below. Innumerable doves lived in the holes in the cliff. And in Lérida there were old crumbling buildings upon whose cornices thousands upon thousands of swallows had built their nests, so that at a little distance the crusted pattern of nests was like some florid moulding of the rococo period. It was queer how for nearly six months past I had had no eyes for such things. With my discharge papers in my pocket I felt like a human being again, and also a little like a tourist. For almost the first time I felt that I was really in Spain, in a country that I had longed all my life to visit. In the quiet back streets of Lérida and Barbastro I seemed to catch a momentary glimpse, a sort of far-off rumour of the Spain that dwells in everyone's imagination. White sierras, goatherds, dungeons of the Inquisition, Moorish palaces, black winding trains of mules, grey olive trees and groves of lemons, girls in black mantillas, the wines of Málaga and Alicante, cathedrals, cardinals, bull-fights, gypsies, serenades—in short, Spain. Of all Europe it was the country that had had most hold upon my imagination. It seemed a pity that when at last I had managed to come here I had seen only this north-eastern corner, in the middle of a confused war and for the most part in winter.

It was late when I got back to Barcelona, and there were no taxis. It was no use trying to get to the *Sanatorium Maurin*, which was right outside the town, so I made for the *Hotel Continental*, stopping for dinner on the way. I remember the conversation I had with a very fatherly waiter about the oak jugs, bound with copper, in which they served the wine. I said I would like to buy a set of them to take back to England. The waiter was sympathetic. 'Yes, beautiful, were they not? But impossible to buy nowadays. Nobody was manufacturing them any longer—nobody was manufacturing anything. This war—such a pity!' We agreed that the war was a pity. Once again I felt like a tourist. The waiter asked me gently, had I liked Spain; would I come back to Spain? Oh, yes, I should come back to Spain. The peaceful quality of this conversation sticks in my memory, because of what happened immediately afterwards.

When I got to the hotel my wife was sitting in the lounge. She got up and came towards me in what struck me as a very unconcerned manner; then she put an arm round my neck and, with a sweet smile for the benefit of the other people in the lounge, hissed in my ear:

'_Get out!_'

'What?'

'Get out of here _at once!_'

'What?'

'Don't keep standing here! You must get outside quickly!'

'What? Why? What do you mean?'

She had me by the arm and was already leading me towards the stairs. Half-way down we met a Frenchman—I am not going to give his name, for though he had no connexion with the P.O.U.M. he was a good friend to us all during the trouble. He looked at me with a concerned face.

'Listen! You mustn't come in here. Get out quickly and hide yourself before they ring up the police.'

And behold! at the bottom of the stairs one of the hotel staff, who was a P.O.U.M. member (unknown to the management, I fancy), slipped furtively out of the lift and told me in broken English to get out. Even now I did not grasp what had happened.

'What the devil is all this about?' I said, as soon as we were on the pavement.

'Haven't you _heard_?'

'No. Heard what? I've heard nothing.'

'The P.O.U.M.'s been suppressed. They've seized all the buildings. Practically everyone's in prison. And they say they're shooting people already.'

So that was it. We had to have somewhere to talk. All the big cafés on the Ramblas were thronged with police, but we found a quiet café in a side street. My wife explained to me what had happened while I was away.

On 15 June the police had suddenly arrested Andres Nin in his office, and the same evening had raided the *Hotel Falcon* and arrested all the people in it, mostly militiamen on leave. The place was converted immediately into a prison, and in a very little while it was filled to the brim with prisoners of all kinds. Next day the P.O.U.M. was declared an illegal organization and all its offices, book-stalls, sanatoria, Red Aid centres, and so forth were seized. Meanwhile the police were arresting everyone they could lay hands on who was known to have any connexion with the P.O.U.M.Within a day or two all or almost all of the forty members of the Executive Committee were in prison. Possibly one or two had escaped into hiding, but the police were adopting the trick (extensively used on both sides in this war) of seizing a man's wife as a hostage if he disappeared. There was no way of discovering how many people had been arrested. My wife had heard that it was about four hundred in Barcelona alone. I have since thought that even at that time the numbers must have been greater. And the most fantastic people had been arrested. In some cases the police had even gone to the length of dragging wounded militiamen out of the hospitals.

It was all profoundly dismaying. What the devil was it all about? I could understand their suppressing the P.O.U.M., but what were they arresting people for? For nothing, so far as one could discover. Apparently the suppression of the P.O.U.M. had a retrospective effect; the P.O.U.M. was now illegal, and therefore one was breaking the law by having previously belonged to it. As usual, none of the arrested people had been charged. Meanwhile, however, the Valencia Communist papers were flaming with the story of a huge 'Fascist plot', radio communication with the enemy, documents signed in invisible ink, etc., etc. I have dealt with this story earlier. The significant thing was that it was appearing only in the Valencia papers; I think I am right in saying that there was not a single word about it, or about the suppression of the P.O.U.M., in any Barcelona papers, Communist, Anarchist, or Republican. We first learned the precise nature of the charges against the P.O.U.M. leaders not from any Spanish paper but from the English papers that reached Barcelona a day or two later. What we could not know at this time was that the Government was not responsible for the charge of treachery and espionage, and that members of the Government were later to repudiate it. We only vaguely knew that the P.O.U.M. leaders, and presumably all the rest of us, were accused of being in Fascist pay. And already the rumours were flying round that people were being secretly shot in jail. There was a lot of exaggeration about this, but it certainly happened in some cases, and there is not much doubt that it happened in the case of Nin. After his arrest Nin was transferred to Valencia and thence to Madrid, and as early as 21 June the rumour reached Barcelona that he had been shot. Later the rumour took a more definite shape: Nin had been shot in prison by the secret police and his body dumped into the street. This story came from several sources, including Federica Montsenys, an ex-member of the Government. From that day to this Nin has never been heard of alive again. When, later, the Government were questioned by delegates from various countries, they shilly-shallied and would say only that Nin had disappeared and they knew nothing of his whereabouts. Some of the newspapers produced a tale that he had escaped to Fascist territory. No evidence was given in support of it, and Irujo, the Minister of Justice, later declared that the Espagne news-agency had falsified his official *communiqué*.*[17] In any case it is most unlikely that a political prisoner of Nin's importance would be allowed to escape. Unless at some future time he is produced alive, I think we must take it that he was murdered in prison.

The tale of arrests went on and on, extending over months, until the number of political prisoners, not counting Fascists, swelled into thousands. One noticeable thing was the autonomy of the lower ranks of the police. Many of the arrests were admittedly illegal, and various people whose release had been ordered by the Chief of Police were re-arrested at the jail gate and carried off to 'secret prisons'. A typical case is that of Kurt Landau and his wife. They were arrested about 17 June, and Landau immediately 'disappeared'. Five months later his wife was still in jail, untried and without news of her husband. She declared a hunger-strike, after which the Minister of Justice, sent word to assure her that her husband was dead. Shortly afterwards she was released, to be almost immediately re-arrested and flung into prison again. And it was noticeable that the police, at any rate at first, seemed completely indifferent as to any effect their actions might have upon the war. They were quite ready to arrest military officers in important posts without getting permission beforehand. About the end of June Jose Rovira, the general

[17] See the reports of the Maxton delegation which I referred to in Chapter 11.

commanding the 29th Division, was arrested somewhere near the front line by a party of police who had been sent from Barcelona. His men sent a delegation to protest at the Ministry of War. It was found that neither the Ministry of War, nor Ortega, the Chief of Police, had even been informed of Rovira's arrest. In the whole business the detail that most sticks in my throat, though perhaps it is not of great importance, is that all news of what was happening was kept from the troops at the front. As you will have seen, neither I nor anyone else at the front had heard anything about the suppression of the P.O.U.M. All the P.O.U.M. militia headquarters, Red Aid centres, and so forth were functioning as usual, and as late as 20 June and as far down the line as Lérida, only about 100 miles from Barcelona, no one had heard what was happening. All word of it was kept out of the Barcelona papers (the Valencia papers, which were running the spy stories, did not reach the Aragón front), and no doubt one reason for arresting all the P.O.U.M. militiamen on leave in Barcelona was to prevent them from getting back to the front with the news. The draft with which I had gone up the line on 15 June must have been about the last to go. I am still puzzled to know how the thing was kept secret, for the supply lorries and so forth were still passing to and fro; but there is no doubt that it was kept secret, and, as I have since learned from a number of others, the men in the front line heard nothing till several days later. The motive for all this is clear enough. The attack on Huesca was beginning, the P.O.U.M. militia was still a separate unit, and it was probably feared that if the men knew what was happening they would refuse to fight. Actually nothing of the kind happened when the news arrived. In the intervening days there must have been numbers of men who were killed without ever learning that the newspapers in the rear were calling them Fascists. This kind of thing is a little difficult to forgive. I know it was the usual policy to keep bad news from the troops, and perhaps as a rule that is justified. But it is a different matter to send men into battle and not even tell them that behind their backs their party is being suppressed, their leaders accused of treachery, and their friends and relatives thrown into prison.

My wife began telling me what had happened to our various friends. Some of the English and other foreigners had got across the frontier. Williams and Stafford Cottman had not been arrested when the Sanatorium Maurin was raided, and were in hiding somewhere. So was John Mc-Nair, who had been in France and had re-entered Spain after the P.O.U.M. was declared illegal—a rash thing to do, but he had not cared to stay in safety while his comrades were in danger. For the rest it was simply a chronicle of 'They've got so and so' and 'They've got so and so'. They seemed to have 'got' nearly everyone. It took me aback to hear that they had also 'got' George Kopp.

'What! Kopp? I thought he was in Valencia.'

It appeared that Kopp had come back to Barcelona; he had a letter from the Ministry of War to the colonel commanding the engineering operations on the eastern front. He knew that the P.O.U.M. had been suppressed, of course, but probably it did not occur to him that the police could be such fools as to arrest him when he was on his way to the front on an urgent military mission. He had come round to the Hotel Continental to fetch his kit-bags; my wife had been out at the time, and the hotel people had managed to detain him with some lying story while they rang up the police. I admit I was angry when I heard of Kopp's arrest. He was my personal friend, I had served under him for months, I had been under fire with him, and I knew his history. He was a man who had sacrificed everything—family, nationality, livelihood—simply to come to Spain and fight against Fascism. By leaving Belgium without permission and joining a foreign army while he was on the Belgian Army reserve, and, earlier, by helping to manufacture munitions illegally for the Spanish Government, he had piled up years of imprisonment for himself if he should ever return to his own country. He had been in the line since October 1936, had worked his way up from militiaman to major, had been in action I do not know how many times, and had been wounded once. During the May trouble, as I had seen for myself, he had prevented fighting locally and probably saved ten or twenty lives. And all they could do in return was to fling him into jail. It is waste of time to be angry, but the stupid malignity of this kind of thing does try one's patience.

Meanwhile they had not 'got' my wife. Although she had remained at the Continental the police had made no move to arrest her. It was fairly obvious that she was being used as a decoy duck. A couple of nights earlier, however, in the small hours of the morning, six of the plain-clothes police had invaded our room at the hotel and searched it. They had seized every scrap of paper we possessed, except, fortunately, our passports and cheque-book. They had taken my diaries, all our books, all the press-cuttings that had been piling up for months past (I have often wondered what use those press-cuttings were to them), all my war souvenirs, and all our letters. (Incidentally, they took away a number of letters I had received from readers. Some of them had not been answered, and of course I have not the addresses. If anyone who wrote to me about my last book, and did not get an answer, happens to read these lines, will he please accept this as an apology?) I learned afterwards that the police had also seized various belongings that I had left at the *Sanatorium Maurin*. They even carried off a bundle of my dirty linen. Perhaps they thought it had messages written on it in invisible ink.

It was obvious that it would be safer for my wife to stay at the hotel, at any rate for the time being. If she tried to disappear they would be after her immediately. As for myself, I should have to go straight into hiding. The prospect revolted me. In spite of the innumerable arrests it was almost impossible for me to believe that

I was in any danger. The whole thing seemed too meaningless. It was the same refusal to take this idiotic onslaught seriously that had led Kopp into jail. I kept saying, but why should anyone want to arrest me? What had I done? I was not even a party member of the P.O.U.M. Certainly I had carried arms during the May fighting, but so had (at a guess) forty or fifty thousand people. Besides, I was badly in need of a proper night's sleep. I wanted to risk it and go back to the hotel. My wife would not hear of it. Patiently she explained the state of affairs. It did not matter what I had done or not done. This was not a round-up of criminals; it was merely a reign of terror. I was not guilty of any definite act, but I was guilty of 'Trotskyism'. The fact that I had served in the P.O.U.M. militia was quite enough to get me into prison. It was no use hanging on to the English notion that you are safe so long as you keep the law. Practically the law was what the police chose to make it. The only thing to do was to lie low and conceal the fact that I had anything to do with the P.O.U.M. We went through the papers in my pockets. My wife made me tear up my militiaman's card, which had P.O.U.M. on it in big letters, also a photo of a group of militiamen with a P.O.U.M. flag in the background; that was the kind of thing that got you arrested nowadays. I had to keep my discharge papers, however. Even these were a danger, for they bore the seal of the 29th Division, and the police would probably know that the 29th Division was the P.O.U.M.; but without them I could be arrested as a deserter.

The thing we had got to think of now was getting out of Spain. There was no sense in staying here with the certainty of imprisonment sooner or later. As a matter of fact both of us would greatly have liked to stay, just to see what happened. But I foresaw that Spanish prisons would be lousy places (actually they were a lot worse than I imagined), once in prison you never knew when you would get out, and I was in wretched health, apart from the pain in my arm. We arranged to meet next day at the British Consulate, where Cottman and McNair were also coming. It would probably take a couple of days to get our passports in order. Before leaving Spain you had to have your passport stamped in three separate places—by the Chief of Police, by the French Consul, and by the Catalan immigration authorities. The Chief of Police was the danger, of course. But perhaps the British Consul could fix things up without letting it be known that we had anything to do with the P.O.U.M. Obviously there must be a list of foreign 'Trotskyist' suspects, and very likely our names were on it, but with luck we might get to the frontier before the list. There was sure to be a lot of muddle and _mañana_. Fortunately this was Spain and not Germany. The Spanish secret police had some of the spirit of the Gestapo, but not much of its competence.

So we parted. My wife went back to the hotel and I wandered off into the darkness to find somewhere to sleep. I remember feeling sulky and bored. I had so wanted a night in bed! There was nowhere I could go, no house where I could take refuge. The P.O.U.M. had practically no underground organization. No doubt the leaders had always realized that the party was likely to be suppressed, but they had never expected a wholesale witch-hunt of this description. They had expected it so little, indeed, that they were actually continuing the alterations to the P.O.U.M. buildings (among other things they were constructing a cinema in the Executive Building, which had previously been a bank) up to the very day when the P.O.U.M. was suppressed. Consequently the rendezvous and hiding-places which every revolutionary party ought to possess as a matter of course did not exist. Goodness knows how many people—people whose homes had been raided by the police—were sleeping in the streets that night. I had had five days of tiresome journeys, sleeping in impossible places, my arm was hurting damnably, and now these fools were chasing me to and fro and I had got to sleep on the ground again. That was about as far as my thoughts went. I did not make any of the correct political reflections. I never do when things are happening. It seems to be always the case when I get mixed up in war or politics—I am conscious of nothing save physical discomfort and a deep desire for this damned nonsense to be over. Afterwards I can see the significance of events, but while they are happening I merely want to be out of them—an ignoble trait, perhaps.

I walked a long way and fetched up somewhere near the General Hospital. I wanted a place where I could lie down without some nosing policeman finding me and demanding my papers. I tried an air-raid shelter, but it was newly dug and dripping with damp. Then I came upon the ruins of a church that had been gutted and burnt in the revolution. It was a mere shell, four roofless walls surrounding piles of rubble. In the half-darkness I poked about and found a kind of hollow where I could lie down. Lumps of broken masonry are not good to lie on, but fortunately it was a warm night and I managed to get several hours' sleep.

CHAPTER 14

The worst of being wanted by the police in a town like Barcelona is that everything opens so late. When you sleep out of doors you always wake about dawn, and none of the Barcelona *cafés* opens much before nine. It was hours before I could get a cup of coffee or a shave. It seemed queer, in the barber's shop, to see the Anarchist notice still on the wall, explaining that tips were prohibited. 'The Revolution has struck off our chains,' the notice said. I felt like telling the barbers that their chains would soon be back again if they didn't look out.

I wandered back to the centre of the town. Over the P.O.U.M. buildings the red flags had been torn down, Republican flags were floating in their place, and knots of armed Civil Guards were lounging in the doorways. At the Red Aid centre on the corner of the *Plaza de Cataluña* the police had amused themselves by smashing most of the windows. The P.O.U.M. book-stalls had been emptied of books and the notice-board farther down the *Ramblas* had been plastered with an anti-P.O.U.M. cartoon—the one representing the mask and the Fascist face beneath. Down at the bottom of the *Ramblas*, near the quay, I came upon a queer sight; a row of militiamen, still ragged and muddy from the front, sprawling exhaustedly on the chairs placed there for the bootblacks. I knew who they were—indeed, I recognized one of them. They were P.O.U.M. militiamen who had come down the line on the previous day to find that the P.O.U.M. had been suppressed, and had had to spend the night in the streets because their homes had been raided. Any P.O.U.M. militiaman who returned to Barcelona at this time had the choice of going straight into hiding or into jail—not a pleasant reception after three or four months in the line.

It was a queer situation that we were in. At night one was a hunted fugitive, but in the daytime one could live an almost normal life. Every house known to harbour P.O.U.M. supporters was—or at any rate was likely to be—under observation, and it was impossible to go to a hotel or boarding-house, because it had been decreed that on the arrival of a stranger the hotel-keeper must inform the police immediately. Practically this meant spending the night out of doors. In the daytime, on the other hand, in a town the size of Barcelona, you were fairly safe. The streets were thronged by Civil Guards, Assault Guards, Carabineros, and ordinary police, besides God knows how many spies in plain clothes; still, they could not stop everyone who passed, and if you looked normal you might escape notice. The thing to do was to avoid hanging round P.O.U.M. buildings and going to *cafés* and restaurants where the waiters knew you by sight. I spent a long time that day, and the next, in having a bath at one of the public baths. This struck me as a good way of putting in the time and keeping out of sight. Unfortunately the same idea occurred to a lot of people, and a few days later—after I left Barcelona—the police raided one of the public baths and arrested a number of 'Trotskyists' in a state of nature.

Half-way up the *Ramblas* I ran into one of the wounded men from the *Sanatorium Maurin*. We exchanged the sort of invisible wink that people were exchanging at that time, and managed in an unobtrusive way to meet in a *café* farther up the street. He had escaped arrest when the Maurin was raided, but, like the others, had been driven into the street. He was in shirt-sleeves—had had to flee without his jacket—and had no money. He described to me how one of the Civil Guards had torn the large coloured portrait of Maurin from the wall and kicked it to pieces. Maurin (one of the founders of the P.O.U.M.) was a prisoner in the hands of the Fascists and at that time was believed to have been shot by them.

I met my wife at the British Consulate at ten o'clock. McNair and Cottman turned up shortly afterwards. The first thing they told me was that Bob Smillie was dead. He had died in prison at Valencia—of what, nobody knew for certain. He had been buried immediately, and the I.L.P. representative on the spot, David Murray, had been refused permission to see his body.

Of course I assumed at once that Smillie had been shot. It was what everyone believed at the time, but I have since thought that I may have been wrong. Later the cause of his death was given out as appendicitis, and we heard afterwards from another prisoner who had been released that Smillie had certainly been ill in prison. So perhaps the appendicitis story was true. The refusal to let Murray see his body may have been due to pure spite. I must say this, however. Bob Smillie was only twenty-two years old and physically he was one of the toughest people I have met. He was, I think, the only person I knew, English or Spanish, who went three months in the trenches without a day's illness. People so tough as that do not usually die of appendicitis if they are properly looked after. But when you saw what the Spanish jails were like—the makeshift jails used for political prisoners—you realized how much chance there was of a sick man getting proper attention. The jails were places that could only be described as dungeons. In England you would have to go back to the eighteenth century to find anything comparable. People were penned together in small rooms where there was barely space for them to lie down, and often they were kept in cellars and other dark places. This was not as a temporary measure—there were cases of people being kept four and five months almost without sight of daylight. And they were fed on a filthy and insufficient diet of two plates of soup and two pieces of bread a day. (Some months later, however, the food seems to have improved a little.) I am not exaggerating; ask any political suspect who was imprisoned in Spain. I have had accounts of the Spanish jails from a number of separate sources, and they agree with one another too well to be disbelieved; besides, I had a few glimpses into one Spanish jail myself. Another English friend who was imprisoned later writes that his experiences in jail 'make Smillie's case easier to understand'. Smillie's death is not a thing I can easily forgive. Here was this brave and gifted boy, who had thrown up his career at Glasgow University in order to come and fight against Fascism, and who, as I saw for myself, had done his job at the front with faultless courage and willingness; and all they could find to do with him was to fling him into jail and let him die like a neglected animal. I know that in the middle of a huge and bloody war it is no use making too much fuss over an individual death. One *aeroplane* bomb in a crowded street causes more suffering than quite a lot of political persecution. But what angers one about a death like this is its utter pointlessness. To be killed in battle—yes, that is what one expects; but to be flung into jail, not even for any imaginary offence, but simply owing to dull blind spite, and then left to die in solitude—that is a different matter. I fail to see how this kind of thing—and it is not as though Smillie's case were exceptional—brought victory any nearer.

My wife and I visited Kopp that afternoon. You were allowed to visit prisoners who were not _*incommunicado*_, though it was not safe to do so more than once or twice. The police watched the people who came and went, and if you visited the jails too often you stamped yourself as a friend of 'Trotskyists' and probably ended in jail yourself. This had already happened to a number of people.

Kopp was not _*incommunicado*_ and we got a permit to see him without difficulty. As they led us through the steel doors into the jail, a Spanish militiaman whom I had known at the front was being led out between two Civil Guards. His eye met mine; again the ghostly wink. And the first person we saw inside was an American militiaman who had left for home a few days earlier; his papers were in good order, but they had arrested him at the frontier all the same, probably because he was still wearing corduroy breeches and was therefore identifiable as a militiaman. We walked past one another as though we had been total strangers. That was dreadful. I had known him for months, had shared a dug-out with him, he had helped to carry me down the line when I was wounded; but it was the only thing one could do. The blue-clad guards were snooping everywhere. It would be fatal to recognize too many people.

The so-called jail was really the ground floor of a shop. Into two rooms each measuring about twenty feet square, close on a hundred people were penned. The place had the real eighteenth-century Newgate Calendar appearance, with its frowsy dirt, its huddle of human bodies, its lack of furniture—just the bare stone floor, one bench, and a few ragged blankets—and its murky light, for the corrugated steel shutters had been drawn over the windows. On the grimy walls revolutionary slogans—'_*Visca* P.O.U.M.!_' '_*Viva la Revolucion!*_' and so forth—had been scrawled. The place had been used as a dump for political prisoners for months past. There was a deafening racket of voices. This was the visiting hour, and the place was so packed with people that it was difficult to move. Nearly all of them were of the poorest of the working-class population. You saw women undoing pitiful packets of food which they had brought for their imprisoned men-folk. There were several of the wounded men from the Sanatorium Maurin among the prisoners. Two of them had amputated legs; one of them had been brought to prison without his crutch and was hopping about on one foot. There was also a boy of not more than twelve; they were even arresting children, apparently. The place had the beastly stench that you always get when crowds of people are penned together without proper sanitary arrangements.

Kopp elbowed his way through the crowd to meet us. His plump fresh-coloured face looked much as usual, and in that filthy place he had kept his uniform neat and had even contrived to shave. There was another officer in the uniform of the Popular Army among the prisoners. He and Kopp saluted as they struggled past one another; the gesture was pathetic, somehow. Kopp seemed in excellent spirits. 'Well, I suppose we shall all be shot,' he said cheerfully. The word 'shot' gave me a sort of inward shudder. A bullet had entered my own body recently and the feeling of it was fresh in my memory; it is not nice to think of that happening to anyone you know well. At that time I took it for granted that all the principal people in the P.O.U.M., and Kopp among them, _would_ be shot. The first rumour of Nin's death had just filtered through, and we knew that the P.O.U.M. were being accused of treachery and espionage. Everything pointed to a huge frame-up trial followed by a massacre of leading 'Trotskyists.' It is a terrible thing to see your friend in jail and to know yourself impotent to help him. For there was nothing that one could do; useless even to appeal to the Belgian authorities, for Kopp had broken the law of his own country by coming here. I had to leave most of the talking to my wife; with my squeaking voice I could not make myself heard in the din. Kopp was telling us about the friends he had made among the other prisoners, about the guards, some of whom were good fellows, but some of whom abused and beat the more timid prisoners, and about the food, which was 'pig-wash'. Fortunately we had thought to bring a packet of food, also cigarettes. Then Kopp began telling us about the papers that had been taken from him when he was arrested. Among them was his letter from the Ministry of War, addressed to the colonel commanding engineering operations in the Army of the East. The police had seized it and refused to give it back; it was said to be lying in the Chief of Police's office. It might make a very great difference if it were recovered.

I saw instantly how important this might be. An official letter of that kind, bearing the recommendation of the Ministry of War and of General Pozas, would establish Kopp's bona fides. But the trouble was to prove that the letter existed; if it were opened in the Chief of Police's office one could be sure that some nark or other would destroy it. There was only one person who might possibly be able to get it back, and that was the officer to whom it was addressed. Kopp had already thought of this, and he had written a letter which he wanted me to smuggle out of the jail and post. But it was obviously quicker and surer to go in person. I left my wife with Kopp, rushed out, and, after a long search, found a taxi. I knew that time was everything. It was now about half past five, the colonel would probably leave his office at six, and by tomorrow the letter might be God knew where—destroyed, perhaps, or lost somewhere in the chaos of documents that was presumably piling up as suspect after suspect was arrested. The colonel's office was at the War Department down by the quay. As I hurried up the steps the Assault Guard on duty at the door barred the way with his long bayonet and demanded 'papers'. I waved my discharge ticket at him; evidently he could not read, and he let me pass, impressed by the vague mystery of 'papers'. Inside, the place was a huge complicated warren running round a central courtyard, with hundreds of offices on each floor; and, as this was Spain, nobody had the vaguest idea where the office I was looking for was. I kept repeating: '_El coronel ——, jefe de ingenieros, Ejercito de Este!_' People smiled and shrugged their shoulders gracefully. Everyone who had an opinion sent me in a different direction; up these stairs, down those, along interminable passages which turned out to be blind alleys. And time was slipping away. I had the strangest sensation of being in a nightmare: the rushing up and down flights of stairs, the mysterious people coming and going, the glimpses through open doors of chaotic offices with papers strewn everywhere and typewriters clicking; and time slipping away and a life perhaps in the balance.

However, I got there in time, and slightly to my surprise I was granted a hearing. I did not see *Colonel* ——, but his aide-de-camp or secretary, a little slip of an officer in smart uniform, with large and squinting eyes, came out to interview me in the ante-room. I began to pour forth my story. I had come on behalf of my superior officer. Major Jorge Kopp, who was on an urgent mission to the front and had been arrested by mistake. The letter to *Colonel* —— was of a confidential nature and should be recovered without delay. I had served with Kopp for months, he was an officer of the highest character, obviously his arrest was a mistake, the police had confused him with someone else, etc., etc., etc. I kept piling it on about the urgency of Kopp's mission to the front, knowing that this was the strongest point. But it must have sounded a strange tale, in my villainous Spanish which elapsed into French at every crisis. The worst was that my voice gave out almost at once and it was only by violent straining that I could produce a sort of croak. I was in dread that it would disappear altogether and the little officer would grow tired of trying to listen to me. I have often wondered what he thought was wrong with my voice—whether he thought I was drunk or merely suffering from a guilty conscience.

However, he heard me patiently, nodded his head a great number of times, and gave a guarded assent to what I said. Yes, it sounded as though there might have been a mistake. Clearly the matter should be looked into. _*Mañana*_—. I protested. Not _*mañana*_! The matter was urgent; Kopp was due at the front already. Again the officer seemed to agree. Then came the question I was dreading:

'This Major Kopp—what force was he serving in?'

The terrible word had to come out: 'In the P.O.U.M. militia.'

'P.O.U.M.!'

I wish I could convey to you the shocked alarm in his voice. You have got to remember how the P.O.U.M. was regarded at that moment. The spy-scare was at its height; probably all good Republicans did believe for a day or two that the P.O.U.M. was a huge spying organization in German pay. To have to say such a thing to an officer in the Popular Army was like going into the Cavalry Club immediately after the Red Letter scare and announcing yourself a Communist. His dark eyes moved obliquely across my face. Another long pause, then he said slowly:

'And you say you were with him at the front. Then you were serving in the P.O.U.M. militia yourself?'

'Yes.'

He turned and dived into the colonel's room. I could hear an agitated conversation. 'It's all up,' I thought. We should never get Kopp's letter back. Moreover I had had to confess that I was in the P.O.U.M. myself, and no doubt they would ring up the police and get me arrested, just to add another Trotskyist to the bag. Presently, however, the officer reappeared, fitting on his cap, and sternly signed to me to follow. We were going to the Chief of Police's office. It was a long way, twenty minutes' walk. The little officer marched stiffly in front with a military step. We did not exchange a single word the whole way. When we got to the Chief of Police's office a crowd of the most dreadful-looking scoundrels, obviously police narks, informers, and spies of every kind, were hanging about outside the door. The little officer went in; there was a long, heated conversation. You could hear voices furiously raised; you pictured violent gestures, shrugging of the shoulders, hangings on the table. Evidently the police were refusing to give the letter up. At last, however, the officer emerged, flushed, but carrying a large official envelope. It was Kopp's letter. We had won a tiny victory—which, as it turned out, made not the slightest difference. The letter was duly delivered, but Kopp's military superiors were quite unable to get him out of jail.

The officer promised me that the letter should be delivered. But what about Kopp? I said. Could we not get him released? He shrugged his shoulders. That was another matter. They did not know what Kopp had been arrested for. He would only tell me that the proper inquiries would be made. There was no more to be said; it was time to part. Both of us bowed slightly. And then there happened a strange and moving thing. The little officer hesitated a moment, then stepped across, and shook hands with me.

I do not know if I can bring home to you how deeply that action touched me. It sounds a small thing, but it was not. You have got to realize what was the feeling of the time—the horrible atmosphere of suspicion and hatred, the lies and rumours circulating everywhere, the posters screaming from the hoardings that I and everyone like me was a Fascist spy. And you have got to remember that we were standing outside the Chief of Police's office, in front of that filthy gang of tale-bearers and _agents provocateurs_, any one of whom might know that I was 'wanted' by the police. It was like publicly shaking hands with a German during the Great War. I suppose he had decided in some way that I was not really a Fascist spy; still, it was good of him to shake hands.

I record this, trivial though it may sound, because it is somehow typical of Spain—of the flashes of magnanimity that you get from Spaniards in the worst of circumstances. I have the most evil memories of Spain, but I have very few bad memories of Spaniards. I only twice remember even being seriously angry with a Spaniard, and on each occasion, when I look back, I believe I was in the wrong myself. They have, there is no doubt, a generosity, a species of nobility, that do not really belong to the twentieth century. It is this that makes one hope that in Spain even Fascism may take a comparatively loose and bearable form. Few Spaniards possess the damnable efficiency and consistency that a modern totalitarian state needs. There had been a queer little illustration of this fact a few nights earlier, when the police had searched my wife's room. As a matter of fact that search was a very interesting business, and I wish

I had seen it, though perhaps it is as well that I did not, for I might not have kept my temper.

The police conducted the search in the recognized Ogpu or Gestapo style. In the small hours of the morning there was a pounding on the door, and six men marched in, switched on the light, and immediately took up various positions about the room, obviously agreed upon beforehand. They then searched both rooms (there was a bathroom attached) with inconceivable thoroughness. They sounded the walls, took up the mats, examined the floor, felt the curtains, probed under the bath and the radiator, emptied every drawer and suitcase and felt every garment and held it up to the light. They impounded all papers, including the contents of the waste-paper basket, and all our books into the bargain. They were thrown into ecstasies of suspicion by finding that we possessed a French translation of Hitler's _Mein Kampf_. If that had been the only book they found our doom would have been sealed. It is obvious that a person who reads _Mein Kampf_ must be a Fascist. The next moment, however, they came upon a copy of Stalin's pamphlet, _Ways of Liquidating Trotskyists and other Double Dealers_, which reassured them somewhat. In one drawer there was a number of packets of cigarette papers. They picked each packet to pieces and examined each paper separately, in case there should be messages written on them. Altogether they were on the job for nearly two hours. Yet all this time they _never searched the bed_. My wife was lying in bed all the while; obviously there might have been half a dozen sub-machine-guns under the mattress, not to mention a library of Trotskyist documents under the pillow. Yet the detectives made no move to touch the bed, never even looked underneath it. I cannot believe that this is a regular feature of the Ogpu routine. One must remember that the police were almost entirely under Communist control, and these men were probably Communist Party members themselves. But they were also Spaniards, and to turn a woman out of bed was a little too much for them. This part of the job was silently dropped, making the whole search meaningless.

That night McNair, Cottman, and I slept in some long grass at the edge of a derelict building-lot. It was a cold night for the time of year and no one slept much. I remember the long dismal hours of loitering about before one could get a cup of coffee. For the first time since I had been in Barcelona I went to have a look at the cathedral—a modern cathedral, and one of the most hideous buildings in the world. It has four crenellated spires exactly the shape of hock bottles. Unlike most of the churches in Barcelona it was not damaged during the revolution—it was spared because of its 'artistic value', people said. I think the Anarchists showed bad taste in not blowing it up when they had the chance, though they did hang a red and black banner between its spires. That afternoon my wife and I went to see Kopp for the last time. There was nothing that we could do for him, absolutely nothing, except to say good-bye and leave money with Spanish friends who would take him food and cigarettes. A little while later, however, after we had left Barcelona, he was placed _*incommunicado*_ and not even food could be sent to him. That night, walking down the *Ramblas*, we passed the *Café Moka*, which the Civil Guards were still holding in force. On an impulse I went in and spoke to two of them who were leaning against the counter with their rifles slung over their shoulders. I asked them if they knew which of their comrades had been on duty here at the time of the May fighting. They did not know, and, with the usual Spanish vagueness, did not know how one could find out. I said that my friend Jorge Kopp was in prison and would perhaps be put on trial for something in connexion with the May fighting; that the men who were on duty here would know that he had stopped the fighting and saved some of their lives; they ought to come forward and give evidence to that effect. One of the men I was talking to was a dull, heavy-looking man who kept shaking his head because he could not hear my voice in the din of the traffic. But the other was different. He said he had heard of Kopp's action from some of his comrades; Kopp was _buen chico_ (a good fellow). But even at the time I knew that it was all useless. If Kopp were ever tried, it would be, as in all such trials, with faked evidence. If he has been shot (and I am afraid it is quite likely), that will be his epitaph: the _buen chico_ of the poor Civil Guard who was part of a dirty system but had remained enough of a human being to know a decent action when he saw one.

It was an extraordinary, insane existence that we were leading. By night we were criminals, but by day we were prosperous English visitors—that was our pose, anyway. Even after a night in the open, a shave, a bath, and a shoe-shine do wonders with your appearance. The safest thing at present was to look as bourgeois as possible. We frequented the fashionable residential quarter of the town, where our faces were not known, went to expensive restaurants, and were very English with the waiters. For the first time in my life I took to writing things on walls. The passage-ways of several smart restaurants had '_Visca P.O.U.M.!_' scrawled on them as large as I could write it. All the while, though I was technically in hiding, I could not feel myself in danger. The whole thing seemed too absurd. I had the ineradicable English belief that 'they' cannot arrest you unless you have broken the law. It is a most dangerous belief to have during a political pogrom. There was a warrant out for McNair's arrest, and the chances were that the rest of us were on the list as well. The arrests, raids, searchings were continuing without pause; practically everyone we knew, except those who were still at the front, was in jail by this time. The police were even boarding the French ships that periodically took off refugees and seizing suspected 'Trotskyists'.

Thanks to the kindness of the British consul, who must have had a very trying time during that week, we had managed to get our passports into order. The sooner we left the better. There was a train that was due to leave for *Port Bou* at half past seven in the evening and might normally be expected to leave at about half past eight. We arranged that my wife should order a taxi beforehand and then pack her bags, pay her bill, and leave the hotel at the last possible moment. If she gave the hotel people too much notice they would be sure to send for the police. I got down to the station at about seven to find that the train had already gone—it had left at ten to seven. The engine-driver had changed his mind, as usual. Fortunately we managed to warn my wife in time. There was another train early the following morning. McNair, Cottman, and I had dinner at a little restaurant near the station and by cautious questioning discovered that the restaurant-keeper was a C.N.T. member and friendly. He let us a three-bedded room and forgot to warn the police. It was the first time in five nights that I had been able to sleep with my clothes off.

Next morning my wife slipped out of the hotel successfully. The train was about an hour late in starting. I filled in the time by writing a long letter to the Ministry of War, telling them about Kopp's case—that without a doubt he had been arrested by mistake, that he was urgently needed at the front, that countless people would testify that he was innocent of any offence, etc., etc., etc. I wonder if anyone read that letter, written on pages torn out of a note-book in wobbly handwriting (my fingers were still partly paralysed) and still more wobbly Spanish. At any rate, neither this letter nor anything else took effect. As I write, six months after the event, Kopp (if he has not been shot) is still in jail, untried and uncharged. At the beginning we had two or three letters from him, smuggled out by released prisoners and posted in France. They all told the same story—imprisonment in filthy dark dens, bad and insufficient food, serious illness due to the conditions of imprisonment, and refusal of medical attention. I have had all this confirmed from several other sources, English and French. More recently he disappeared into one of the 'secret prisons' with which it seems impossible to make any kind of communication. His case is the case of scores or hundreds of foreigners and no one knows how many thousands of Spaniards.

In the end we crossed the frontier without incident. The train had a first class and a dining-car, the first I had seen in Spain. Until recently there had been only one class on the trains in Catalonia. Two detectives came round the train taking the names of foreigners, but when they saw us in the dining-car they seemed satisfied that we were respectable. It was queer how everything had changed. Only six months ago, when the Anarchists still reigned, it was looking like a proletarian that made you respectable. On the way down from Perpignan to Cerberes a French commercial traveller in my carriage had said to me in all solemnity: 'You mustn't go into Spain looking like that. Take off that collar and tie. They'll tear them off you in Barcelona.' He was exaggerating, but it showed how Catalonia was regarded. And at the frontier the Anarchist guards had turned back a smartly dressed Frenchman and his wife, solely—I think—because they looked too bourgeois. Now it was the other way about; to look bourgeois was the one salvation. At the passport office they looked us up in the card-index of suspects, but thanks to the inefficiency of the police our names were not listed, not even McNair's. We were searched from head to foot, but we possessed nothing incriminating, except my discharge-papers, and the carabineros who searched me did not know that the 29th Division was the P.O.U.M. So we slipped through the barrier, and after just six months I was on French soil again. My only souvenirs of Spain were a goatskin water-bottle and one of those tiny iron lamps in which the Aragón peasants burn olive oil-lamps almost exactly the shape of the terra-cotta lamps that the Romans used two thousand years ago—which I had picked up in some ruined hut, and which had somehow got stuck in my luggage.

After all, it turned out that we had come away none too soon. The very first newspaper we saw announced McNair's arrest for espionage. The Spanish authorities had been a little premature in announcing this. Fortunately, 'Trotskyism' is not extraditable.

I wonder what is the appropriate first action when you come from a country at war and set foot on peaceful soil. Mine was to rush to the tobacco-kiosk and buy as many cigars and cigarettes as I could stuff into my pockets. Then we all went to the buffet and had a cup of tea, the first tea with fresh milk in it that we had had for many months. It was several days before I could get used to the idea that you could buy cigarettes whenever you wanted them. I always half-expected to see the tobacconists' doors barred and the forbidding notice '_No hay tabaco_' in the window.

McNair and Cottman were going on to Paris. My wife and I got off the train at Banyuls, the first station up the line, feeling that we would like a rest. We were not too well received in Banyuls when they discovered that we had come from Barcelona. Quite a number of times I was involved in the same conversation: 'You come from Spain? Which side were you fighting on? The Government? Oh!'—and then a marked coolness. The little town seemed solidly pro-Franco, no doubt because of the various Spanish Fascist refugees who had arrived there from time to time. The waiter at the café I frequented was a pro-Franco Spaniard and used to give me lowering glances as he served me with an aperitif. It was otherwise in Perpignan, which was stiff with Government partisans and where all the different factions were caballing against one another almost as in Barcelona. There was one *café* where the word 'P.O.U.M.' immediately procured you French friends and smiles from the waiter.

I think we stayed three days in Banyuls. It was a strangely restless time. In this quiet fishing-town, remote from bombs, machine-guns, food-queues, propaganda, and intrigue, we ought to have felt profoundly relieved and thankful. We felt nothing of the kind. The things we had seen in Spain did not recede and fall into proportion now that we were away from them; instead they rushed back upon us and were far more vivid than before. We thought, talked, dreamed incessantly of Spain. For months past we had been telling ourselves that 'when we get out of Spain' we would go somewhere beside the Mediterranean and be quiet for a little while and perhaps do a little fishing, but now that we were here it was merely a bore and a disappointment. It was chilly weather, a persistent wind blew off the sea, the water was dull and choppy, round the harbour's edge a scum of ashes, corks, and fish-guts bobbed against the stones. It sounds like lunacy, but the thing that both of us wanted was to be back in Spain. Though it could have done no good to anybody, might indeed have done serious harm, both of us wished that we had stayed to be imprisoned along with the others. I suppose I have failed to convey more than a little of what those months in Spain meant to me. I have recorded some of the outward events, but I cannot record the feeling they have left me with. It is all mixed up with sights, smells, and sounds that cannot be conveyed in writing: the smell of the trenches, the mountain dawns stretching away into inconceivable distances, the frosty crackle of bullets, the roar and glare of bombs; the clear cold light of the Barcelona mornings, and the stamp of boots in the barrack yard, back in December when people still believed in the revolution; and the food-queues and the red and black flags and the faces of Spanish militiamen; above all the faces of militiamen—men whom I knew in the line and who are now scattered Lord knows where, some killed in battle, some maimed, some in prison—most of them, I hope, still safe and sound. Good luck to them all; I hope they win their war and drive all the foreigners out of Spain, Germans, Russians, and Italians alike. This war, in which I played so ineffectual a part, has left me with memories that are mostly evil, and yet I do not wish that I had missed it. When you have had a glimpse of such a disaster as this—and however it ends the Spanish war will turn out to have been an appalling disaster, quite apart from the slaughter and physical suffering—the result is not necessarily disillusionment and cynicism. Curiously enough the whole experience has left me with not less but more belief in the decency of human beings. And I hope the account I have given is not too misleading. I believe that on such an issue as this no one is or can be completely truthful. It is difficult to be certain about anything except what you have seen with your own eyes, and consciously or unconsciously everyone writes as a partisan. In case I have not said this somewhere earlier in the book I will say it now: beware of my partisanship, my mistakes of fact, and the distortion inevitably caused by my having seen only one corner of events. And beware of exactly the same things when you read any other book on this period of the Spanish war.

Because of the feeling that we ought to be doing something, though actually there was nothing we could do, we left Banyuls earlier than we had intended. With every mile that you went northward France grew greener and softer. Away from the mountain and the vine, back to the meadow and the elm. When I had passed through Paris on my way to Spain it had seemed to me decayed and gloomy, very different from the Paris I had known eight years earlier, when living was cheap and Hitler was not heard of. Half the *cafés* I used to know were shut for lack of custom, and everyone was obsessed with the high cost of living and the fear of war. Now, after poor Spain, even Paris seemed gay and prosperous. And the Exhibition was in full swing, though we managed to avoid visiting it.

And then England—southern England, probably the sleekest landscape in the world. It is difficult when you pass that way, especially when you are peacefully recovering from sea-sickness with the plush cushions of a boat-train carriage under your bum, to believe that anything is really happening anywhere. Earthquakes in Japan, famines in China, revolutions in Mexico? Don't worry, the milk will be on the doorstep tomorrow morning, the _New Statesman_ will come out on Friday. The industrial towns were far away, a smudge of smoke and misery hidden by the curve of the earth's surface. Down here it was still the England I had known in my childhood: the railway-cuttings smothered in wild flowers, the deep meadows where the great shining horses browse and meditate, the slow-moving streams bordered by willows, the green bosoms of the elms, the larkspurs in the cottage gardens; and then the huge peaceful wilderness of outer London, the barges on the miry river, the familiar streets, the posters telling of cricket matches and Royal weddings, the men in bowler hats, the pigeons in Trafalgar Square, the red buses, the blue policemen—all sleeping the deep, deep sleep of England, from which I sometimes fear that we shall never wake till we are jerked out of it by the roar of bombs.

The End